Also by Fr

Gabriel's Chalice
A Novel
Frank A. Ruffolo

ALL THREE BOOKS OF THE SERIES
THE
TRIHEDRAL
OF CHAOS
A Trilogy of Love...
and Hate
From The Author of Gabriel's Chalice
FRANK A. RUFFOLO

“...the story pulls you in. There are a few small twist that make you question what will happen next. Look forward to see if there will be anymore stories to add to the series.” ~ Ella Gram

JACK STENHOUSE MYSTERIES

The Shadow of Death
The Saturnalian Affect

Frank A. Ruffolo

This book is a work of fiction. With the exception of recognized historical figures, the characters in this novel are fictional. Any resemblance to actual persons, living or dead, is purely coincidental.

Printed in the United States of America
Cover Design: Linkville Graphics'
Editor: K.R. Morrison

Linkville Press
linkvillepress.wix.com/home
linkvillepress@gmail.com

ISBN-13: 978-1507740439
ISBN-10: 1507740433

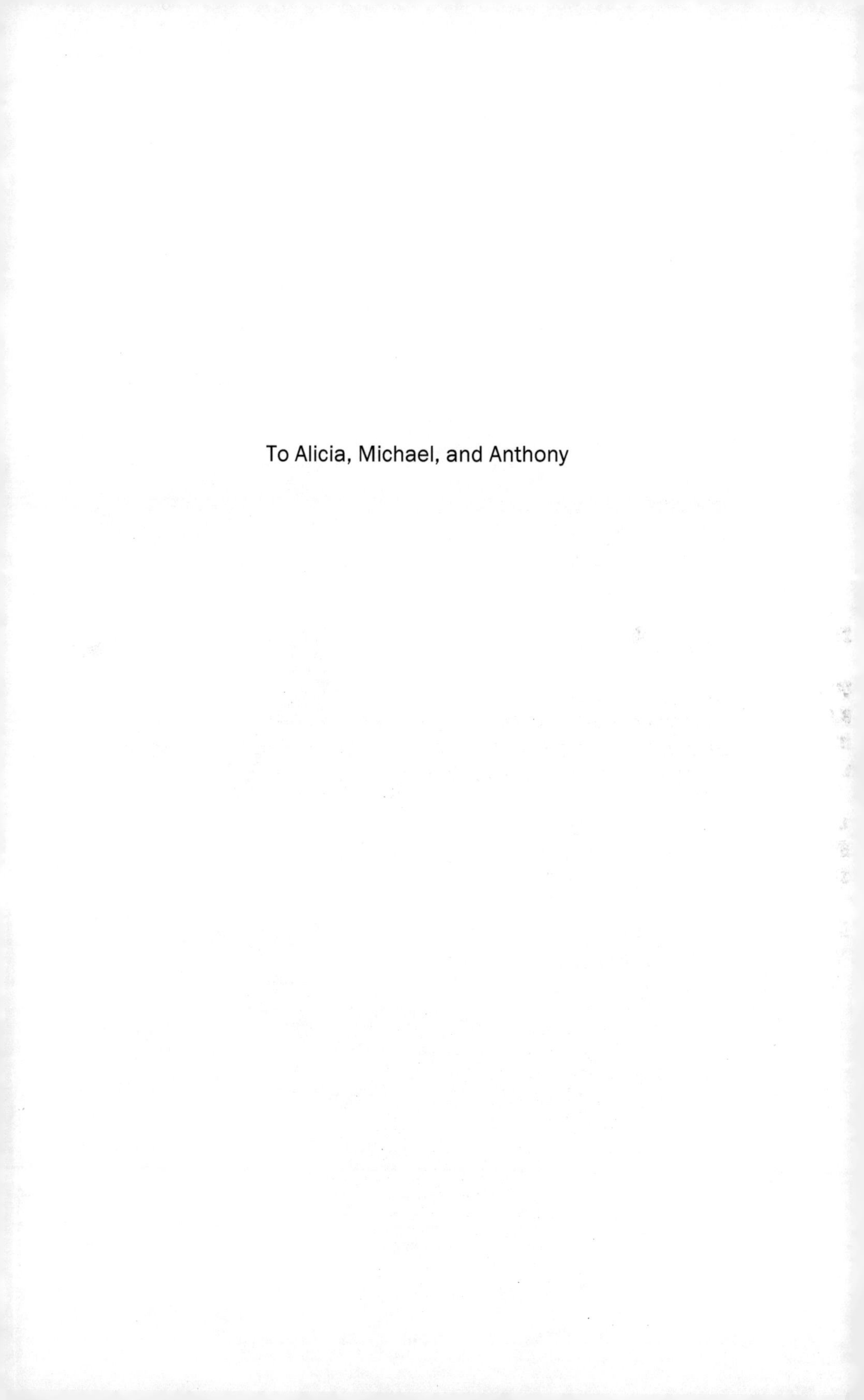

To Alicia, Michael, and Anthony

Foreword

Jack Stenhouse, a player and Fort Lauderdale's leading homicide detective, is haunted by THE SHADOW OF DEATH as he searches the steamy streets of Fort Lauderdale to solve a murder on the beach, under the watchful eye of his boss and the oppressive heat of South Florida. With his stripper girlfriend, Didi, a woman with a nickname to fit her attributes, Jack must determine why beautiful women are dying from the bite of the black mamba, a snake found only in Africa.

In THE SATURNALIAN AFFECT, Jack and Didi move from the hot summers of South Florida to the concrete jungle of the Big Apple. As the new man at the First Precinct, Jack's first assignment is to track down a serial killer who only targets his victims during the pagan festival of Saturnalia.

Will the Saturnalian affect cloud his judgment? Will this Florida boy be able to withstand the cold and snow of New York City? You need only turn the page to find out if Jack is up to these tasks.

Now, if you dare, enter the mysterious world of Jack Stenhouse.

THE SHADOW OF DEATH

CHAPTER ONE

It is a typical August sunrise on Fort Lauderdale Beach; the orange rays poke through purple thunderstorms percolating offshore. At only 7:30 in the morning, the 85-degree air is so thick to breathe that you must cut a slice of it like a New York cheesecake. While lovers and joggers parade along the shoreline, a man combs the sand with his metal detector, looking for hidden treasure.

After almost an hour of scouring the beach, suddenly a high-pitched squeal emits from the screen: a hit, a gold ring just a few inches from the surface. In wild desperation, the man drops to his knees to clear the sand away from his newfound bounty.

Suddenly, he jumps back in horror.

He's found a gold ring all right, but unfortunately, the owner is still wearing it.

A ringing telephone interrupts the quiet of the morning. Jack Stenhouse, one of Fort Lauderdale's finest detectives, is sleeping next to his newest hooker/stripper girlfriend.

Jack, a twenty-year veteran of the Fort Lauderdale Police Department, was born and raised in Broward County, Florida. His eyes are his best feature, a shade grayer than blue, but a stare from them would stop a clock. And at six-foot-one, one hundred eight-five pounds, he looks ten years younger than his early forties.

He is not currently married, having been divorced three times, and thanks to the vasectomy he had while in college, there are no little Jacks running around. As he puts it, the reason for having the vasectomy is that he is too lazy to buy condoms, and that he doesn't want to experience the bullshit agony of parenthood.

Jack's vices, which ruined his three marriages, are bimbos, hookers, and strippers.

Reaching for the telephone, Jack's tone of voice expresses his annoyance at having been woken up from a sound sleep.

"Yeah?" he grumbles. "This *better* be good."

He listens silently for a while and then, sighing deeply, replies, "Damn. Let me do my three S's. I'll be there as soon as I can."

Wide awake now, Jack hangs up the phone and looks over at Didi, his main squeeze, who happens to have the perfect name for a girl with breasts to match. When he slaps Didi on the ass, she wakes up with a jolt.

"Gotta go, Babe. Duty calls."

"How the hell am I gonna get home, Jack?" Didi asks sleepily.

Naked as a jaybird, Jack walks over to his pants, which are lying on the floor, and reaches into the front pocket. Pulling out three ten dollar bills, he throws them on the bed and stares down at the naked Didi, thinking all the while of the front bumper of a '58 Caddy.

"Take a cab and buy some breakfast. I gotta shit, shower, shave, and then hit the road. Lock up when you leave, okay? I'll take you to dinner tonight."

Jack heads for the shower while Didi rolls over and tries to go back to sleep.

After twenty minutes, Jack heads out the door while Didi heads into the shower, having given up on sleep. Her double D's make it into the bathroom long before the rest of her.

Didi is in her late thirties, and as the saying goes, "built like a brick shit house." As she lathers up in the shower, Jack walks down the stairs from his condo in downtown Fort Lauderdale and then climbs into his '68 Hemi Road Runner.

The Road Runner is Jack's "baby." It has a four-barrel carburetor and four on the floor, with headers and a dual glass pack exhaust. When the car starts up with a roar, he gives the horn a quick beep-beep, waking up most of his neighbors, and leaves two rubber patches on the parking lot surface as the Road Runner screams onto Broward Boulevard.

A couple of blocks later, Jack turns down a side street toward Las Olas Boulevard, then makes a left turn toward the beach. At A1A, he turns right and quickly pulls off the street into a public parking area amid a sparkling display of flashing blue lights.

Jack carefully parks the Road Runner, but before exiting the vehicle, he takes off his Italian leather shoes and socks, puts one sock into each shoe, then tosses the mated pairs onto the front passenger seat of the vehicle. After locking the door, he rolls up his trousers to keep them dry, and then walks toward the crowd on the beach.

With a yellow flowered Hawaiian shirt over his pants to hide his 9mm, Jack looks more like a tourist than a detective. As he approaches the crowd, a couple of uniformed police officers turn and watch Jack as he approaches them barefoot. Snickering, one of them calls out, "Hey, look! Here comes Surfer Joe!"

Jack flashes them half a peace sign while walking toward Sergeant Jackson, the officer in charge of the crime scene.

"Hi, Wayne. What do we have here?"

Sergeant Wayne Jackson points to a visibly-shaken Stu Glassman and waves the man over to them.

"Mr. Stewart Glassman, one of the regular treasure hunters here on the beach, made the discovery."

Turning toward the older man, Jack introduces himself. "Mr. Glassman, I'm Detective Stenhouse. Can you tell me what happened?"

"Well, Detective, I've been treasure-hunting here for over five years, and this is horrible."

"Yes, we know, Mr. Glassman. Please go on."

"Well, as I was walking along the beach scanning the sand, my metal detector signaled that there was a ring about six inches below the surface. When I dug in the sand, I saw that it was still on someone's finger. That's the hole where I found it."

Jack walks over to a small hole in the sand and sees the hand of what appears to be a young woman, with a large sapphire ring on her finger.

While he examines the hand, the police department's Crime Scene Investigation (CSI) unit arrives. Before turning the scene over to them, he calls out, "I need you guys to bag all the sand around this excavation so it can be sifted for evidence."

As the crime scene team goes to work, they slowly uncover the body of a young attractive female wearing nothing but a ring and sporting a recently-etched tattoo of a coiled snake on the small of her back, just above her buttocks.

While watching the scene unfolding before him, Jack has a thought, and turns to Sergeant Jackson. "Let's bring the work crew into the station for questioning. Don't they have to comb and level the beaches here every morning?"

"10-4, Jack. Will do."

With that task assigned to the sergeant, Jack re-addresses Mr. Glassman.

"Mr. Glassman, please take my card and call me if you remember anything else about what happened today. One of those uniformed officers over there will take your statement. Thanks for your cooperation."

After pointing Mr. Glassman in the direction of the nearest police officer, Jack says to Wayne, "As soon as the coroner releases the body, I'm going to follow him back to the morgue to observe the autopsy. I want to get the time of death, and anything else he can tell me. It's a shame, a pretty girl like that, no ID. This is going to be a rough one."

While waiting for the coroner to arrive, Jack stares at the ocean. Another beautiful sunrise over Fort Lauderdale Beach displays its beauty, with the sun breaking through offshore thunderstorms and turning the sky orange and yellow.

The local TV news trucks pull up and break his reverie, too soon for Jack's liking. Turning to look at the woman lying in the sand, he has a puzzling thought. *Boy, she looks familiar. Where the hell have I seen her before?*

CHAPTER TWO

In a Sunny Isles Beach penthouse condo, Sean LeDue is awakened by the sunshine invading his bedroom. The CEO and owner of Mamba Imports, LLC, an importer of fine art, is also the operator of LeDue Art Gallery on Las Olas Boulevard. He feels the effects of an overwhelming hangover as he slowly exits his bedroom. Entering the living room, he gingerly steps around the arms and legs of the people sleeping on the floor, mostly half-naked women, and heads into the kitchen for a much-needed jolt of caffeine. However, once he's in the kitchen, the thought of having to deal with the coffee maker causes him to opt for a cold Pepsi instead, which gives him a caffeine jolt and a sugar jolt at the same time.

As he waits for his hangover to slowly subside, he hears Rosa, the housekeeper, letting herself in at the front door. Knowing what will surely come next, he holds his breath, then hears what he knew was coming.

"*Mr. LeDue, what the hell happened here?!*"

Approaching Rosa as she stands at the door, he responds, "I had a few friends over."

"Yeah, and they're still here! Look, I don't mind cleaning your house and washing various women's laundry, but *this* is out of hand!"

Holding up a finger to beg Rosa to wait a minute, he walks into the bedroom and quickly returns with a one-hundred-dollar bill.

"Feeling any better?" he asks.

Smiling, Rosa takes the bill and tucks it down the front of her blouse and into her bra.

"Feeling fine, Mr. LeDue. Want some coffee?"

Rosa places her purse on the dining room table and heads into the kitchen, where she makes a beeline for one of the lower cabinet doors. Opening the door, she pulls out a large pot, then grabs a serving spoon and walks into the living room, banging the spoon against the pot like a drum.

"Okay, people! Up and out!"

The loud banging quickly awakens everyone, causing them to jump up and gather their belongings while trying not to bump into each other.

With Sean laughing beside her, Rosa observes the scrambling of half-asleep people, and imagines, *This is what it must have been like to work for a Roman Emperor!*

When the telephone begins to ring, she carefully weaves her way through the madness to pick it up.

"LeDue residence... Yes, please hold on."

Handing the phone to Sean, she walks back into the kitchen to begin making coffee.

"Yes?" asks Sean into the phone. "Oh, hi, Tom."

"Have you seen the morning news?"

"No, I just got up."

"Well, you need to check it out right now!"

When Tom abruptly ends the call, Sean grabs the remote control and turns on the widescreen TV in the living room.

"...and we have further reports from Fort Lauderdale Beach. The body of a nude young woman was found buried on the beach just north of Las Olas Boulevard. Police found no ID on this woman and there are no reports of anyone missing who fits her description. The only clue they have so far is that the victim has a fairly new tattoo of a coiled snake on her lower back, at the base of her spine."

Stunned, Sean turns off the TV. The coiled snake is his company logo, and many of his female employees have a similar tattoo.

Needing privacy, he walks into his bedroom and picks up the telephone on his nightstand.

"Hey! This is Sean. Look, I'm not paying you for nothing. The incident on the beach this morning needs to go away quietly, understood?"

After hanging up the phone, he walks into the bathroom to take a cold shower before beginning his day.

With blonde hair, blue eyes, and more money than God, Sean LeDue's attitude is that his shit doesn't stink. He also believes that if he throws enough money at his problems, they will all go away.

What a fool.

At the beach, the crime scene team was lucky. They managed to finish their analysis of the scene before the offshore thunderstorms rolled onto the beach, forcing the cops, and the local news crews with their mobile satellite antennae stuck in the air like stalagmites, to run for cover.

Fortunately, Jack had left the beach a few minutes earlier, before the rain started. He had waited for the medical examiner to pronounce the time of death and release the body, then he walked back to his Road Runner, where he put his socks and shoes back on and rolled his pants legs down.

Catching sight of the ambulance that is transporting the "Snake Lady" to the morgue, Jack follows close behind, intending to observe the autopsy. Within ten minutes, both he and the ambulance pull up to the back entrance of the medical examiner's office.

After parking the Road Runner, Jack runs inside to escape the rain that is now falling in sheets, and joins the ambulance crew as they wheel the body down the long hallway to the morgue. There, he finds Sergeant Wayne Jackson and Doctor Indra Ghosh, who will perform the autopsy.

"Wayne, what the hell are you doin' here? This case was transferred to me."

"Just checking to see what's happening. It's not often that we find a body buried at the beach."

"So you have nothing better to do than to watch an autopsy? I thought you were supposed to interview the crew that levels off the beach?"

"Yeah, the crew is coming into the station this morning. I guess I better get over there. Look, if anything turns up, let me know, okay?"

"Sure, you do the same."

Jack aims a questioning look at Sergeant Jackson's back as he watches him walk away, but when the sergeant is out of sight, he shrugs off his uneasy feeling and turns his attention to the medical examiner, who is positioning the mystery lady's body on the autopsy table.

After waiting patiently for Doctor Ghosh to finish his preliminary examination, he approaches the doctor to ask about his initial observations.

"So what did you find out, Doc?"

"Well, we have a very attractive young woman here, a natural blonde, twenty-three to twenty-five years of age, about five-feet-six inches tall, and one hundred twenty pounds or so, with store-bought breasts. There's a bluing of the lips, fingers and toes, which indicates oxygen deprivation, but there are no outward signs of trauma or distress. We'll have to do a toxic screen on her blood, but at this time, I see no obvious evidence of foul play."

The doctor continues to scan the body, front and back, and also checks for rape, with no positive results. Then, while examining the body again, he lingers in the area around the head and motions for Jack to join him.

"Look at her neck, behind the right ear. See the two small puncture wounds? It looks like a snake bite."

Jack bends down to take a closer look.

"So what are you saying? A rattler did this?"

"I won't know anything definite until the results of the toxicology screen come back."

After the M.E. flips the body over again, they spend a few minutes examining the snake tattoo at the base of the woman's spine. Then the doctor reaches for a small magnifying glass.

"Jack, it looks like this tattoo was done within forty-eight hours of her death, and I know who did it. This particular artist always puts his initials into his work, and I've seen other bodies with his tattoos. Here, look at the head of the snake.

You can see the letters, 'TJ.' He's the owner of Lauderdale Ink on the east end of Las Olas."

Doctor Ghosh writes up some notes, then asks for Jack's help in turning the body onto its back so he can begin his internal exam by opening up the corpse, like a frog in a high school science lab. He starts the process by sawing into the sternum and spreading the ribs apart to get to the heart and lungs.

"Doc, no matter how many of these I've seen, I still get a little queasy."

Laughing while he checks the heart, he calls to Jack.

"Hey, we have some visual damage here. Could have been cardiac infarction, commonly known as cardiac arrest."

"A heart attack? That's kind of unusual in someone this young."

"Well, the toxic screen will show if any drugs are present, but from what I'm seeing, yeah, it is kind of unusual."

"Okay, Doc. Let me know when the tox screen comes back, or if you find out anything else. There's a tattoo artist I have to talk to."

Before leaving the doctor to complete his work, Jack takes a photo of "Jane Doe" with his cell phone, then exits the building.

On the way to speak with TJ at Lauderdale Ink, Jack stops for a quick fast food breakfast. As he eats his McMuffin and drinks his coffee, he mulls over the way his life has been going lately, and comes to the conclusion that South Florida is not for him anymore. He needs more action, more jazz, so he decides to start sending his resume to police departments in larger cities. He intends to try Chicago and New York first, just to see what type of reaction he gets.

Sean LeDue is on his way to the art gallery he owns on Las Olas Boulevard. Because Fort Lauderdale Police have not yet released any detailed information about the discovery at the beach, he's confident that none of his employees would know who was found there. While he drives, he contacts his insurance company to arrange for a counselor to come into the art gallery to speak to his employees about the incident. That way, he expects it will make them think that he has their well-being at heart, while he really doesn't give a shit about any of them. Sean is only worried about his business, and he wants to get as much productivity out of his employees as possible.

CHAPTER THREE

It is late morning when Jack pulls up in front of Lauderdale Ink, and the outside temperature is already close to ninety degrees. The morning rain shower didn't reduce the temperature; it just steamed up the road, increasing the humidity to an unbearable level. Walking from the car to the tattoo parlor produces beads of sweat across Jack's forehead. As he sweats, he thinks to himself, *Well, if I die and go to hell today, it'll give me a chance to cool off. I'm* really *tired of this heat!*

The blast of cold air that hits him as he walks into the tattoo parlor is a godsend, along with the pretty, multi-tattooed young lady who greets him as he flashes his ID.

"Morning. I'm Detective Stenhouse, and I need to speak to TJ. Is he in?"

The pretty young lady rolls her eyes and takes a deep breath.

"He's in the back, in his office. I'll tell him you're here."

When she walks through a door at the back of the tattoo parlor, Jack takes a moment to survey his surroundings.

The place has ceramic tile floors, a granite countertop, granite-topped tables, an espresso coffee machine, and a lounge area with a widescreen TV. Not your stereotypical, dingy tattoo parlor.

"Detective Stenhouse?"

Turning toward the voice, Jack quickly sizes up the tattoo artist, who is looming before him. He is bald, about six-foot-six inches tall, and close to two hundred fifty pounds, with various earrings and piercings. He's wearing a leather vest with a white V-neck tee shirt over jeans and combat boots.

From where Jack stands, he can see that tattoos cover both of the man's arms, including his exposed neck and chest area.

At six-foot-one inch tall, Jack is not a small man, but he feels like a dwarf next to this guy. When he extends his hand, he hopes it won't be crushed.

"TJ? I'm Detective Stenhouse, Fort Lauderdale Police."

TJ shakes Jack's hand with a very calm, firm grip. "What can I do for you, Detective?"

"Is there a place we can talk privately?"

TJ guides Jack into his office, where he closes the door behind them. Confirming that the door is closed, Jack takes out his cell phone and works the buttons until it displays Jane Doe's photo, then hands the phone to TJ.

"Do you recognize this woman?"

"Why, yes, I do. That's Cindy. She was here two days ago. I put a snake on her lower back."

"Well, Cindy was found dead this morning, buried on the beach. Can you tell me anything about her?"

"Wow, that's awful!" He lowers his head in shock, and the big man sheds a small tear. "That is a first for me. She was a beautiful woman. Why would anyone do that?

"Oh, sorry, Detective. Lost it there for second. Let me see what I have; I try to keep records of all my clients. If you give me a minute, I'll pull up her information on my computer."

Sitting down at his desk, TJ works the keyboard to access his client files.

"Here she is. Cynthia Walsh. She wanted to be called Cindy. She lives in Plantation and works for LeDue Gallery on Las Olas, right up the road from here. Or at least she used to. The snake is some kind of corporate logo thing. She said most of the female employees there have one, and she was one of the last ones to get it. She was very nervous about getting marked."

"Did she seem upset about anything else?"

"No, kinda flirty, very outgoing. She was well-endowed and liked to show it. She seemed a little trampy to be working for an art gallery, though. I tattooed a few women from there, and a couple of them seemed out of place."

"How do you mean, 'out of place'?"

"Oh, I don't know, I don't go to art galleries, but I always thought that the people who worked at those kinds of places would be more reserved and demure."

"Cindy wasn't?"

"No, she came across like a bimbo."

Jack knew bimbos, and TJ was right. You normally don't see bimbos at an art gallery, especially on Las Olas Boulevard.

"Thanks, TJ. Can you get me the names of the other women you worked on from that gallery?"

"Sure, no problem. I'll print their information out for you, along with Cindy's."

Within a couple of minutes, Jack has a list of four women that TJ has tattooed with the snake logo.

After thanking TJ for his cooperation, Jack hands him a business card and tells him to call if he remembers anything that he may have forgotten, then leaves the tattoo parlor.

When Jack enters the Road Runner, he immediately turns on the ignition and cranks up the vehicle's air conditioning. While waiting for it to get cold, he considers his next move, and decides that he needs to stop at the LeDue Gallery. However, before he can put the car into drive, he receives a call on his cell phone.

"Hello? *What?* Another body? Where? ... I'm on my way."

He grabs a red, flashing strobe light from his dashboard and places it on the roof of his car, enjoying the advantage of his law enforcement position to dodge traffic on his way to investigate the city's crimes.

This latest crime isn't the only thing on his mind, however, as he speeds to the Broward Convention Center. Mumbling aloud, he complains, "This is really getting old. I can't *stand* this heat anymore!"

CHAPTER FOUR

When Sean arrives at his art gallery on Las Olas, he immediately notices that all of his female employees are visibly shaken, presumably because they've heard the news reports about the snake tattoo on the dead woman, even though the body on the beach has yet to be identified.

He immediately herds all the employees into a group in the center of the gallery and locks the front door so they won't be disturbed.

"I've gathered you all together to talk about the news that I'm sure you've already heard this morning. I called the police station on the way in and they told me that a Detective Stenhouse has been assigned to investigate the case of the woman on the beach. I gave them my phone number and told them about our snake logo, and they said they'd pass the information on to the detective. He should be in touch with me later today. I also arranged for a counselor to come into the gallery this morning to talk to anyone who wants to discuss their feelings about this incident, and I'll be available if anyone wants to talk to me privately. I would like all of you to stay here until the detective and the counselor arrive, but if you feel you need to go home for the day, please make yourself available for questioning by the police at a later time. I gave them my word that we would cooperate with their investigation."

At the sound of a knock at the door, heads turn to see a middle-aged woman holding an attaché case in one hand, while peering through the glass door with the other.

Sean walks to the door and unlocks it, then slowly opens it inward.

"Yes? Can I help you? We're having a staff meeting this morning."

"Yes, you can help me. I'm Doctor Linda Sanders. I was sent here by America Insurance Company for emergency crisis counseling."

"Oh, good! That was quick! Doctor, come right in."

At the loading dock area of the Broward Convention Center, two Fort Lauderdale Police cruisers are parked near a large garbage truck. When Jack pulls up alongside the cars, he is greeted by a uniformed officer.

"Hey, Jack! Been busy today?"

"Yeah. What do ya have here, numb nuts?"

"The driver over there, from Lauderdale Waste Recycling, found a body in the paper recycling dumpster. Lucky for him, he saw the body before he dumped it into his truck. His name is James Reynolds. He's been working for LWR for ten years."

Jack walks over to the driver, who is standing in front of his truck.

"Mr. Reynolds, my name is Detective Jack Stenhouse. Can you tell me what happened?"

"Well, we were given instructions to look in all the dumpsters before we pick them up, because about six months ago, one of our drivers picked up a dumpster behind a supermarket that a homeless guy was sleeping in. He wasn't injured, but he lawyered up and cost the company a small fortune. So before I picked up the dumpster here, I got out of the truck to see if anyone was inside, and there she was. I called 911, and now, here you are. Look, I'm late with my route. Can I leave now?"

"Sure, just give your statement to one of those officers, and take this business card. If you remember anything else, give me a call immediately."

Jack walks over to the dumpster, but before peering inside, puts on the pair of protective gloves that he grabbed from the glove box before exiting his vehicle.

The dumpster is filled almost to the top with various waste paper products, but lying on top of everything is a beautiful young woman who looks almost like Sleeping

Beauty, except that she is wearing hip hugger jeans and a bikini top.

Jack lifts the body slightly to take a look at the woman's back, and sees the snake tattoo that he had a sneaking suspicion he would find there. Laying the body back down, he examines the area behind the woman's ears and sees the same puncture marks that are on Cindy's body back in the morgue.

When the police crime scene team arrives, Jack moves away from the dumpster to let them do their thing, but before getting back into his car to continue on his way to the LeDue Gallery, he returns to take a photo of the body with his cell phone camera.

Once he's back in the car, he places a call to Doctor Ghosh to tell him that a second young woman is coming into the morgue with the same marks on her body that are on the morgue's current resident, and he also inquires about the tox screen results, but the M.E. replies that he does not expect any reports until morning.

Ending the call, Jack leaves the convention center and drives toward Las Olas Boulevard, a trendy, tree-lined shopping district with boutiques, galleries and restaurants where people can window shop or sit in outdoor cafés drinking lattes and eating quiche.

With parking at a premium on Las Olas, Jack pulls into the lot behind the LeDue Gallery and walks around to the front of the building. The door to the gallery is locked, but he sees people milling about inside. When he knocks, a young woman unlocks the door.

"Hello. Please excuse us, we don't usually have the door locked. We're under a little stress this morning. Can I help you?"

Jack displays his ID and police badge. "I'm Detective Stenhouse with the Fort Lauderdale Police. Is Mr. LeDue in?"

"Yes, yes. Please come in."

The woman guides him to an office at the back of the building.

"Mr. LeDue, there's a policeman here to see you," she calls through the closed door.

Opening the door slightly, Sean asks, "Can I help you, officer?"

"Yes, I'm Detective Stenhouse. I need to speak with you."

"Okay, come in, please."

Sean waits for Jack to enter the office, then closes the door behind him and offers him a seat in one of the two chairs that are situated in front of a large desk, while he seats himself in the plush chair behind it.

Not one to waste time with pleasantries, Jack begins his questioning without delay.

"Mr. LeDue, do you know Cynthia Walsh?"

"Yes, I do, she's one of the hostesses here at the gallery, but she's not at work today. Why are you asking about her? Hey, wait a minute; she isn't the woman they found on the beach, is she?"

"Yes, she is."

Pulling his cell phone from his pocket, Jack searches through the saved photos on his device, and when he finds the one he wants, he shows it to Sean.

“We found another young woman this morning. Do you know who this woman is?"

"Oh, God, that's Lisa! Lisa Stevens!"

"Another hostess?"

"No, she was an administrative assistant. Wow! I can't believe this!"

"Did she also work here at the gallery?"

"No, no, she worked for my company, Mamba Imports, LLC, at another location."

"Did the two women know each other?"

"Yes, they worked together at auctions and showings."

"Why would both of them have a snake tattoo on their lower backs?"

"Oh, um, that's our company logo. Some of our employees like to display it as a tattoo."

"Mr. LeDue, I'm investigating both of these deaths as homicides. Do you have any idea why someone would want these young ladies dead?"

"Ah, no. Uh, no. Not that I know of."

"Okay, Mr. LeDue. I'll need you to give me all the information you have on these two women, and I'll also need you to be available to the police for further questioning. Since you and your company are the only link we have right now to both of them, you'll need to stay in town until we've completed our investigations.

"Detective, I'll cooperate with you as much as I can. Now sit right there, and I'll get you their personnel files."

When he waits, Jack begins to think. His first impression of Sean LeDue is that he seems nervous and uneasy, and although he can't put his finger on it, something doesn't seem right. He decides to give Mamba Imports, LLC, a thorough investigation.

After a few minutes, Sean returns to the office with two files, one for Cindy and one for Lisa. Handing both of them to Jack, he says, "Here you go, Detective. If there is anything else you need, feel free to call me."

"Thank you, and I will call. I'll also need to speak to some of your employees here, as well those at Mamba Imports."

"Well, because we heard about the snake tattoo on the news, I gave most of my employees the day off today, but you can come back any time. Just call ahead, and we'll make the arrangements."

"Will do, Mr. LeDue, will do."

The two men shake hands, then Sean escorts Jack out of the gallery.

When he's sure that Jack has left the building, Sean returns to his office, closes the door, and makes a phone call.

"This is Sean. You need to keep a close eye on this Detective Stenhouse. I want you to keep track of everything that's going on, and I want to know everything that he finds out. That's why you're on the payroll."

The moment he hangs up from that call, he makes a second one.

"Scott, it's Sean. Did you see the news this morning? Lisa and Cindy were found dead. I need you here right now! We need to talk."

On the other end of the line, Scott Simms is in shock. When the call from Sean ends, he rushes out of his apartment and heads to the art gallery as fast as he can.

Scott is extremely upset. More upset than he ought to be.

CHAPTER FIVE

Late in the afternoon, Jack's phone rings at his desk at police headquarters on Broward Boulevard.

"Jack, it's Doctor Ghosh. I have some news for you."

"I'll come right over. I'll be at your office in about ten minutes."

Jack hangs up and quickly walks away from his desk.

"Hey, Jack! Where ya goin'?"

"Just doin' my job, Wayne. Headin' over to see Doctor Ghosh."

"Hey, let me come with ya."

Sergeant Jackson begins to walk across the office to join Jack, but he is stopped by their boss, Captain Jeffers.

"Where the hell are you going, Wayne?"

"I thought I'd join up with Jack to see what's new at the morgue."

"Oh, yeah? Did you solve the carjacking yet? No? Then leave Jack alone and get back to work!"

"But, Captain..."

"But? No buts! In fact, get your butt into my office!"

Jack drives to the morgue while Wayne gets a lecture.

At the art gallery, Scott Simms is sitting in Sean LeDue's office while he waits for Sean to get off the phone. When Sean hangs up, he looks over at Scott.

"What the hell is going on, Scott? First Cindy, then Lisa?"

"I, ah, don't know. I don't know!"

"Look, you worked with them last. Anything I should know? Drugs, maybe?"

"No, no. No drugs. The photo shoot went well."

"Yeah? Well, you need to recruit another crew immediately. I have commitments to make!"

"Maybe we should delay until the cloud clears."

Pulling a DVD from his desk drawer, Sean flashes it at Scott and shouts, "No delays! Get it done, or the cops get *this*!"

Jack walks down the long hallway to Doctor Ghosh's office, knocks on the door, and walks in.

"So what's up, Doc?" He snickers. "I always wanted to say that."

Ignoring the lame joke, Doctor Ghosh responds, "Jack, I've got more news for you. First, Jane Doe number one was about four weeks pregnant. Second, there was a contusion on the back of the second Jane Doe's head. It wasn't a fatal blow. There was no sign of concussion, but it probably knocked her out. Third, both of them had the same tattoo on their lower backs and the same puncture wounds on their necks. However, the puncture wounds were not made by a snake. They are not curved under the skin, but go in straight. Also, both of the victims appear to have suffered from either heart failure or another type of thrombosis. There is considerable damage to both of their hearts, and both of their lungs have been compromised. I did a toxicology screen on the second victim, and I'll compare it to the results from the first one."

"They would be Cynthia Walsh and Lisa Stevens."

"These two women?"

"Yeah, they both worked for Sean LeDue, an art dealer on Las Olas."

"Well, Jack, we still don't have a definite cause of death for either one of them; however, the evidence we do have points to homicide. Someone wanted those puncture marks to appear as if they were made by a snake bite."

"Well, that's just great. Now I have to get into the mind of a killer and reason why he did what he did. Maybe he just likes snakes. Look Doc, it's my job to find out who and why, and I need you to find out how."

"Jack, there's more. I did a rape examination on both women. Neither of them appears to have been raped, but semen was present with Lisa, the second victim, and as I said earlier, the first victim, Cindy, was pregnant. I took a sample of the semen and ran a DNA check. I can have results on that in a couple of days, if I rush it."

"Thanks, please do." Running a hand through his hair, Jack continues, "Doc, I'm done for the day. If you find out anything new, give me a call. If not, I'll touch base with you in the morning."

Turning away from Doctor Ghosh, Jack leaves the M.E.'s office and walks back to his car. He finds that he cannot get Cindy's face out of his mind.

As he drives out of the parking area, he remembers that he has a dinner date with Didi.

Suddenly, his cell phone rings. "Yeah? This is Jack."

"Hi, Hon. Just calling to remind you about our dinner date. I'm workin' today at Shangri La, and I get off at six. Pick me up there, okay?"

"Sure, no problem. Maybe I'll get there early and watch you for a while."

"You're bad, Jack. See you later."

Jack smiles as he heads home to do his three S's before he meets Didi. He also wants to take a few minutes to update his resume so he can send out job queries as soon as possible. Jack does not want to remain in South Florida any longer than possible.

At Shangri La, Didi is getting ready to go on stage. She has been working the pole at the club since her college days at the University of Miami in Coral Gables. At first she worked there to pay for tuition, but the money was so good, and she was so good at what she did, that she kept going back, even after she got her business degree. The motivating factor for her unusual career choice is a desire to quickly build a nest egg large enough to enable her to retire early and move away from Florida, up to the Big Apple.

What she doesn't know, is that Jack also wants to move out of Florida.

CHAPTER SIX

With two of the S's done, Jack steps out of the shower and towels off. Grabbing the shaving foam, he lathers up his face, then wipes the condensation from his bathroom mirror. He shaves quickly, hits the deodorant and the aftershave, and then pulls on a black V-neck tee shirt, over which he straps his shoulder holster. Before pulling on a pair of black Dockers, he holsters a .38 snub nose with the serial number ground off over his right ankle, then dons a pair of black leather sneakers and a tan sports coat that was in style five years ago. Patting his shoulder holster, Jack is comforted by the untraceable gun that he always carries, just in case he needs it.

Before leaving the condo for Shangri La, a premier gentlemen's club on Federal Highway, Jack turns his laptop on so he can update his resume. He intends to email it out in the morning, hoping that he'll get some hits sooner rather than later.

At about 5:30 p.m., Jack pulls into the Shangri La parking lot, taking up two spots so no one can park next to him.

At the front door, he is stopped from entering by a commotion involving an over-served customer. As he watches two bouncers escort the customer out of the building, the drunk suddenly breaks free and lays out one of the men with a quick overhand right. Then, turning like a fugitive from an Ultimate Fighter Octagon match, the drunk puts a quick knee to the jaw of the other bouncer, and lays him out as well.

Never one to stand aside, Jack sizes things up and quickly steps behind the patron, grabbing the drunkard by the hair and smashing his nose into the side of the building, instantly stunning him. Then, he takes out his 9mm and smashes it up against the side of the bleeding man's head, causing him to drop to the ground. As the drunkard lies there incapacitated, Jack helps the first bouncer up while he re-holsters his weapon.

Looking around, Jack notices the club manager, who arrived in the middle of the commotion. He flashes his badge at him and says, "Better call 911 to get the EMTs out here. Sorry I got blood all over your wall."

Leaving the manager to tidy up, he walks inside the club and heads straight for the bathroom. He needs to clean off any blood splatters before he enters the lounge area to watch Didi onstage, caressing the pole.

When he finally walks into the lounge, he finds Didi walking toward him. She has already changed out of her costume and is ready to go to dinner. Sadly, he realizes that he missed her entire performance.

Greeting Jack with a smile, Didi asks, “Where we goin' for dinner, Jack? I'm hungry!"

"Hi, Doll! I tried to get here in time to watch you, but some shit-for-brains had to be taken care of first. How's Japanese sound?"

"Great! Let's go."

The EMTs pull up before they can reach the parking lot, so Jack takes a moment to detail the evening’s events, then he escorts Didi to his Road Runner and they drive off toward the Intracoastal Waterway, to one of those Japanese restaurants where the chef cooks the food right at your table.

Scott Simms’ evening isn’t going very well. He is in his studio apartment in Hollywood Beach, doing his best to finish off a liter of scotch while trying to ignore the incessant ringing of his telephone. When it finally stops, he sighs deeply in the ensuing silence and gulps down another scotch.

While he is pouring himself yet another glass, the phone rings again, but this time it doesn’t stop. Reluctantly, he picks it up.

"Hello?" Hearing no answer, he says again, "Hello?" After a pause, he hears, "Scott, Cindy is gone and now Lisa is gone. You're the only one left. Get my drift? I need the tape."

"How do I know you won't kill me after I give it to you?"

"Ha! That's the best part, Scott. You don't. But I *will* kill you if you don't. You got forty-eight hours. I'll call you again to remind you, and to make arrangements to pick it up."

The phone call ends abruptly, but not Scott's drinking. It continues all evening until he passes out.

When Jack and Didi walk into the Japanese restaurant, all eyes turn toward Didi and her double D's. Wearing a black mini cocktail dress and six-inch heels, she could make an atheist go to confession. Jack loves the attention; arm candy never hurt anyone. The hostess escorts them to a large table, where they will sit with six other diners. As they wait for the hostess to fill the remaining seats, Didi moves her hand under the table to find Jack's knee.

"So tell me, how did your day go today? Were you involved with the investigation of that woman they found on the beach?"

"Actually, there were two women today, one on the beach, and one in a dumpster. Both of them were lookers."

"Oh, Jack, that's terrible!"

"Yeah, and the first one on the beach was pregnant. Her name was Cynthia Walsh."

"My God! *Cindy*?"

"You knew her?"

"Yeah! She used to wait tables at Shangri La!"

"Damn! That's where I saw her. When did she leave there?"

"Oh, about four weeks ago. Some guy came in and offered her a job as a hostess and also promised her some movie work. She said it was some fancy art dealer. Jack, she always wanted to be an actress."

"Do you remember what the guy looked like?"

"No, I can't see much from the stage, the lights are too bright. He did walk with a limp, though."

"That art dealer wasn't named Sean LeDue, was he?"

"Cindy didn't mention a name. All she said was something like... Mamba? That's all I can remember."

Jack plants a kiss on Didi's lips. "Perfect, Babe! That's just what I needed."

Didi moves her hand up Jack's thigh, but he pulls it away.

"Later, Babe."

As the hostess returns to the table, followed by their fellow diners, Jack's cell phone rings. It's Doctor Ghosh.

"Jack here, and this better be good."

There is silence on Jack's end as he listens intently.

"Okay, how late will you be there? Nine it is. Thanks, Doc."

"Leaving again, Jack?" Didi pouts and leans over, pressing her breasts against Jack's shoulder.

"Yeah, but we got time to eat dinner and knock boots at my place before I have to leave." Whispering in her ear, he adds, "And then I'll be back for round two."

Didi smiles at him while everyone else around the table introduces themselves, and the chef begins to describe what's on the menu.

CHAPTER SEVEN

After their delicious dinner, Jack pays the bill, then frowns as he glances at his watch. Turning to Didi, he announces, "Babe, I didn't realize it was so late. Since it's now 8:35, I won't have time to drop you off before I meet with the M.E., so I guess you'll have to come with me. Ever been to the morgue?"

"The *morgue*?"

"Yeah, it shouldn't take long. Anyway, I like havin' you around."

Ten minutes after roaring out of the parking lot, they arrive at the receiving entrance of the morgue, and Jack and Didi head down the hallway to Doctor Ghosh's office. The doctor is surprised to see a woman walking in ahead of Jack, and stands up quickly to greet her. Reaching out his hand, he introduces himself.

"Well, hello, there! I'm Doctor Ghosh."

"Put your tongue back in your mouth, Doc, you're drooling all over your carpet. This is Deidra Lee."

Didi ignores Jack and grasps the doctor's hand, saying, "Pleased to meet you, Doctor. Please call me Didi."

Motioning to the doctor to grab his attention, Jack informs him, "We were at a restaurant eating dinner when you called, and I didn't have time to drop Didi off. So tell me, what have you found?"

Back in business mode, the doctor replies, "Well, there are two things, Jack. First, both women were killed by a neurotoxin that paralyzed their muscles, including their hearts. They probably died within four to six minutes of receiving the toxin."

"What type of toxin was it?"

"Some kind of snake venom, very potent. There was probably enough toxin in each of their systems to kill an elephant."

"Which snake was it? A rattler?"

"No, you couldn't get that much venom from five rattlers. It was probably a black mamba, one of the quickest and deadliest snakes in Africa. They call it the Shadow of Death."

"Where would you get that venom here in Florida? Oh, wait, wasn't there a guy who held snake shows here a while ago, where people came to watch him milk venom from cobras and rattlers?"

"You mean Doctor Benjamin Handel? Yes, I remember that he had a serpent show here until his building burned down about ten years ago. I heard that he still lives on his farm in west Broward County, off Alligator Alley. He doesn't hold shows there, but he does run a business harvesting venom for antidotes. If anyone has black mambas, I suppose it would be him. He supplies the world with antivenin."

"That's great information, Doc. I'll go out to see him tomorrow."

"There's more, Jack. My crew pulled an all-nighter last night, and we got a hit on the DNA sample we took from Lisa. It belongs to a guy named Scott Simms. He's currently out on parole after serving a prison sentence for making and distributing child pornography. When he turned state's witness, he got a reduced sentence. I contacted his probation officer and found out that he works for Mamba Imports, an art import and export business."

"Man, this is tying together very nicely! I'll have some uniforms pick him up." Glancing at Didi, he says, "Looks like I'm going to be busy."

On their way back to the condo, Jack calls Captain Jeffers to pass on the information he received from Doctor Ghosh, and to ask the captain to send a couple of uniformed cops to pick up Scott Simms as soon as possible.

Upon hearing Jack's report, Captain Jeffers wastes no time and immediately orders two uniformed officers to contact Scott's probation officer and meet him at Scott's studio apartment.

Scott is fast asleep on the sofa in a drunken stupor, so he doesn't respond when one of the police officers knocks on his door later that night. In the resulting silence, the probation officer impatiently steps up to the door and pounds on it, shouting, "SCOTT! OPEN UP!"

At that, the officers hear a rustling noise inside the apartment, and then a voice cries out, "GO AWAY, OR I'LL CALL THE COPS!"

In unison, the trio responds, "WE *ARE* THE COPS! OPEN UP, OR WE BUST IT DOWN!"

In his half-drunken state, Scott shouts back obscenities, bellowing out a verb and then a pronoun.

Because of hurricane building codes, the door of this first floor apartment opens out to prevent strong winds from blowing it in, so the cops know that busting it down won't be easy. One of the officers walks back to their police cruiser and quickly returns with a crowbar. But before continuing with their plan, the officers shout through the closed door one more time to ask Scott to cooperate.

"HEY, SCOTT! ARE WE DOIN' THIS THE EASY WAY, OR THE HARD WAY?"

Scott's response is a loud profanity shouted through the closed door. Alcohol makes everyone a little braver, but much more stupid.

At Scott's retort, the officers shrug their shoulders and move into action. One of them shoves the crowbar between the door and the doorjamb and forces the door open. Then the three of them charge into the apartment, only to find Scott half asleep on the sofa. Grabbing his shirt, one of the officers yanks Scott off the sofa and places him on the floor, where he cuffs his hands behind his back and lifts him onto his feet in one sweeping motion.

"Mr. Simms, you know that not following a police officer's instructions could violate your probation, don't you?" asks the probation officer brusquely.

Still a sleepy drunk, Scott mumbles incoherently as the trio escorts him out of his apartment.

CHAPTER EIGHT

Before driving Didi to her own place the next morning, Jack emails his resume to police departments in Chicago and New York. Both departments are currently looking for experienced homicide detectives, so he has his fingers crossed.

When Jack finally arrives at work this morning, it's a little later than usual, so before stopping at his desk, he walks into Captain Jeffers' office.

"Morning, sir. Did we pick up Scott Simms last night?"

Glaring at Jack, the captain retorts, "Glad you could make it in, Jack. We started half an hour ago. Yeah, he's in lockup, but we can't hold him for more than twenty-four hours without charging him with something."

"Look, I know he's involved in those two homicides. I just need to figure out his connection to them."

Sighing noisily, the captain replies, "I'll have him brought to Interrogation Room Two. You can talk to him there."

"Thanks, Captain. I'll be waiting."

Shaking his head, Captain Jeffers calls down to the lockup to order Scott Simms to be brought into Interrogation Room Two.

As Jack heads out of the captain's office, he mumbles to himself, “I hope I don't have to put up with his shit much longer.”

Jack lets Scott squirm alone in the interrogation room while he alternately reads the arrest record from the night before and studies Scott through the one-way mirror in the adjacent room. When he feels that Scott is sufficiently restless, he enters the room and sits across the table from him.

"Did you have a nice rest, Mr. Simms?"

Scott is seriously hung over from his drinking binge and can barely open his eyes for fear he will bleed to death.

"Hey, man. Can I get some coffee and a Coke?"

"Sure, in a minute. I need some answers first."

With the homicide case files in front of him, Jack pulls out two photos, one of Lisa and one of Cindy, and places them face up on the table in front of Scott.

"Do you know these two women?"

As he looks at the photos, Scott becomes very nervous. Pointing at each photo in turn, he states, "Yeah, that's Lisa, and that's Cindy. They used to work for Mamba Imports."

"'Used to'? They were recently murdered, Scott. What do you know about that?"

Scott stares at the floor to avoid eye contact, then responds, "Sean LeDue told me they were found dead yesterday. It was such a shock!"

"Really? Tell me, Scott, why would an art gallery owner hire a convicted filmmaker and distributor of child pornography?"

Lowering his head in shame, Scott just confesses like he was talking to his parish priest. "Look, I was the cameraman for those films, that's all, and I'm not proud of what I did. I turned state's witness, but I was convicted along with my former boss. Mr. LeDue is my boss now, and he doesn't mind hiring people who are on probation, or on parole. Now I take videos of art auctions and post photos of LeDue's new inventory on his website. I also manage the inventory and his warehouse."

"Where do Cindy and Lisa fit into all of that?"

"They were hostesses at auctions and dinner parties that LeDue held for buyers at his showroom and gallery."

"Did you ever work directly with them, or go out with them socially?"

Scott stares off into space, stopping the conversation.

"Scott! Pay attention! Did you hear the question?"

"No. I mean yes. I worked with them at auctions. I didn't see them socially."

"Mr. Simms. Can you explain how your semen was found on, or shall I say in, Lisa's body?"

Running his fingers through his hair, Scott replies, "Yeah, okay, we were dating. It was getting serious, and now she's dead."

"Do you know why anyone would want to kill her? Did she have any enemies?"

"Look, charge me with something, or let me go. I got nothin' else."

Jack stands up and walks out of the interrogation room with the two case files. After closing the door, he enters the adjoining room and finds Captain Jeffers and Sergeant Jackson observing Scott through the one-way mirror. Joining them at the mirror, the three of them watch as two guards escort the suspect out of the room.

When Scott is out of view, Jack turns to his boss and declares, "Captain, I know he's hiding something. I need to talk to him at least one more time."

"Well, Jack, you're in luck. Since he may be in violation of his parole, we can keep him here for a couple of days until the D.A. lets us know the status of his case."

"Great! Then I'm going to take some time now to drive out west to speak to the snake guy. I'll catch up with you later."

Jack climbs into his Road Runner and heads for Alligator Alley, the east-west road that stretches out to the far reaches of western Broward County. After a forty-five minute drive, he turns north onto a government road and approaches a group of buildings alongside a large, walled-in area. He pulls the Road Runner up to the front entrance of the main building and walks into a small lobby, where he is greeted by a receptionist behind a small, sliding glass window.

"Hello. Can I help you?"

Jack displays his badge and ID card. "Yes, I'm Detective Jack Stenhouse, Fort Lauderdale Police. I need to speak with Doctor Handel."

"Oh? I'll check with Doctor Handel."

After the receptionist leaves her post, Jack looks around the room and notices that there are photos of various types of snakes on each wall of the lobby, with one prominent photo showing Doctor Handel holding a king cobra. As Jack examines the photo, a door opens, and Doctor Handel walks into the room.

"Detective Stenhouse, I'm Benjamin Handel."

Exchanging a quick handshake with the doctor, Jack is taken aback by his firm grip. "Wow, that's some grip, Doc."

"Thanks. It stops me from being bitten. Come on in."

Jack follows the doctor to his office, where he is motioned over to a table and two chairs in the lounge area of the office as the doctor softly closes the door behind them.

"Have a seat, Detective."

Jack sits at the small table while the doctor takes the chair next to him and asks, "What can I do for you?"

"Doctor Handel, there were two homicides in Fort Lauderdale yesterday, and both murder victims had what the medical examiner discovered to be high levels of a neurotoxin injected into the arteries in their necks. He said the amount injected into each victim would probably have killed an elephant. I'd like to know if that neurotoxin was from snake venom."

"Well, there is only one species of venomous snake that could produce that much venom, and that would be the black mamba."

"Interesting, but where would someone get black mamba venom in South Florida? I thought they were found only in Africa."

"I have a couple of black mambas here as part of my collection. That species has the unique ability to keep producing venom, strike after strike. And the medical examiner is most correct. Those serpents can certainly deliver enough venom to kill an elephant."

"You haven't had any thefts or burglaries lately, have you?"

"Actually, we had a break-in about two weeks ago, but I think it was done by a bunch of kids. They spray-painted the walls, broke some windows, and stole a couple of computers. We are on Seminole Indian land out here, so I reported it to their Tribal Council, but since the Indians have limited resources, they referred it to Fort Lauderdale. A Sergeant Jackson came out and took a statement, but he basically said there wasn't anything they could do. He helped me straighten up, though, and we didn't find any venom missing."

"Do you mind if I take a look at the area that was vandalized?"

“Sure, no problem. Follow me.”

Doctor Handel escorts Jack to his lab at the back of the building and guides him over to a commercial-sized refrigerator. The doctor explains that the refrigerator contains drawers holding vials of venom that are labeled and stored in alphabetical order by snake species.

Opening the refrigerator door, the doctor locates the drawer containing *polylepis dendroaspis*, the scientific name for black mambas, but after pulling open the drawer, he gasps audibly.

"That's odd!"

"What's wrong, Doc?"

"I usually keep four bottles of this venom on hand for when I get calls for antivenin, or when it’s needed for various types of medical research. They’re currently researching snake venom as a cure for hypertension. Well, the four bottles are here, but one of them is empty!"

"Didn't you check all of your stock after the break-in?"

"Yes, I checked the bottles. All of them were present, but I didn't check the contents of each bottle."

"How much venom does each bottle contain?"

"Detective, you could kill a couple of elephants with the contents of one of these black mamba vials. Inject someone with one quarter of the contents of one vial and they would be dead within minutes, especially if you introduced the venom into a major artery."

"Well, then, I guess it wasn’t kids who broke in here. Maybe the mess that was left behind was a cover-up for the theft of the venom. Listen, can I have the empty vial?"

"Yeah. I’m guessing you have a good idea of where the venom ended up."

Ignoring that comment, Jack hands Doctor Handel his business card.

“Doctor Handel, if you find anything else missing, please give me a call immediately."

Jack shakes the doctor's hand again, and as he leaves the building, Doctor Handel examines every bottle of snake venom in his inventory.

On the trip back to police headquarters, Jack has a nagging feeling that something is not right. Why would someone break into a snake business and steal venom if they wanted to kill someone? Wouldn't it be easier just to buy a gun and shoot the person dead? Jack decides that he needs to speak to Scott Simms again very soon, and he also wants to get the empty venom vial to the police forensics department. Flooring the Road Runner, he screams down the "Alley" back to Fort Lauderdale.

CHAPTER NINE

Once again, Jack stares at Scott Simms through the two-way mirror. He's letting Scott sit in the interrogation room alone again, hoping that the prisoner's solitary thoughts will make him nervous.

Captain Jeffers addresses Jack as he joins him in the observation room.

"Jack, we have to let him go. Mr. LeDue spoke with the D.A., and they decided there's no cause to press charges about Scott's relationship with the deceased."

“Give me fifteen minutes alone with him."

"You got five."

Jack enters the interrogation room and sits down across the table from Scott. "Morning, Scott. Want some coffee?"

"No, I just want to get out of here. Mr. LeDue visited me and said you would be letting me go. He's even paying for the door you guys broke down at my place."

"Look, Scott. You said you worked with Cindy and Lisa. Someone obviously wanted them dead. They died after being injected with enough snake venom to kill an elephant, and we think there's more of that venom out there. Tell me what you know."

Scott stares at the floor and shakes his head. "I can't. Not here, not now."

"Scott, take my card and call me. I don't think you want to end up like Lisa."

Jack leaves Scott alone again and returns to the observation room, watching as Scott continues to sit quietly at the table, staring at the floor. After a few minutes, a guard opens the interrogation room door and allows Scott to leave. Jack peeks out the door of his room and watches as Scott walks toward the officer who will begin the process of releasing him from police custody.

Sighing, Jack walks back to his desk and sits down, lost in thought. When Sergeant Jackson approaches him, he doesn't notice him until he speaks.

"How's the investigation going, Jack?"

"Oh, hey, Wayne. I need to talk to you about Doctor Handel. You were out at his place a couple of weeks ago, right? Tell me about it."

"Nothin' to tell. A bunch of kids came in, tore the place up, sprayed some graffiti on the walls, and took a couple of computers."

"Handel said you helped him straighten out the place and do a quick check to see if anything was missing."

"Felt sorry for the guy. I knew we wouldn't find who trashed the place, so I stayed a few minutes to help him get settled."

"Yeah, well, snake venom was taken. The same venom that killed our two victims. Enough venom to kill a couple of elephants, so he says."

Wayne begins to sweat profusely and pace back and forth. "Well, we didn't notice that anything was gone at the time. All of the venom was in its place. Listen, Jack, I gotta go. Good luck with your investigation."

Jack, wondering what just happened, watches Wayne Jackson leave the room, then he picks up the phone to place a call to Sean LeDue.

A man walks up to his desk as he is dialing and asks, "Detective Stenhouse?"

"That's me." Jack puts the phone down. "You are?"

"Frank DiCarlo. I smooth the beaches down in Fort Lauderdale. I gave a statement to one of your officers, and he said to come here and see you if I remembered anything else."

"That's right. Have a seat, Mr. DiCarlo. What do you have to tell me?"

"Well, I started my shift around three in the morning the day you found that body on the beach. I smooth out the sand and clean up the beach for the next day. There is usually no one on the beach that early, but that morning, I remember seeing a man walking up the beach, from the water to A1A. His dress slacks were rolled up so he wouldn't get them wet."

"Can you remember what he looked like? I could get an artist in here to do a sketch."

"No need. He just walked out of here as I came in."

Jack's eyebrows shoot up into his hairline and he jerks his head around. "The guy in the brown suit?"

"Yeah, that's the guy. In fact, I think he had on the same slacks."

"Thank you, Mr. DiCarlo. You've been a great help."

After Frank leaves the police station, Jack leans back in his chair, mulling over what just took place. *Wayne seems to be popping up all over this investigation. I'm going to have to question Scott Simms and Sean LeDue again.*

Breaking his reverie, Jack reaches for the phone and dials Sean LeDue.

"Hello, Mamba Imports," sings a young, female voice.

"Sean LeDue, please."

"May I tell him who's calling?"

"Detective Stenhouse, Fort Lauderdale Police."

"Thank you, Detective. Please hold."

At the art gallery, the receptionist walks over to Sean to let him know that he has a phone call.

"Mr. LeDue, Detective Stenhouse is on line one."

"Thank you, Stacy."

Sean walks into his office and closes the door behind him before he picks up the phone and punches line one.

"Good afternoon, Detective. What can I do for you?"

"Mr. LeDue, I need to speak with you again, and also with any of your employees who worked with Lisa and Cindy."

"Well, we'll all be at my warehouse showroom tonight. We're having a cocktail party to exhibit some new art objects that I just imported, and there will be an auction the following evening. Why don't you stop by? Let's say, eight o'clock? You can talk to my staff informally at the party. The warehouse is just off Perimeter Road, north of Fort Lauderdale Airport. Bring a date, if you like. Dress will be semi-formal."

"Thank you, Mr. LeDue. I'll see you later."

When Jack hangs up the phone, he immediately calls Didi.

"Hey, Babe, dress it up tonight, we're going to a cocktail party! I'll pick you up at seven-thirty."

Before Jack can rise from his desk to leave the station, he hears Captain Jeffers calling his name.

"*Jack!* Get into my office!"

CHAPTER TEN

"Sit down, Jack. I have another case I need you to work on right away. Vice has been working with Interpol and Scotland Yard on a case involving pornography exported out of the country to Europe, and they've traced the shipments to South Florida. They told us that the actresses in the flicks have snake tattoos on their lower backs, just like our two victims, so I need you to visit Mamba Imports."

"Well, actually, the timing's great! Sean LeDue just invited me to attend a cocktail party tonight at Mamba so I can interview a few of his employees. Captain, Scott Simms was the cameraman for that child porn ring video he was arrested for, and now he's doing film work for Sean LeDue. That's way too coincidental."

"Yeah, it sure is. We need to get proof of a connection, though, and someone on the inside would be a big help. Sergeant Jackson has been moonlighting as a security guard for Mamba, but we can't use him. He's currently under a quiet departmental investigation, because he hasn't been very cooperative in sharing what he knows about Mamba. We've also found out that there have been some large deposits into his bank account recently. I hate to ask this, Jack, but do you think you can get Didi to help us out?"

Momentarily speechless, Jack inquires icily, "You mean, put her in harm's way?"

"Listen, Jack. If Cindy and Lisa were making movies for Sean LeDue, he's going to need new actresses. I just want you to ask Didi to seem interested in Mamba's operation tonight, and to ask a few questions. You'll be right there with her, so there shouldn't be any problems. I'm working on getting someone from the department inside Mamba, but it may take a while. We're looking at a couple of graduates of the police academy who have undercover experience, but who haven't been seen by Wayne yet." The captain paced back and forth, contemplating his next sentence. “We could really use Didi’s help, Jack. By the way, I just got search warrants approved for Lisa’s and Cindy's apartments. They lived in the same complex but in different buildings. First thing in the morning, I want you to join the crime scene team while they search the apartments."

Jack’s cell phone rings as he leaves the captain's office. "Jack here."

"Hello, Jack. It’s Doctor Ghosh. The forensic techs have been sifting through the beach sand that was collected from around Cynthia's body, and they found a button, probably from a man's suit."

Nodding in agreement, Jack quickly responds, "Hmm, that’s interesting. I'm going to a cocktail party at Mamba Imports tonight, and I’d like to take that button with me to see if I can find a match there. I'll head over to your office now to sign it out. See you soon, Doc."

Jack climbs into his Road Runner and points it in the direction of the medical examiner’s office. After this stop, he will still have time to head home, change, pick up Didi, and then go to the party.

Evidence is starting to come together, and Jack couldn't be more pleased.

At Mamba Imports, Scott has been sitting in his boss’ office for over an hour, waiting for a meeting with Sean. When Sean finally appears, he closes the office door, sits down in the chair behind his desk, and stares at Scott with a scowl on his face. After a few minutes of uncomfortable silence, he begins speaking in an unusually quiet voice.

"I've been on the phone all afternoon, Scott, talking to my contacts downtown. What do you know about Cindy's pregnancy? And how long have you been doing Lisa?"

Surprised by Sean's direct questions, Scott decides that honesty is probably the best policy right about now, so he responds without hesitation.

"Lisa and I have been dating for a while. Cindy--that's news to me."

Now, Sean's voice is no longer quiet.

"Are you an *idiot*? I hired you to film movies that I could sell in Europe, and I supplied you with those two porn queens to star in them! One phone call from me to your probation officer, and you're back in jail for selling and distributing pornography! Why didn't you know that Cindy was pregnant? And how am I going to deliver the next movie without a cast?" He stood up, towering over Scott like an old oak tree. "Listen, you got your right leg busted up in jail last time. If you don't get me more actresses soon, I'll have your other leg busted up! You got that? Look—be on the lookout and watch yourself. That Detective Stenhouse is going to be snooping around at the party tonight. Be prepared for him, Scott. I make much more money exporting sex than art, but the art part of my business provides the money to make the porn, so you need to make a good impression tonight. Now, get out of here, and start setting things up for the party!"

Scott jumps up out of his seat and exits the office quickly. After he leaves, Sean runs his hand across his forehead, then calls his secretary. "Sherri! Go find Wayne Jackson, and have him come in here!"

A few minutes later, Wayne casually walks into Sean's office.

"You called me, Mr. LeDue?"

"Yes. Your buddy, Detective Stenhouse, will be at the party this evening, and he will probably be asking questions. Keep an eye on him. Also, Scott has become a liability to me. I'm interviewing new videographers in the morning, so I will no longer require his services. After the showing tonight, you need to take care of that problem."

CHAPTER ELEVEN

Jack is dressed casually this evening, wearing a tan sports jacket over a lightweight, black V-neck sweater, and black pants. He is ready to leave his condo for Didi's apartment in Dania Beach, two blocks from the ocean. She lives in a small, one-bedroom duplex, in a building with a small courtyard in front, and virtually no parking nearby.

His cell phone rings as he walks out his front door.

"This is Jack."

"Detective Stenhouse, this is Deputy Inspector Gene Rawlings, First Precinct, New York City Police. We need a seasoned homicide detective, and your resume fits our shopping list. I'd like you to come up to New York to speak with us, and to tell me why I should hire you."

Jack's heart does a double-flip, as he tries to remain cool and collected as he cashes. His ticket to the big time! "Inspector, I assure you that your search has ended. However, I'm right in the middle of a double homicide. As soon as I wrap things up here, I'll be happy to fly up there to talk with you."

"It's not that girl they found on the beach, is it? It's all over the news up here."

"Yeah, that's the one, but another victim is being tied to it. Do you have an email address where I can contact you?"

"Sure, it's dirawlings1p, at nypd dot org."

"That's great, Inspector, and thank you."

Jack hangs up, writes the email address down so he won't forget it, and heads over to Didi's. On the way, he mulls the same question over and over again in his mind. *If I get the job in New York, will Didi go up there with me?*

At Didi's apartment, he parks on the sidewalk, halfway into the courtyard, and walks up to her door, giving it a couple of hard knocks. Didi peers through the spy hole in the door and is surprised to see Jack, because he's early. When she opens the door, she's half naked.

"Jack, you're way too early. I'm only half dressed."

Jack walks past Didi, sits on the sofa in the living room, and says with a smile, "Well, that's one way to see you naked."

Walking over to Jack, Didi gives him a quick kiss on the cheek and states, "You know you can see me naked anytime you want, Jack." Then she turns around and walks into her bedroom to finish dressing for the evening, while Jack remains on the sofa.

Jack had every intention of waiting patiently on the sofa for Didi to finish dressing, but he knows that he needs to speak with her before they leave for the party. And after a few moments, he rises and walks into the bedroom.

He finds Didi in the bathroom, dressed only in her bra and panties, putting on her makeup.

"Hey, gorgeous! Can we talk for a minute? I need a favor from you tonight."

"Anything, Jack. What is it?"

"Don't be too quick to agree. You know that I'm still investigating those two murders, but what you don't know is that the investigation has led us to a pornography ring. Captain Jeffers asked me to request your help during the party tonight. He wants to know if you would assist us by talking to the gallery owner and making him think you're interested in becoming their new porn star. It seems that Lisa and Cindy, our two victims, were both part of the action there, so now those scum bags are short of 'talented ladies'. Babe, you've got more talent than you know, so would you be willing to help us out?"

"Of course I'll help you, Jack. You really know how to flatter a girl! However, you know diamonds work better."

"Yeah, from your lips to God's ears. Babe, I need you to dress appropriately for this situation tonight. You'll need to display your 'talents' so you can try to get as much information from them as you can. I'll be close by all night for protection and support."

"No problem. Now get out while I get dressed. I want to surprise you."

Jack leaves the bedroom and returns to the living room, thinking about diamonds. While he waits on the sofa, he turns on the TV and watches Fox News for the twenty minutes it takes Didi to make her grand entrance.

When she re-enters the living room, she's dressed in a bright red vinyl micro mini-dress that's cut low in the front and back, and looks like it was painted on. Her shoes are bright red patent-leather six-inch heels, and her long, reddish-brown hair is draped over her shoulders and flows down her back like a gentle waterfall. Her dress barely covers her large double D's, and they look like they're about to escape at any minute.

"Holy shit!" Jack stands up in amazement. "You look ...DAAAMMMNN! ... Are you wearing any underwear?"

"Nothing at all. Is this appropriate enough?"

"Wow! Now I don't want to go anywhere at all!"

Smiling brightly, Didi takes Jack's hand and practically drags him out to the car.

When Jack opens the passenger-side door, Didi slithers in, but Jack remains standing there, staring at her. Didi breaks his trance by grabbing the car's door handle and closing it. Jack quickly walks around the car and climbs into the driver's seat.

"Now, Jack, keep your eyes on the road. I want to get there in one piece, okay?"

Jack stares at her thighs, then her boobs. Shaking his head, he fires up the Road Runner, beeps the horn twice, and hauls ass.

After a fifteen-minute ride, they turn onto the road that loops around Fort Lauderdale International Airport and then pull into the parking lot of the Mamba Imports warehouse. The lot is almost full, but Jack manages to find a spot at the back of the lot.

As they walk up to the building, Jack stumbles over the curb while staring at Didi out of the corner of his eye.

"Where did you get that dress?"

"Bought it just for you," Didi purrs.

As Jack opens the door to the lobby of Mamba Imports, he addresses Sergeant Wayne Jackson, who is standing next to the door.

"Moonlighting, Wayne?"

"Yeah. Hi, Jack. I need the extra money; child support is killing me. I work security here, a lot of expensive art stuff."

With no comment, Jack leads Didi past Sergeant Jackson, then he reaches into his pocket and pulls out the button he signed out from Doctor Ghosh's office earlier in the day. Although the button seems to match Wayne's suit, there are no buttons missing from the sergeant's suit jacket this evening.

Before entering the main gallery area, Jack and Didi stop just inside the doorway. While surveying the crowd, Didi turns to Jack and whispers, "See that guy in the corner? He looks like the one who talked to Cindy at the club!"

"Really? Go on over there and grab his attention. I'll be right here."

As she begins to step away from Jack's side, Didi suddenly feels a light smack on her ass, so she turns and flashes Jack half a peace sign before continuing on her way.

While his woman melts into the crowd, Jack tries to keep her in sight, but he is soon distracted by a voice behind him.

"Welcome, Detective Stenhouse."

Turning toward the voice, Jack spots Sean LeDue standing behind him, with a very attractive young woman on his arm. He has the feeling that he has met the woman before.

"Evening, Mr. LeDue. And who is this lovely lady?"

"Detective Stenhouse, I'd like you to meet Miss Laura Connelly."

"My pleasure, Miss Connelly. Have we met before? You look very familiar."

"Why, yes, Detective. I work for Doctor Handel as his receptionist."

"Small world! What are you doing here?"

"Sean and I are... well, he invited me."

"You two are an item, huh? Well, that's a surprise."

"We met at his art gallery a few months ago, and we've been seeing each other ever since."

"I see. Well, Mr. LeDue, I'm going to mingle around and ask a few questions here and there. It was nice seeing you again, Laura."

While Jack walks around the crowd, he keeps an eye on Didi, who is talking to Scott at the other end of the room. After a while, he walks directly up to them and interrupts their conversation.

"Mr. Simms! We meet again."

At the sight of Jack, Scott hastily reaches into his suit pocket and hands a business card to Didi.

"Call me if you're interested. You'd be perfect."

Turning to Jack, Scott whispers, "We need to talk, but not here. There are too many ears here, and at the station, too. Meet me tonight at the downtown bus terminal, around midnight." Looking around, he spies Sergeant Jackson walking toward them and hurries away from Jack and Didi as fast as he can.

When Wayne reaches the couple, he comments, "Everything okay, Jack? And Didi, WOW!"

"Put your tongue back in your mouth, Wayne. Yeah, everything's just fine. Didi, I think we're done here. Let's go."

"Aw, Jack, the party hasn't started yet."

"Wait till we get back to my place. I'll show you the *real* party."

On the drive back to the condo, Jack thanks Didi for her help at the party, then takes a deep breath before asking her the question that's been gnawing at him all evening.

"Didi, I need to ask you something. If I made a career change and transferred to another city, would you come with me?"

Placing her hand on Jack's knee, Didi sighs, "Jack, I'd follow you to the moon."

CHAPTER TWELVE

Later that night, Jack quietly rolls out of bed, hoping he doesn't wake Didi. He steps over the red vinyl dress lying on the floor and leaves a note on the dresser to remind her where he's going. Then he dresses quickly and leaves the condo, hopping into his Road Runner for the trip to the bus terminal to meet Scott.

The bus terminal is a lonely place at midnight, so Jack takes a seat against the far wall in order to have a complete view of the empty terminal. Except for a couple of homeless guys milling about outside, he sees no one else. At one o'clock, he calls Didi to make sure she knows he's still at the terminal.

With only his thoughts to keep him company, he reflects on the evening's events, beginning with Scott Simms offering Didi a role in the pornographic movies that he's filming for his boss. Jack knew the job offer was all but inevitable, thanks to the outfit Didi was wearing at the party, but it provided Jack with everything he needed in order to link the pornography ring to Sean LeDue.

At one-thirty, tired of waiting for Scott to show up, Jack calls the police station to get Scott's address, then drives over to the cameraman's apartment to see if he can find out why he blew off their meeting.

The drive is short, and the streets are quiet at this time of the morning. After parking his beast in the apartment building's parking lot, Jack strides up the sidewalk to Scott's unit and immediately notices its brand-new door. He knocks several times but receives no response. Taking a closer look around, he notices that there is a light shining from under the closed door. Curious but cautious, he walks around to the back of the building to find out if he can see anything through the unit's first-floor windows. He counts three apartments over and stops near a set of sliding glass doors. The vertical blinds are closed, but a small amount of light is sneaking through, and he's able to peer through a small space between the blinds like the captain of a submarine squinting through a periscope.

As he looks through the blinds, he spots a foot lying on the floor. The sliding glass doors are locked, so he runs back to his car to get the lug nut wrench from his trunk, which he uses to break the glass.

The tempered glass shatters in a million pieces, enabling Jack to push enough of the blinds aside to see Scott Simms lying in a pool of blood on his kitchen floor. From Jack's vantage point, it appears that Scott bled out after being slashed in the neck, but not before he left a message on the tile floor in his own blood: 5352CUP.

Remaining outside the apartment, Jack calls 911, then sits on the grass to wait for the cavalry to arrive. While he waits, he calls Didi again to let her know that he expects to be home in about two hours and that he'll drive her home as soon as he arrives.

After hanging up with Didi, Jack's mind turns back to the scene inside the apartment. *5352CUP--what the hell does that mean?* He plays the case over and over inside his head: *Cindy, Lisa, Wayne, Scott, Sean, and now 5352CUP.*

After turning the crime scene over to the CSI techs, Jack calls Captain Jeffers' cell phone.

"Hi, Captain, sorry to wake you. I know it's only four o'clock in the morning, but I need you to meet me downtown as soon as you can. I have new information on the porn ring and the two murders."

Jack rushes back to his condo to keep his promise to Didi before meeting with the captain. When he arrives, Didi is waiting.

"Morning, Babe. Ready to go?"

"All set. What happened, Jack?"

Stifling a yawn while rubbing his eyes, Jack replies, "I found Scott dead in his apartment after he didn't show for our meeting. We gotta leave right now, though. I'll drop you off at home, then I need to head downtown."

"Scott is the guy from last night, right? That's really creepy! I was just talking with him!"

"Yeah, death seems to be following me like a shadow."

Jack puts the blue lights on his dashboard and speeds to Dania to drop off Didi, then races across town to the Fort Lauderdale police station.

When he walks into the squad room, he finds Captain Jeffers already there, waiting for him. Over the rim of his coffee cup, the captain asks, "What's going on, Jack? Why am I here this early?"

Grabbing the nearest chair, Jack sits down heavily.

"When Didi and I were poking around at the Mamba Imports party last night, we saw Wayne Jackson there, who was apparently poking around, too. It's interesting that Wayne was there last night, because before the party, I stopped at Doctor Ghosh's office to pick up a button that they found in the sand near Cindy's body, and that button looks like it could be a match for the buttons on the suit Wayne was wearing last night. And to make it even more interesting, one of the beach cleanup crew members ID'd him as being on the beach the morning Cindy's body was found."

Grimacing, the captain exclaims, "Damn! One of ours is involved in this crap?"

"Maybe. And by the way, Didi really came through for us last night. She managed to get Scott Simms alone, and just like we thought he would, he propositioned her to do some pornographic film work. When Scott saw me there he wasn't happy, but he said he wanted to tell me something that he couldn't talk about before. He said there were too many ears at the police station and also at Mamba, and he asked me to meet him at the bus terminal at midnight. I waited a while, but he never showed, so I drove to his apartment and found him there, dead. His throat was cut, and there was blood everywhere. But before he died, he managed to write a message on the floor in his own blood: 5352CUP. I have no idea what that means, do you?"

"No, not at all, Jack. Bounce it around with some of the other detectives. So, it looks like you had a very busy evening. I'll inform Internal Affairs about a possible connection to Wayne and get them to pick him up this morning for questioning. We know he's been moonlighting at Mamba, so we're going to have to squeeze him to find out what he knows about Mamba's operation and about what happened to Scott. I want you to go with them to pick him up. It'll give you an opportunity to take a look around his house. Hell, maybe he'll even start talking about Mamba when he sees you. I'll let you know when the boys from I.A. are ready to leave." Glancing at his watch, he exclaims, "Shit, they're not even awake yet!"

While waiting for the other detectives to arrive at the station, Jack munches on a candy bar and gulps down some coffee from the vending machine to help him stay awake and focused.

When detectives Robert Stacy and Tom Harris enter the squad room at the end of their shifts, he calls them over to his desk.

"Hey, guys, I got a clue from a crime scene last night that I need help deciphering. If we work together, maybe we can figure it out. You game?"

"Yeah, sure," replies Detective Stacy. "What do you have?"

"A murder victim scrawled this on the floor in his own blood."

With a black magic marker, Jack walks over to an easel pad, flips it over to an empty page and writes, 5352CUP.

"Any ideas, guys?"

"Didi's bra size?" grins Harris.

"Very funny, asshole."

"I don't have a clue, Jack," states Harris solemnly. "Maybe there's a cup in locker number 5352 somewhere. At the airport or the bus terminal?"

"Hey, that's a start. Stacy, why don't you check it out and see if you can find a locker with that number."

Hearing a commotion in the squad room, Jack glances around and declares, "Harris, I think I'm about to be called into Captain Jeffers' office; two suits just walked in. Can you run that clue by Forensics for me? There's a guy down there who likes cracking word clues."

Two minutes later, Captain Jeffers' voice fills the squad room as he yells out Jack's name. But before he can respond to his boss' call, he is stopped by Detective Harris' hand on his arm.

"We'll start working on this clue for you, Jack, but our shift ends at seven this morning. We'll call you if we get any hits."

CHAPTER THIRTEEN

After spending time with his new main squeeze Laura Connolly at the Indian Casino in Hollywood, entertaining potential buyers from Dubai through hours of dinner, gambling, and finally, breakfast, Sean LeDue returns home exhausted at eight-thirty the next morning. When he walks into his kitchen to make himself a pot of coffee, he is relieved to find the cell phone he thought he lost sitting innocently on the kitchen counter. Picking the phone up, he immediately checks for messages, noting three missed phone calls from Wayne Jackson and a voicemail message. Replaying the voicemail message, he hears, "Mr. LeDue, your problem has been neutralized."

Sean saves the message for future leverage.

Later that morning, Jack follows the police cruiser containing two officers from Internal Affairs as they drive through Broward County to Sergeant Jackson's house in Sunrise. When they arrive, they pull into the circular driveway and park. The trio approaches the door, but before they can knock, it is opened by Wayne Jackson, who stands silently in the doorway. He glances at the officers' IDs, then steps aside to allow them to enter, with Jack taking up the rear.

In the hallway, one of the I.A. officers states, "Sergeant Jackson, you are under investigation for improper conduct. You need to come down to the station with us for questioning."

"Whoa, are you arresting me?" Wayne asks. "Jack, what's going on?"

"Go with them, Wayne, nice and easy, or *I'll* arrest ya. Got it?"

Wayne wisely decides to cooperate with the two Internal Affairs officers, who escort him to their car and drive off, leaving Jack at the house to snoop around.

Upon entering the living room, the first thing Jack notices is a fifty-five inch widescreen T.V., and when he enters the kitchen, he is surprised to see new, hi-tech stainless steel appliances sparkling under the fluorescent lights.

In the master bedroom, he opens Wayne's closet and rifles through the clothing, stopping when he finds a luxurious brown suit.

"Wow, handmade Italian!" In wonder, he mumbles to himself, "How did you afford all of this, Wayne?"

Taking out the button from the beach crime scene, he holds it up to the suit and finds that, although it matches perfectly, none of the suit jacket's buttons are missing. Puzzled, he checks the inside of the jacket, where a suit's extra buttons are usually found, and finds that one of them is gone. However, it doesn't appear as though the button had gotten caught on something, or had fallen off from being worn out; it was cut off, cleanly. He re-checks the buttons on the outside of the jacket, but none of them appears to have been re-attached.

Taking the suit jacket off the hanger, Jack leaves the house, locks the door behind him, and heads back to the station.

Rush hour is just beginning, and the morning drive back downtown is hell on wheels. The usual fifteen-minute drive takes close to forty-five minutes. When Jack finally arrives at the police station's parking lot, he takes up two spots so no one will park near his ride, then heads upstairs carrying Wayne's suit jacket.

As soon as he enters the office, he makes a beeline for Captain Jeffers.

"Captain, this is the jacket from Wayne's handmade Italian suit, and it matches the button from the crime scene." Holding the jacket out, he asks, "Notice anything odd?"

The captain examines the suit jacket, then looks at Jack blankly.

"The button they found was cut off this suit, but none of the other buttons appears to have been replaced; all of them are the originals. Someone planted that button on the beach."

"Well, maybe I.A. will get Wayne to talk to us today."

"Look, Captain. I know Wayne is involved in this mess, but I don't know how just yet. If I.A. comes up empty, I want to arrest him on suspicion of murder. That'll keep him locked up here until he lawyers up. Maybe I can get some answers out of him before then."

A knock on the captain's door interrupts them.

"Jack, I got something on your clue," the newcomer says as he steps inside.

"And who are *you*?" Jack snaps.

"Name's John Lennon. No, don't say anything, I can't sing worth a lick. I like breaking codes, so I work in Forensics."

"Okay, spit it out, man."

"Well, if you're a golfer, you would split your clue up like this: 535 2 cup. It indicates the distance from the tee to the hole: 535 yards to the cup. I did some research on local golf courses, and a course in Plantation has a hole with a par five, at 535 yards."

With a glance at the captain, Jack says, "John, you're with me. Let's go golfing."

The golf course is nearby, about seven miles west of the station, and Jack gets there in less than ten minutes. He turns south on Pine Island Road and follows the signs to the entrance.

"Okay, John. Which hole is it?"

"Number five."

"You got it. Hold on!"

With siren blazing and lights flashing, Jack pulls the Road Runner onto the cart path and hauls ass to the fifth hole, scattering golfers in all directions. When they reach the fifth green, Jack stops the car and they both get out.

"Okay, we're here, John. Now what?"

"I'm guessing that your victim left a clue somewhere near here, or he wouldn't have written down the cup number."

"Don't they re-position the cups on these greens from time to time?" Jack asks, not really expecting an answer.

Walking over to the cup on the green, he takes out the flag as a foursome drives their carts toward the hole. Flashing his badge toward them, he tells John to keep them off the green and states, "We'll be out of your way soon, gentlemen."

Kneeling down to examine the bottom of the cup, he notices something shiny through the drain holes. Placing his fingers through the holes, he pulls the cup out of the green and spies a small package wrapped in plastic. Surprised, he carefully pries out the package and replaces the cup in the green, then straightens up and brushes grass from his pants while calling out to the golfers, "It's all yours, guys! Sorry for the delay."

Followed by John, Jack walks quickly back to his car, where he carefully unwraps the package.

"What do we have there, Jack?"

"Well, well, well. It's one of those mini DVD's. You have equipment at the lab to view this, right?"

"Sure do. Let's go."

Arriving at the forensics lab in record time, Jack follows the technician to the lab's DVD player, into which he inserts the disk he found at the golf course. As the DVD screen comes to life, they are surprised to see that they're watching a porn flick starring Cindy Walsh, Lisa Stevens, Laura Connelly, and... Sergeant Wayne Jackson. The movie lasts about thirty minutes, and when it's over, an image of Scott Simms fills the screen.

"My name is Scott Simms. I filmed this video, and if you're watching it, I'm probably dead. I'm recording this to let everyone know that Sean LeDue has been exporting illegal pornography, and that I've been involved with filming and distributing it. I also want to tell everyone that Wayne Jackson is the one who 'took care of' Cindy Walsh. When he got her pregnant, she tried to blackmail him about the pregnancy and about his involvement in Sean's business, but Wayne didn't want anyone to know that he was involved in illegal pornography, so he took care of that 'problem'. In addition to that, Wayne threatened my life when he found out that I was recording this DVD. I hope that all this information is used to correct our misdeeds."

Jack takes the disk out of the DVD player and runs upstairs to Captain Jeffers' office, hoping that they still have Wayne in the building for questioning. Barging into the office without knocking, he begins talking in rapid bursts.

"Captain! You need to look at this disk. We need to keep Wayne in custody! It looks like he killed Scott Simms, and maybe Cindy Walsh! I'm going to need a search warrant for his house, and I'll also need people to check the dumpsters at the stores near the house, as well as the dumpsters at Scott's apartment complex. There was so much blood at Scott's place that some of it must have gotten on Wayne's clothing!"

"Oh, crap! Okay, good thing Wayne is still with I.A. in Interrogation Room Three. I'll get the search warrant, and I'll also get the D.A to take a look at this disk. Go and give our sergeant the good news. He's going to be with us for a while."

Leaving the captain's office, Jack walks down the hall to Interrogation Room Three, where he walks in on the officers from I.A.

"Excuse me, guys, but I need to speak with one of you outside."

The senior officer joins Jack in the hallway, where Jack quickly fills him in on what Wayne has been up to. After hearing the details, the officer re-enters the room and informs Wayne that they won't be releasing him just yet. Meanwhile, Jack heads back to Captain Jeffers' office to check on the warrant, and to schedule the crime scene unit for dumpster diving sessions.

CHAPTER FOURTEEN

Satisfied that he can make a case against Wayne Jackson after viewing the DVD from the golf course and the information Jack has gathered so far, the D.A. initiates the process of charging Wayne with the first-degree murder of Scott Simms.

By law, Wayne can be held for twenty-four hours for questioning before he can lawyer up and stop talking; however, after being read his Miranda rights, he decides to cooperate with the investigation.

Assured now that Wayne's interrogation will continue, Jack heads back to Wayne's house, search warrant in hand, followed by John Lennon and the crew from the crime scene unit. Jack intends to rummage through the house while the CSI team splits up to search the dumpsters behind the drug store and the gas station on University Drive, just two blocks away.

The first room Jack heads for is Wayne's bedroom. When he enters the room, he looks around slowly. Spotting a desktop computer, he turns it on and sits down to wait for the computer to boot up, relieved that it does not require a password.

Most of the files Jack sorts through seem to be harmless, until he finds a file named Mamba. Upon opening that file, he begins to read several entries involving Cindy, Lisa and Scott. One entry states that Scott has been shooting his own films on the side and selling them to Sean's clients behind Sean's back. It seems that Wayne has been playing both sides. While working for Sean, he was also helping Scott rip off their boss.

Jack shuts down the computer and takes it out to his car. He is satisfied that he has found enough evidence for now, and he wants to bring the computer to police headquarters so they can search it more thoroughly.

On the way to the station, he stops at the nearby drug store, where one of the CSI teams is going through the store's trash. Pulling up alongside a large trash container, Jack powers down the driver's side window and calls out, "Any luck, John?"

John Lennon's head pops up briefly from inside the dumpster.

"We found nothing at the gas station. But hey, wait a minute, I think I got something here." Pulling something out of the trash pile, he holds it up and says, "Well, look at this. It's a pair of exercise shorts and a shirt, and they're both full of blood splatters. If this isn't Scott's blood, then we have another murder on our hands."

"Great! Bag them. I got Wayne's computer with me, and I'm heading back downtown. I'll meet you there."

Jack spins the Road Runner in a donut before roaring out of the parking lot and zipping south on University Drive. Weaving in and out of traffic, he places the blue light on his dashboard to avoid being pulled over by the Plantation police, and within minutes pulls into the police station's parking lot, once again taking up two spots so that no one will ding his beloved Road Runner.

Carrying Wayne's computer under his arm, he walks up the stairs and heads directly for the captain's office.

"Hey, Captain! The CSI team found some bloody clothing in a dumpster near Wayne's house. If we get a match, Wayne's toast."

"Great! That will solve one out of three murders, but what about the other two?"

"I'm working on them. I also found some incriminating stuff on his computer, but I want to talk to him again."

"Okay, I'll get him out of lockup, but you need to hurry. He's going to be booked and moved to county jail in about an hour."

Jack leaves Wayne's computer in the captain's office, then waits in the interrogation room. Within a few minutes, the two men are staring at each other in the closed room. With a withering glance at the demoralized police officer, Jack asks, "What the hell's going on, Wayne? How the hell did you get into this mess?"

After a brief silence, Wayne replies, "Alimony and child support wreak havoc on a bank account, Jack. That's all I can say at this point."

"Crap, man! We have a DVD that Scott made, and we found bloody clothes in a dumpster near your house! The D.A. is going to pursue this, Wayne, but if the DNA matches yours and Scott's, a trial won't even be necessary."

A prolonged silence ensues during which neither man says anything, then Wayne sighs.

"Okay, Jack. Here it is. Sean LeDue had a film set built at the warehouse where Scott filmed Sean's porn movies, but Scott started to moonlight there, using the set to film some 'special movies' that he would sell to Sean's clients on the side. I stood guard while Sean was filming to make sure they weren't disturbed. But one of the actresses was a freak. Cindy would do anything, with anyone, or anything. Animal, vegetable, or mineral, it didn't matter to her. A couple of times, Lisa would join in the fun on the set, and they'd all have a really good time. One night, I got caught up in the action after I thought they were done with the movie, but I didn't realize that Scott was still filming. There were also a couple of times when I picked up the girls at their apartments and drove them to the shoot and back, and Cindy invited me in and we knocked boots. Well, I ended up getting her pregnant and Cindy started bragging to Laura and Lisa about how she was going to blackmail me by threatening to show my kid what I've been doing. She had a big mouth, and she also knew that Laura was doing Sean, so along with blackmailing me, she started accusing Scott, Lisa and Laura of ripping off Sean. I tried to get her to shut up, but she didn't care. She said Laura was involved in Scott's little enterprise because of the movies she was making for him and that Sean should know about it. I think she was hot for him."

Wayne stops talking as the door opens and John from Forensics enters the room. He whispers something to Jack, who listens intently, then solemnly shakes his head as John exits, leaving them alone again.

"Wayne, the clothing we found is covered with Scott's blood, and they also found your DNA on them. What happened there, asshole? And what do you think your son is gonna think about his dad when all this comes out?"

Running his fingers through his hair, Wayne grimaces.

"Sean wanted Scott gone, man. He said Scott was a problem that needed to be solved, and when I found out that Scott made that damn DVD to cover his ass and incriminate me in Cindy's murder, I also needed to get rid of him. But I didn't kill Cindy or Lisa. My kid, that's a bitch, but at least he'll know I stood up for myself against that little creep, and that I'm cooperating with you now."

Nodding with interest during the sergeant's admissions, Jack continues.

"I didn't think you were involved with the women, but we found a button in the sand near Cindy's body that came from one of your suits. It was one of those extra buttons they put inside suit jackets, and it was cut off the suit. There was no indication that any of the buttons on the outside of the jacket where re-sewn on, so someone tried to implicate you in Cindy's murder. Were Lisa, Laura, or Scott ever at your house? And by the way, why were you at the beach the morning after Cindy's murder? A maintenance guy saw you there."

"Yeah, they were all at my house one night after a long shoot. I invited them over for breakfast." Smiling weakly, he adds, "I make a mean omelet."

With a sigh, he continues, "My bet is that Laura's the snitch. She probably went to Sean before Cindy could get to him, and told him what was going on behind his back. And about the beach thing, Sean called me on my cell phone and said he wanted to talk to me in private. Said to meet him at the beach. When he didn't show, I took a stroll along the water. Who knew I'd be walking over Cindy?"

At that moment, two officers and an attorney from the D.A.'s office enter the room.

"Wayne Jackson, you are charged with the murder of Scott Simms. You have the right to an attorney."

Responding impatiently, Wayne declares, "Fuck the attorney! Let's get this over with. Jack, when you need my help, you know where I'll be."

Jack lingers in the room alone after Wayne is led out in handcuffs. At the table, his mind is working overtime. *Well, it looks like I can shut the books on one murder, but now I have to solve the others. I have a feeling that Sean LeDue is involved somehow, but I'm going to need hard evidence in order to implicate him. I think Laura would be a good place to start.*

CHAPTER FIFTEEN

"Hey, Captain, got a minute?"

"Yeah, come in, Jack. What happened with Wayne?"

"Well, I managed to get a confession out of him. He murdered Scott, all right, but I think it was Sean LeDue who killed Cindy and Lisa, with help from his girlfriend, Laura Connelly. She's Doctor Handel's receptionist, and she may have access to the doctor's snake venom. I need to visit the snake man's office again to get a set of fingerprints from Miss Connelly."

After a short pause, Jack continues. "But hey, wait a minute...I just got another idea. Why don't we release a phony story to the press that we are questioning a suspect in Cindy's and Lisa's murders? It may put Sean and Laura at ease long enough to let their guards down."

The captain agrees with Jack's suggestion and immediately begins to draft a statement that his office will release the next morning, stating that they have a suspect in custody in the murders of Cindy Walsh and Lisa Stevens.

Satisfied that his plan is going into effect, Jack tells the captain that he's going down to Forensics to see if they were able to get any evidence off the button and the vial from the snake man, and that he will pay a visit to Laura and Doctor Handel the next day.

Upon entering the Forensics Lab, Jack finds John peering through a microscope.

"How's our resident Beatle doing?"

John looks up and shakes his head in disgust at the comment.

"What d'ya need, Jack?"

"Were you guys able to pull prints off the button and the vial?"

"Yeah, we got a small, partial print off the button, and a good one off the vial that matches the one from the button. We ran the print through our database, but nothing showed up."

"Hmm. I think I know who it belongs to, and I hope I'm about to find out for sure. Thanks."

The next morning, Jack listens to an all-news radio station on his way to Doctor Handel's place, and chuckles when he hears the phony story about Sergeant Wayne Jackson being a suspect in the murders of two local women.

Sean LeDue is sitting at his desk, listening to the same radio station while waiting for his first appointment of the day to arrive. For the past few days, he has been concentrating on replacing his recently-deceased filmmaker. When he hears that the police have taken Wayne in for questioning, he is convinced that he has gotten rid of all his problems. With Scott, Cindy, and Lisa already gone, he believes that Wayne's arrest is now icing on the cake.

When his secretary calls him on the intercom to announce his applicant's arrival, he sits back in his chair and smiles, confident that his business ventures will soon resume.

"Mr. LeDue, your first interview is here."

"Send him in, send him in."

Laura Connelly is the first person Jack sees when he walks into the lobby of Doctor Handel's compound. Greeting her, he says with a smile, "Hello there, Laura. We meet again."

"Oh, good morning, Detective Stenhouse. I just heard the good news on the radio. Kind of puts the Fort Lauderdale police in a bad light, though, that one of your own may be a murderer."

"Well, stuff happens. Is Doctor Handel in?"

"He's out back, rounding up snakes for milking. It'll be a few minutes before he can come out. Can I get you anything? Coffee, soda?"

"I'll take coffee, but not in a Styrofoam cup. I hate the way coffee tastes in those things. Make it black, no sugar."

"Sure, no problem."

Laura hands a large mug of lukewarm coffee to Jack. He grabs it by the handle, careful not to touch the same area that Laura touched. He takes a sip while waiting for the doctor.

"Detective Stenhouse! Why are you here again?"

Jack has to think fast and not tip his hand to Laura, so he makes up an excuse to go into the doctor's office.

"Just wanted to let you know about the progress we've made about your missing venom. Let's go into your office to talk."

Once inside the office, Doctor Handel gestures to the small table and chairs.

“Have a seat, Detective.”

"No, thanks. I wanted to let you know that we identified the perpetrator, and to thank you for your help. But don't tell anyone about this yet--we haven't apprehended the thief."

"I'm glad you think I was helpful, even though I really didn't do anything."

"Oh, you were more helpful than you know.” Taking a large gulp of coffee, he ends his visit by saying, “Take care, Doc, and let me know if you have any more trouble out here."

In the hallway outside the doctor's office, Jack takes time to finish his coffee, then hides the mug under his sport coat before he reenters the lobby. As he waves goodbye to Laura, he mumbles under his breath, "See you again soon, bitch."

Jack drops the coffee mug off with John in Forensics, then settles in at his desk to wait for John's call. It doesn't take long for the phone to ring.

"Detective Stenhouse."

"Jack, it's John from Forensics. We have a match! The prints on the cup match the prints on the vial and the button."

"Thanks, John!"

Jack hangs up the phone and walks quickly over to the captain. "Captain, I got a match. Laura Connelly's prints are on the button *and* the vial."

With a sigh of relief and a pat on the back, Jack's boss suddenly becomes tolerable. "Good work, Jack! I'll get in touch with the D.A.'s office and have them issue an arrest warrant for Laura Connelly. Get some lunch and be back here later this afternoon. She should be here by then."

Puzzled at the sudden respect, Jack responds, "Thanks, Captain."

Wanting to make the most of his unexpected free time, Jack decides to grab a box lunch at Shangri La and watch Didi perform. But before heading over there, he stops at his condo to send an email to Deputy Inspector Rawlings in New York. He wants to re-state how much he is looking forward to meeting with him.

When he's finally on his way to the gentlemen's club, he hopes that this time he won't be bothered by an over-served patron.

CHAPTER SIXTEEN

As he sits next to the stage and watches Didi slithering around the pole, Jack thinks that it can't get any better than this: a BLT, a beer, and a little T and A. Didi puts on a good show, and the tips are flowing.

After finishing his lunch, he downs the last few ounces of his beer. He has risen from his seat before noticing that Didi is crawling over to him on her hands and knees. When she reaches him, she leans over the edge of the stage and gives him a long, wet kiss.

"See you later, Stud."

Smiling, Jack turns to the guy sitting next to him. "Stare all you like, Slick. She goes home with me."

With a high-five from the customer, he leaves the club and returns to the real world.

Captain Jeffers calls out to Jack as he strolls through the office toward his desk.

"She's waiting for you in Interrogation Room One."

Seizing the case files from his desk, Jack walks toward the interrogation room to speak with Laura Connelly. Upon entering the room, he sits across from Laura and opens his file folder, silently placing photos of Cindy Walsh and Lisa Stevens on the table in front of her.

"Either of them look familiar to you?"

Laura turns away, trying to avoid the photos. "Why have you brought me here?" she stammers. "I thought you had your killer!"

"Yeah, well, everything isn't what it seems. You see, Laura, Wayne *is* a killer. He murdered Scott Simms. You remember Scott, don't you? He remembered you. He got you on video a couple of times. In fact, I have one of your movies right here. Want to see it?" After a brief silence, Jack continues, "No, I guess you don't."

"What do you want from me?"

"Want? I don't want anything from you. I have all I need. I have your fingerprints on a button that was found at Cindy's crime scene. I have your fingerprints on an empty vial of snake venom. I have two victims who were killed by snake venom, and I have proof that the people you are connected with are involved in an illegal pornography ring. All I need to do is charge you with two counts of murder, and then I can go home."

She stands up, her voice shrill and shaking, and blurts, "Hey, wait a minute! You can't prove anything! You have no evidence on me, or I'd already be charged. Either charge me now or let me go. I'm not going to say anything else until I get a lawyer."

"Okay, go ahead and lawyer up. The D.A. is preparing your charges, though. Illegal porn and murder one, two counts. We got you directly connected to one of the murders, and with a motive. Lisa and Cindy were cheating and robbing your boyfriend, so you thought you'd help him by getting rid of his problems. And oh, yeah, we have you on that DVD. Quite a good performance, there. You're looking at the death penalty, if you're lucky. If not, you'll be an old, ugly lady by the time you get out. *If* you get out. Think about that for a while."

Jack remains silent for a few moments to allow Laura to stew, then he continues.

"But you know what? I don't think you did this yourself. You're not strong enough to handle two dead bodies. It would be a shame to lose your life over something you didn't do, but hey, it wouldn't be the first time someone got prosecuted for something they didn't do. So go ahead, lawyer up."

Granting Laura time to call her lawyer, Jack returns to Captain Jeffers' office.

"Boss, I don't think we have enough evidence to pick up LeDue yet. It's one person's word against another's right now."

"Remember when I said I was working on putting someone on the inside at Mamba Imports?" Captain Jeffers picks up the phone and dials the front desk.

"Send her in, please." Hanging up the phone, he hands a personnel file to Jack.

"Tell me what you think."

Jack reviews the background information.

Twenty-two years old, 5' 10" tall, black belt in karate, graduated from the University of Miami in three years with a degree in Criminal Justice, runner-up at the Miss Florida pageant, graduated from the police academy last year at the top of her class. After graduation, was assigned to the Fort Lauderdale Police Department, but was quickly placed on loan with the Vice Squad in Tampa to go undercover to bust a prostitution ring.

"Wow! Seems pretty qualified."

"Glad you think so, Jack. Meet Maria Assante."

Turning toward the door, Jack's jaw drops.

"Captain," he says, "If this is what the police force looks like now, I may never retire!" Extending his hand in greeting toward his fellow officer, he grins, "Welcome aboard, Maria!"

The new arrival, with long black hair, beautiful blue eyes, and legs that just won't quit, looks like she'd just stepped off the silver screen. Unexpectedly, though, she returns Jack's grip with a firm handshake.

Despite being surprised by the tight grip on his hand, Jack continues to stare at the vision before him. Without thinking, he blurts out, "Maria, why would anyone with your obvious attributes want to be a cop? You could make so much more money doing just about anything else!"

Captain Jeffers quickly interjects, "Sorry, Maria. Detective Stenhouse is a dog."

Conspicuously ignoring Jack, Maria responds, "Detective Stenhouse has a reputation that precedes him, Captain. There's nothing to be sorry for; I can handle men like him." With her hands on her well-shaped hips, Maria holds Jack's stare and demands, "Well, Detective?"

"Jack. Call me Jack, since we'll be working together on the same case."

"Okay, *Jack,* but my eyes are up here, got it? Now, police work is in my family. All of my brothers are cops in Chicago, and this is what I want to do for a living. You have a problem with any of that?"

"No, no problem. Besides, you can probably kick my ass."

"Damn right I could."

Interrupting the exchange between his two detectives, Captain Jeffers explains, "Listen, Jack. Maria has already been hired by LeDue, and she starts tomorrow. We gave her a temporary snake tattoo so she can show Sean that she's eager to get started in his business."

Studying her thoughtfully, Jack asks, "Maria, do you know what you'll be asked to do?"

"Jack! I already filled her in and showed her Scott's DVD," retorts the captain testily.

Asserting herself into the escalating exchange, Maria declares, "I'm ready to do whatever needs to be done here. I'm no pansy!"

"Okay, then I'd like to get to know you before we start working together," declares Jack. "Why don't you join me and my girlfriend, Didi, for dinner tonight so I can give you more details about the case and we can talk? Say seven, at the cheesecake place on Las Olas Boulevard?"

"Sounds good. I'll see you then, Jack."

Maria turns to leave the office, knowing that Jack is ogling her while she walks out of the room. When the two men are alone again, Jack exchanges glances with his boss.

"She's wasting her talents here, Captain."

"Yeah, well, what are you gonna do? She actually wants to be here, for cryin' out loud. But you have to admit, for undercover work, who the hell would think she's a cop?"

Handing Maria's file back to Jeffers, Jack walks out of the captain's office and is immediately approached by an assistant from the district attorney's office.

"Stenhouse, Laura's lawyer came in, and we talked. She wants a deal. She'll give up LeDue, but she wants no jail time for herself. Wayne is also trying to cut a deal. He realizes he's toast, but he wants a reduced sentence in exchange for providing testimony against LeDue. At this point, because we don't have any firm evidence against LeDue, the best we can do is charge him with tax evasion, so I contacted the Feds. They opened an investigation to look into that, just in case it's all we get."

"Is Laura still in Interrogation?"

"Yeah, she's waiting for a reply about a deal."

"What's your feeling about it?"

"We can probably get her on aiding and abetting, but she's attractive and she'll produce some tears at trial; say she was forced into helping LeDue. Juries tend not to convict pretty defendants, so if she gets a good lawyer, she's free."

"Well, let's go and see what she can tell us about LeDue."

Jack and the assistant D.A. walk into the interrogation room to speak with Laura, who has been joined by her attorney. Jack stares silently at Laura for several minutes, then speaks firmly.

"Okay, Laura, we're all ears. What do 'ya have for us?"

Before she can say anything, her lawyer pipes up.

"We turn state's witness and Laura goes free. No jail time."

"Yeah, we heard that, but it depends on what she has on LeDue and how involved she is in all this."

"No jail, or no info."

Jack turns to the assistant D.A., who nods his head. "Okay, spill it," Jack demands.

Laura's lawyer quickly whispers into her ear, eliciting a nod of Laura's head. Then, she leans back in her chair and stares at Jack for several seconds before speaking.

"I found out from Cindy that she and Scott were ripping off Sean and selling porn directly to some of his clients. Wayne knew about it, but said nothing, and Lisa, well, she wasn't really involved in this. She did some movies, but she was just in the wrong place at the wrong time."

Urging her on, Jack asks, "How did this escalate to murder?"

"Sean was really pissed about Scott and Cindy double-crossing him, so he wanted both of them dead. I told him that I had access to snake venom that mimics heart failure, that it was very potent, and that he wouldn't need a lot of it. When he heard that, he wanted me to get him some, and he said he had the perfect way to administer it. It turns out that Sean's a diabetic and he injects himself with insulin every day, so he has a supply of disposable needles on hand at all times, the perfect device for injecting venom. The night he killed Cindy, he asked me to go with him because he needed someone to help him with the body, so I stayed in the car while he went up to her apartment. It was the perfect setup. The entrance to her apartment was around the side of the building, next to a canal, and no one saw him go in. But just as he had finished injecting Cindy with enough serum so it wouldn't be detected, Lisa, who lived in the same complex and had a key to Cindy's place, happened to stop by. She walked in as Sean was taking the clothes off Cindy's body on the kitchen floor. Sean was quick, though. Before she could scream, he grabbed a small pot from the drying rack next to the sink and knocked her out. Then, he injected Lisa with the rest of the snake venom. When he called me on my cell phone, I joined him in the apartment, and he told me what happened. I helped him put the hypodermic needle, the empty vial of snake venom, and the pot into a large zip lock bag that we found in Cindy's apartment. After poking some holes into the bag, we took both bodies out to his car, and he threw the bag into the canal behind the building. Then, we drove around awhile, eventually putting Lisa in a dumpster and burying Cindy at the beach."

Jack asks, "Do you know anything about a button that was found near Cindy's body at the beach?"

"Oh, yeah, the button. Before all this happened, Sean asked me to cut a button off of Wayne's suit. He wears that suit all the time, but he's really careless about the jacket; leaves it lying around all over the place. At the time, I wondered why he wanted a button, of all things, and why he wanted me to place it into a plastic bag before I gave it to him, but I didn't ask. When I saw him drop the button into the sand around Cindy's body, I remembered that it had my prints on it, and I got scared."

Pausing, Laura sips from a glass of water, then continues.

"After we got Cindy covered up, Sean called Wayne and asked him to come down to the beach for a 'meeting.' Then we left. The next morning, I replaced the missing vial of snake venom in Doctor Handel's refrigerator with an empty vial. That's it. Oh, wait; one more thing. Wayne killed Scott on

Sean's orders, but if it wasn't for the DVD that Scott made about Sean's operation and Wayne's involvement in it, Scott would probably have hired someone to get rid of Wayne, too. The rest you know."

With a glance at the assistant D.A., Jack asks, "How do you know about the DVD?"

"Scott told me he was going to cover his ass. When the D.A. mentioned a DVD earlier, I assumed it was the one that Scott made. But you know, LeDue told me that he made a DVD about Scott to keep him honest, so I guess there's a couple of DVD's floating around."

Jack sits back with a sigh. "That's quite a story you've told us, Laura. Everyone made a DVD, huh? But at this point, you haven't given us any proof that Sean was involved in these crimes. I'll have a dive team search the canal to see if we can recover the plastic bag, but it's up to the D.A. now. His office will decide if you get a deal or not. I'm done here."

Jack leaves the interrogation room and walks over to his desk to schedule the dive team for the next day. After setting that up, he leaves the office.

An afternoon thunderstorm has done nothing to cool off the summer heat, and by the time Jack gets to his car, beads of sweat are rolling down his forehead. While thinking about dinner that evening with Didi and Maria, he turns the AC on high and pulls onto Broward Boulevard, mumbling, "I hate this heat, and I hate Florida."

With two quick beeps of the horn, he heads home.

CHAPTER SEVENTEEN

The cheesecake restaurant on Las Olas is as busy as usual, so Jack and Didi stake a place near the hostess' desk while they wait for Maria to arrive. As they watch people coming and going, Didi suddenly sees someone she recognizes, and smirks.

"Jack, that's Commissioner Daniels from Fort Lauderdale. He's running for the empty School Board seat."

"Yeah, so?"

"Well, he's a very good tipper. Watch this."

Didi opens one more button of her blouse, and in her tight, hip-hugger jeans, she saunters over to Daniels, who's making his way through the crowd towards the door. With all the men's eyes turned toward Didi's cleavage, she surprises Commissioner Daniels with a loud greeting.

"Larry, honey! Are you going to leave without saying hello?" Didi wraps her arms around the commissioner, gently rubbing her best assets across his chest.

"Why, ah, Didi! Um, what a surprise." Grabbing her shoulders, he pushes her away, stammering, "Um, look, you need to leave. My wife will be out of the restroom at any moment."

"Ohhh, are you sure she wouldn't want to meet the woman who gets your motor running before you go home?"

Didi smiles and gives the commissioner a deep kiss, thrusting her tongue halfway down his throat. Startled, the commissioner looks past her and sees his wife walking out of the restroom. He frantically tries to pull away, but Didi's not through with him yet. Before leaving him, she gently touches his cheek and purrs, "See you around, stud."

When Didi rejoins Jack, she finds him laughing hysterically. They watch as the commissioner's wife grabs her husband by the arm and yanks him out of the restaurant, only to have him crash into Maria as she walks in through the door. When the commissioner's wife spies yet another gorgeous woman entangled with her husband, she screams out, “IS THIS ANOTHER ONE OF YOUR TRAMPS?”

Maria looks puzzled, but mumbles an apology to the flustered man. As she breaks away from the retreating couple and walks up to Jack and Didi, all the men's eyes are now ogling the two gorgeous women.

Jack quickly notices that Maria is dressed very differently from when he met her earlier in Captain Jeffers' office. She's now wearing high heels, skinny jeans, and a sleeveless knit top that looks two sizes too small.

"Hi, Jack." She thrusts a thumb over her shoulder, toward the door. “For some reason, I feel that you were responsible for THAT."

"No, it wasn't me, it was actually Didi!" Jack puts his arm around his reason for living. “Didi, this is Maria, the new cop I told you about."

"Hi, Maria. It's nice to meet you."

"Nice to meet you, too. Listen Jack, I need to freshen up before we're seated. Didi, do you want to join me?"

"Sure."

Allowing Didi to walk ahead of her, Maria turns quickly to Jack and whispers, "Damn! If I was going to switch sides, she'd be the first!"

As both women walk off, Jack is left alone, with all the men's eyes now staring at him.

Sean LeDue is working late tonight. He's in his office at the art gallery, dialing the number of his new videographer.

"Lance, this is Sean. Listen, I have a new hostess starting tomorrow morning. Her name is Maria, and she's a real looker. Be at the gallery around nine. Before you arrive, I'm going to fill her in on her hostess responsibilities and lay out the foundation for her new ‘movie career.' When you get here, you can bring her over to the warehouse to meet her co-stars."

Captain Jeffers has been trying to leave the office for a while, but just as he's finally ready to call it a night, the door to his office opens and the assistant D.A. walks in.

"Captain, Wayne Jackson wants to cut a deal. He says he can get Sean LeDue to confess."

“What kind of a deal is he looking for? And how is he going to get LeDue to confess when he's locked up in jail for murder?"

"Right now, he's looking at life with no parole, but he wants the charge reduced to manslaughter, with a twenty-five year sentence. He'd be eligible for parole in fifteen years."

"Yeah? But I still want to know how he's going to get LeDue to confess."

"I'm working on that. When I get it figured out and a plan approved, I'll let you and Jack know. By the way, we put Laura on house arrest as a material witness in the case and moved her to a safe house. She told LeDue that she had a family emergency and that she'd be out of town for a while. She'll be watched 24/7.”

"Great. Good luck with all that. Now, if you'll excuse me, I'm already late for dinner, and my wife is not a happy camper."

At the restaurant, the hostess has been holding Jack's table while he waits for the two bombshells to return from the restroom. When the group is ready, she takes them to a booth at the back of the restaurant. When the waiter appears, Jack orders a bourbon and coke and the women ask for margaritas.

Once their drink orders arrive, Jack raises his glass in a toast.

"To Maria! Welcome aboard, and may the bad guys beware!"

The waiter stands at the table while they clink their glasses together and drink to the toast, then he takes their food orders. After he leaves, Jack gets down to business.

"Maria, Captain Jeffers told me he already gave you the files on Cindy, Lisa, and Scott, so let me fill in the blanks. Sean LeDue runs an art gallery on Las Olas, and he imports and exports high-dollar art objects to very wealthy clients, but he also films and sells pornography videos on the side. We learned that Cindy and Lisa were hired as hostesses for LeDue's art gallery and auctions, and that they were also actresses in his adult videos, and that Scott is, or *was*, his videographer and Sergeant Wayne Jackson provided security protection for the operation.

"Recently, Laura Connelly, LeDue's girlfriend, discovered that Cindy and Scott were working together to undercut Sean's prices by producing their own porn and selling it to Sean's clients, and that Wayne Jackson was concealing the entire operation from Sean. When LeDue found out about this little enterprise, he decided to get rid of everyone who was involved, and Laura helped him. We got a confession from Laura about her part in all of this, so now we need you to get inside Mamba Imports to collect proof of Sean's involvement. Right now, the D.A. only has enough information to charge him with tax evasion."

"So I'm to be the new temptress?"

"Well, you do have the qualifications, and you sure do *not* look like a cop."

"How are we going to get LeDue to admit to the murders?"

"Laura said he threw the murder weapons into the canal near Cindy's apartment, and a dive team is going to search there in the morning. If we can't get any DNA linking LeDue to the crime, we still got nothing. By the way, Didi was propositioned by Scott to start a new career with him in the 'movies,' but that's a dead issue now. No pun intended."

Maria turns to Didi and asks, "How did you get involved in all of this?"

"Well, that's an interesting story," Didi says as she glances at Jack. "Captain Jeffers asked for my help at a cocktail party that Sean invited us to. That's the only reason

Jack's allowing me to participate in this discussion. I was supposed to start a conversation with Scott to get him interested in me for his movies, but as it turns out, I didn't have to do much talking, because Scott was all over me like white on rice. Besides, I knew Cindy, the woman they found at the beach. We used to work together at Shangri La, me on the stage, and her waiting tables."

With a lift of an eyebrow, Maria says, "Really? You work the pole? I always wanted to do that! Can you teach me?"

With a laugh, Didi replies, "Sure, I can get into the club early any morning. We can meet there any day you want." Reaching into her purse, she locates a pen and paper and writes down her phone number. Handing the paper to Maria, she declares, "Give me a call anytime, and we'll set it up."

Jack has been uncharacteristically quiet during this turn in the conversation, but at this point, he can contain himself no longer.

"Didi, you *have* to let me know when you set a date for this, because I *really* want to be there!"

After dinner, Jack drops Didi off at her apartment and heads toward his condo, but when he looks at his watch, he notes that it's much too early to end the night. So instead of driving home, he points his Road Runner toward the Himmarshee district on Second Street, to a tavern where cops hang out after their night shifts.

Jack parks behind the tavern, then walks around to the front and enters, but before he reaches the bar, he hears someone calling from the back, "Hey, it's Surfer Joe!"

Jack takes a bow and then flashes the Florida state bird. He orders when he reaches the bar.

"Hey, gimme a bourbon and coke, and make it a double."

"A Jack for Jack. Comin' right up, man!"

Sitting at the bar is one of Jack's fellow officers, Detective Robert Stacy. Turning toward the new arrival, he remarks, “Man! Did you see that Maria babe the captain was displaying today?”

“Yeah. What a waste of talent, being a cop! With a body like that, she could do anything she wants, and she chooses *this* line of work? Go figure.”

Frank, another fellow officer, continues, “Where you been, Jack? Haven’t seen you around here for a while. Didi keeping you busy?” He shakes his head and gives a low whistle. “Damn, she could keep me busy anytime! How do you do it, Jack?”

“Vitamins! I take lots of vitamins with my bourbon!”

“Vitamins, or Viagra?” he smirks.

Smiling widely, Jack takes a drink while Frank slaps him on the back.

“Hey, Jack, did you hear about Commissioner Daniels and his wife?”

Chuckling, Jack remembers the scene at the restaurant.

“No, what did our shit-for-brains commissioner do now?”

“Not Daniels, his wife. A neighbor called 911 tonight, and when the uniforms showed up, they found that Daniels’ wife had beat the shit out of him. He didn’t press charges, but they had to call the EMTs and rush him to the hospital.”

“Couldn’t happen to a nicer guy. Didn’t she beat him up before? One of these times, she’s gonna kill that idiot.” Jack picks up his glass. “Here’s to Commissioner Daniels, a pimple on the face of progress!”

CHAPTER EIGHTEEN

Jack arrives at work late the next day, after being held up at the condo by a call from a captain at the New York Police Department. The call was productive, and it looks like his career move is on track.

When he finally gets to the station, he is greeted by a stern Captain Jeffers.

"So nice of you to join us today, Jack. I'm sorry your job is cutting into your social life, but I have another case for you to work on."

"Captain, I still haven't finished the LeDue case!"

"Yeah, well, crime marches on. We found a homeless guy, shoeless and very dead, underneath the Andrews Avenue Bridge. There are a lot of yachts tied up along the New River, and some of them have people living in them. Check them out; find out if anyone saw or heard anything. From what we've been told, this guy had been living near the bridge for a while." Handing the case file to Jack, he states, "Get down there today and snoop around. Let me know what you find out."

"Captain, can't a uniformed unit do this?"

"Budget cuts, Jack, budget cuts. Everyone is doubling up--no new hiring. All I can do is replace positions due to attrition. Look, check out some of the river residents and also the security camera on the high-rise condo next to the park near the bridge. Maybe you'll get lucky. He was probably killed by another homeless guy who needed shoes. Oh, and as for LeDue, Maria should get some information today, and the D.A. is working with Wayne on something. I'll keep you updated. Now, get down to the river."

At the same time Jack is heading toward the river, Maria is walking into LeDue Art Gallery, about a mile away from the Andrews Avenue Bridge. She is immediately greeted by a receptionist at the front desk.

"Welcome to LeDue Art Gallery. May I help you?"

"Yes, I have an appointment with Mr. LeDue."

"May I tell him who's here?"

"Yes, Maria Assante."

"Just one moment, please."

The young receptionist walks into Sean's office at the back of the gallery to let him know that his appointment is waiting. Within seconds, Sean walks out to the front lobby to greet Maria.

“Good morning, Maria! You're right on time and I must say, you look great for so early in the morning!"

"Thank you! I do clean up nicely, don't I?" She flashes her straight, white teeth at him and pushes out her chest.

With a smile, Sean declares, "Come with me into my office; I'll explain your duties."

While Maria follows LeDue, the other employees stare at their new co-worker.

For her first day on the job, Maria is wearing black high heels with a short black skirt and a tight white blouse. She has left the top three buttons of the blouse undone in order to show enough cleavage to make things interesting.

Even though Maria is dressed skimpily, she is still a cop, and a small transmitter has been hidden in her bra, enabling a crew of undercover cops in the “telephone company” van parked across the street to monitor her situation constantly, and to listen to and record everything that is being said.

After they enter Sean's office, he closes the door behind them and motions for Maria to take a seat in the chair in front of his desk. When she sits down, she notices that her skirt is riding halfway up her thigh, so she separates her knees slightly, just to see how fast she can get things moving.

"Well, Maria, I read the background information your parole officer gave me, and I want you to know that there are other employees here, in my organization, who have troubled backgrounds. You see, I like to give everyone a chance to turn their lives around. But you need to know that we are involved in the import and export of high-dollar-amount paintings and art objects to extremely rich clients. In your position, you will act as hostess to these clients at the art auctions and cocktail parties that we periodically hold at our warehouse location, as well as here at our art gallery."

As Sean LeDue continues to describe the work that he will expect of Maria as one of his employees, she begins to cross and uncross her legs, displaying more of the attributes that she was apparently hired for. Sean is acutely aware of what Maria is doing, and considers her actions as justification for him to explain her "other" duties.

"Maria, most of our clientele are very wealthy, and some of them have, shall we say, 'unique' needs. We want to keep all of our customers happy, so we also cater to those special needs, some of which are artfully-made videos of young women in adult situations, which I have been told you have no objection to."

Maria uncrosses her legs, stands up and, placing both of her hands on LeDue's desk, she leans forward, cleavage and all.

"Let's get something straight, *Sean*. First, I need you to look me in the *eyes*. You've been staring at my chest and up my dress since I walked in here. You read my file, so you know what I'm capable of. Second, I do not crap where I eat, get it? Third..." She stops, reaches out and grabs Sean LeDue by the chin and pulls his head up. "My eyes are up here! Third, if you want me to hook, or as you say, play 'hostess,' I charge one thousand dollars per trick. Fourth, as far as being your new porn queen, I get a commission there, too. Do you have a problem with any of that?"

Maria thrusts her thumb up into the pressure point under Sean's chin, just behind the back of his lower jaw to force his head upwards. As he grimaces in pain, Sean is taken aback at first, but quickly recovers and responds casually to Maria's question.

"No, no problem. Everything you want can be worked out."

Satisfied with that answer, Maria releases her grip and sits back down.

Sean continues as if nothing has happened. He knows that he can make a lot of money off of her, even though she may be tough to control.

"My new videographer, Lance Cutler, will be here in a few minutes to take you to our main warehouse and introduce you to the other cast members. But first, let's fill out your new-hire forms. Then, I'll introduce you to our staff here at the art gallery."

CHAPTER NINETEEN

There is no parking near the Andrews Avenue Bridge over the New River, so Jack pulls the Road Runner up over the curb and parks on the brick path beside the water. When he walks past a forty-foot sailboat, he sees a man sitting on the deck, drinking a cup of coffee. Jack approaches the sailboat dockside and presents his badge and I.D.

"Good morning, sir. I'm Detective Jack Stenhouse with the Fort Lauderdale Police. Are you the owner?"

"Yes, I am."

"Can I come aboard? I have a few questions."

"Sure, Detective. Welcome aboard. Would you like some coffee? I just brewed it."

"Thanks. Black, no sugar."

The sailboat owner walks into the galley to get a cup while Jack climbs on board. As he waits for the owner to return with his coffee, Jack makes himself comfortable at a small table near the stern.

When the owner reappears with a mug of strong coffee, he asks, "How may I help you, Detective?"

"I need to ask you a few questions, but first, I need to get your name. Then, I need to know if you reside here permanently."

"Name's James Dupree, and this is my home; I live here year-round. Dock rent is cheaper than a mortgage, or even renting an apartment nowadays. If a hurricane comes, no problem, I just head north."

"Sounds good. Mr. Dupree, were you on board here two nights ago?"

"Yes, I was. Why?"

Jack shows him a photo of the homeless man who was found dead under the Andrews Avenue Bridge.

"Do you recognize this man?"

"Yeah, that's Old Willy. He hangs out under the bridge. What's wrong with him?"

"Willy was his name?"

"Well, that's what we call him along the river. Nice old guy."

"Well, Willy was murdered two nights ago, and the only thing we know about it is that when he was found, his shoes were missing."

"Wow, who would kill him? He's a harmless old man!"

"Maybe someone wanted his shoes?"

"Well, I didn't hear anything unusual, but people walk up and down the river pretty much every night. You can check with the crew of the Intrepid II, two boats up. The captain there helped Willy out from time to time. He'd give him small chores to do in exchange for food and some cash."

Jack finishes his coffee, then reaches into his pocket for one of his business cards.

"Thanks for your information, Mr. Dupree. Here's my card. If you can think of anything else, please give me a call."

"Will do, Detective, and good luck. So sorry about Willy!"

Back on shore, Jack walks over to the Intrepid II. It's still morning in Fort Lauderdale, but the temperature is already eighty-three degrees. The trees and the breeze along the river are helping to keep the temperature down somewhat, but Jack knows that within the hour, it will probably reach ninety. He is hoping that he can get out of the heat before then, and he inwardly curses the high temperature as he walks along the footpath.

The crew of the Intrepid II is on board the ship, cleaning up from the night before. The yacht is a charter boat, used mainly for wedding receptions and dinner cruises along the Intracoastal Waterway. As Jack approaches, he calls out to a man who's wiping down the railings.

"Good morning! Is the captain on board?"

"Who's asking?"

"Detective Stenhouse, Fort Lauderdale Police."

"Just a second." Turning, the crewmember shouts, "Captain! You're wanted on deck!"

A head pokes out of the bridge, then a man descends the stairs and walks to the stern of the boat. Nodding in Jack's direction, the crewman states, "Captain, this gentleman wants to speak with you."

Looking over at Jack standing on the shore, the captain says, "I'm Captain Gerrard. And you are...?"

"Detective Jack Stenhouse." Flashing his I.D. badge, he asks, "Can I come aboard?"

The captain takes his time inspecting Jack's I.D., then motions him toward the gangway. Once he's aboard, he asks, "What can I help you with, Detective?"

"Did you know a guy named Old Willy?"

"Yeah, he's a little old guy. Lives under the bridge."

"Well, I'm sorry to be the bearer of bad news, but someone murdered him two nights ago."

Shaking his head in disgust, he says, "Oh, no! That poor guy! He was homeless, you know."

"Yes, I know. Listen, I understand that you knew Willy and that you helped him out a bit. Can you tell me how he was usually dressed? Was he in the habit of wearing shoes regularly?"

"Yes, he always wore shoes, and I just gave him a new pair recently."

"Really? Go on."

"I felt sorry for the old man, so I used to give him some light chores to do aboard ship, and since there's always leftover food after a cruise, I'd also feed him or slip him a couple of bucks. When I noticed his shoes were falling apart, I gave him a new pair."

"Captain Gerrard, when Willy was found, he was missing his shoes. We think they may have had something to do with his murder."

"Shit! You don't think he got killed for those things? He liked them a lot; they lit up when he walked." Suddenly a thought comes to him. "Hey, wait a minute! I saw another homeless guy hanging around recently, and he was giving Willy a hard time. I chased him away at the time, and I think he hangs out at the other bridge now, the one past the old Fort Lauderdale newspaper building. Man, if he's wearing Willy's shoes..."

"Thanks, Captain. I'll let you know."

Jack climbs back on shore and heads to the nearby bridge. Within a couple of minutes, he spots a man wearing a pair of brand new shoes sleeping under some cardboard boxes. Approaching warily, he kicks at the man's feet.

"Hey, you! Wake up!"

The man shifts under the cardboard and mumbles, "Go away and leave me alone. I'm not bothering anyone."

"Fort Lauderdale Police, sir. Stand up and turn around."

"Hey, I'm not doin' nothing! Why you botherin' me?"

Not taking any chances, Jack pulls out his 9mm.

"Look, turn over on your stomach, spread your legs and put your hands behind your back. NOW!"

"Okay, okay!"

After the man complies with Jack's directions, he cuffs him, pulls him up off the ground and escorts him back toward the Intrepid II. As they walk along the riverfront, Jack notices that the man's shoes are lighting up with each step. When they are alongside the ship, Captain Gerrard spots them.

"That's the guy who was bothering Willy, Detective, and hey! Those are Willy's shoes!"

Jack turns to his cuffed sidekick. "You want to tell me about these shoes?"

"What? That ole fart didn't need these shoes. I'm the king of this river, and I *need* new shoes. He wouldn't give 'em to me, so I took 'em."

"Yeah? Well, when you took them, he must have hit his head somehow, 'cause he died."

"Well, I told you he didn't need these shoes."

Jack uses his cell phone to request a uniformed unit to take in his suspect. As they wait for a cruiser to arrive at the river, Jack has time to think. *I'm working on a triple murder case with an illegal porn tie-in, and Jeffers has me doing this bullshit as well. I can't wait to get the hell out of South Florida. And damn, it's way too hot here!*

CHAPTER TWENTY

Back at the station, Jack is at his desk, busy finalizing the paperwork on the Andrews Avenue Bridge murder, when his thoughts are interrupted by his ringing telephone. Picking up the receiver, he answers absently, "Detective Stenhouse speaking."

"Jack, this is John from Forensics. The dive team recovered some evidence from the canal behind Cindy's apartment, but there was no usable DNA. They found a plastic bag containing an empty vial, a disposable hypodermic needle, and a small pot. The pot matched the bruise on Lisa's head, and they found traces of venom in the vial and needle, but there's nothing directly linking LeDue to the evidence."

"Damn! Even if we get a warrant and find needles in his condo that match the one from the canal, it'll only be circumstantial." He pinches the bridge of his nose and blows out a breath in frustration. "We still have no actual evidence against LeDue, just the hearsay testimony of Scott and Laura. The one thing we need to do now is to get LeDue to 'fess up somehow. Thanks, John."

Following orders, Lance has driven Maria to Mamba's headquarters near the airport, where they have entered the building via the loading dock behind the warehouse. He introduced Maria to the receiving clerk and the warehouse personnel, then gave her a tour of the main warehouse, the auction hall and, finally, the private studio. As they were touring the facility, the "telephone company" van has pulled up across the street from the warehouse and has set up shop.

Still inside the private studio, Lance is explaining Maria's special duties.

"Maria, this is the studio where we shoot the films for our more discreet clients. They each have individual needs and desires, and we try to accommodate all of them. Occasionally, they may want to 'star' in their own production. While we try to comply with all desires, we have one rule: no underage participants, unless they pay us a whole lot extra."

"Hmm, a porn czar with a heart...sort of. You're gonna make me cry, Lance. So I'm supposed to do *anything* they want? Well, for me, there's no anal and no animals. If they want any of that, you can find someone else to get their freak on."

"No problem, Maria. We want you to be as comfortable as possible."

"Good. Hey, I heard that Mamba was in the news recently. A few of your employees were killed, right? What's up with that?"

"I wasn't here at the time. In fact, I replaced the last filmmaker. Mr. LeDue said it was done by a disgruntled employee who has since been arrested."

"Really? Well, as long as he's no longer around, I guess it's okay. When do I get to strut my stuff?"

"Well, it looks like you're already strutting," Lance says with a sneer. "Actually, we're shooting a film tomorrow night. It's scheduled to be an all-girl cast, unless the client wants something unique. But there's also a cocktail party tonight, where you'll meet the clients who requested that film. Be back here at seven o'clock, and I'll introduce you to your co-stars. The clients will be here at nine p.m., so you can start strutting your stuff for them then. We'll shoot the film tomorrow night, after an auction that Mr. LeDue is holding here at the warehouse, where you'll be a hostess. Mr. LeDue will fill you in on what you need to do for that. Come on, let's get back to the gallery."

After the pair drives off, the "telephone company" van remains at the warehouse for a few minutes, then departs.

With his paperwork on the Andrews Avenue Bridge case finally finished, Jack stretches and rises from his chair, intent upon getting a cup of coffee. But before he can take a step, he hears the captain calling his name, and reluctantly detours to his boss' office.

"I just finalized the case on the homeless guy who was murdered under the bridge."

"That's not why I called you in, Jack."

Jeffers closes the door behind them. "Sit down, Jack. The D.A. has come up with a scheme to trap LeDue."

"I'm guessing this involves Wayne."

"Yeah, it does, and wait till you hear *this*. They're going to announce to the public that Wayne has been formally charged with the murders of Cynthia Walsh, Lisa Stevens, and Scott Simms, and that he has confessed to all of them."

"How is that going to get LeDue?"

"Let me finish. I think it's a risky plot, but they hope the announcement will put LeDue off guard, since he will probably assume that he's now off the hook. Now, here's what's risky. During Wayne's transfer from the county jail to a more permanent facility upstate, they're going to stage an automobile accident involving his transfer van on I-95. That's when Wayne will 'escape.' You know there's no direct evidence linking LeDue to the murders, so the only way we can convict him now, because of our 'beyond the shadow of a doubt' bullshit, is to get a direct confession from him. Before Wayne gets in the van, we're going to hook him up with a wire from the D.A.'s office. Then, after the 'crash' and his escape trick, we're going to help him double back into town so he can confront LeDue at his art gallery and get him to admit to the killings on the record. In exchange for his cooperation, Wayne's attorney negotiated with the D.A. for a reduced sentence of manslaughter in the murder of Scott Simms."

"Oh, yeah, 'bullshit' is correct. But Captain, you went along with this crap?"

"Had to. The mayor got involved, and he wants this thing ended."

"When's all this going to happen?"

"The phony escape happens tomorrow morning about five a.m. They're going to shut down I-95 and create a big mess."

Running his fingers through his hair, Jack declares, "One way or another, Captain, I want to be on the back-up team when Wayne talks to LeDue."

"You're there, Jack, and I want Maria there, too, on the inside. I'll fill her in about all this when she reports to me later today."

Anticipating that his work day tomorrow will be a long one, Jack leaves the office early. On the way home, he decides to give Didi a call, hoping to spend some time with her before he has to call it a night. She picks up on the first ring.

"Hey, Babe! Are you up for a late lunch, early dinner?"

"Sure, Jack!"

"Great. I'm gonna pick up some Chinese and be right over. I want to talk to you about something."

"Is there anything wrong?"

"Nope, just an early dinner and some good conversation. See ya soon."

Puzzled, Didi hangs up the phone and walks into her bedroom to fix herself up before Jack arrives. She is nervous about why Jack wants to come over to talk. He *never* wants to talk.

A knock at the door too soon after Jack's phone call surprises her.

"Yes? Is that you, Jack?"

A muffled voice beyond the door responds, "Hurry up, Babe! The food's getting cold and the beer's getting warm!"

Slipping into a bathrobe, she rushes to open the front door.

"Sorry, Jack." she apologizes. "Here, let me help you."

Didi grabs the cold six-pack as Jack carries in a bag containing cartons of egg drop soup, egg rolls, and sweet and sour pork and places it on the table in the kitchen. Jack opens the cartons and passes them out, while Didi pops open two beers and hands one to Jack.

With a suspicious look at Jack, Didi says, "Okay, you're here. Now, what do you want to talk about? You're not breaking up with me, are you?"

Jack almost chokes on the beer he's drinking.

"Hell, no! Didi, I'm tired of South Florida. It's too damn hot here. Plus, Captain Jeffers is an ass. I sent my resume out to a couple of police forces out of state, and I got a call from a deputy inspector in charge of the First Precinct in New York City, and another one from a captain at the Chicago police department. They're both looking for experienced homicide detectives, and they're interested in me. As soon as this LeDue thing is over, I'm going to use some vacation time to go up to New York to interview for the NYPD job. I've been keeping the New York inspector up-to-date on the progress of my current case, and he's holding the job open until I can get there. If I get the job, I want you to come to New York with me."

Didi stares at Jack in open-mouthed astonishment.

"Better shut your mouth, Babe, you're gonna catch flies."

In response, Didi stretches across the table and gives Jack a kiss. "Of course I'll come with you!" After a slight pause, she adds in a sultry voice, "Jack, is this your way of telling me that you love me?"

This time, it is Jack who is staring at Didi with an open mouth.

"Yeah, I guess so. It looks that way. Yeah."

Didi smiles brightly. "You realize that this means there won't only be talking after we eat, right?"

Groaning, Jack replies, "Not today, Babe. I gotta leave soon; big day tomorrow."

Almost gagging on his eggroll, Jack can't believe he just said no.

CHAPTER TWENTY-ONE

After Lance drops her back at the art gallery, Maria watches until he is out of sight, then calls Captain Jeffers on her cell phone before entering the building.

"Captain, this is Assante. There's going to be a cocktail party at Mamba's headquarters later tonight, and I have to be there. Tomorrow night, there will be an auction for some wealthy clients, and after that, we shoot a film. I'll be doing double duty, first as a hostess at tonight's party, then as a porn star tomorrow night. You can raid the place tomorrow, while they're filming. I'll let you know if anything changes before then."

"Okay, that works for us, Maria. Listen, we're going to have Wayne Jackson make a surprise visit to Mamba tomorrow, to try to get LeDue to confess. Try to catch the news in the morning; it's going to be a setup by the D.A. Wayne will be wearing a wire when he gets there, so be on the lookout for him. You saw his case file, so you know what he looks like. We'll brief him on what you're doing there."

"Okay, sir. Bye for now."

When Maria enters the gallery, she is met by Sean, who guides her into his office and explains her duties for the next two evenings. After their talk, Sean allows Maria to leave work a few hours early so she can shop for some "appropriate" clothing for her new position.

While Maria was talking with Sean, Captain Jeffers was calling the D.A.'s office and asking to speak to the assistant working on the LeDue case.

"Good afternoon, this is Captain Jeffers. We need to make a slight change in our plans for tomorrow. I just found out that LeDue won't be at the art gallery tomorrow night. Instead, he'll be holding an auction at Mamba's warehouse near the airport. We need to get Wayne into that auction, with the wire on. After the auction, they're going to shoot a porn flick, so with everyone together in one place, it'll be the perfect time to raid them. Are you all set for the escape?"

"Everything's in place. Just watch the TV news in the morning. We'll bring Wayne over to your station late tonight. You'll need to hold him there until we're ready to set the trap."

"Okay, see you tomorrow."

As the sun begins to set that evening, Jack is feeling, well, "anxious," so he hops in his car and calls Didi on the way to her apartment.

"Hey, Hon, it's Jack. I changed my mind."

"Oh, no! I'm sorry, but I'm with Maria right now, and we're shopping for some new outfits; she wants my 'professional' opinion. I may get some new stuff for myself, as well."

The idea of the two women trying on clothes together almost makes Jack run off the road.

"Need any help with zippers and stuff?"

"No, Jack, we're fine. Just calm yourself down; I'll call you tomorrow. Maybe we can do dinner and breakfast. Byeee."

Hanging up the phone, Jack envisions Didi's proposition, but reality soon strikes. *Damn! I'm going to be busy tomorrow with Wayne and LeDue, and all that other bullshit! Guess dinner and breakfast will have to wait for another day. Or maybe I can just get breakfast.*

Maria quickly finds two outfits for her big reveal at Mamba that evening. For the cocktail party, she bought a halter top dress in spandex, along with a push-up bra. The bra promises to add two cup sizes to an area that she doesn't need to embellish. For the auction and her supposed movie debut, she bought a tight-fitting zebra-print mini dress in rayon. She knows that if these dresses don't turn heads, nothing will, but she also knows that she could probably turn heads even if she only wore a potato sack. With six inches added to each of those dresses, she anticipates that she'll stop traffic at both events.

After their shopping spree, during which Didi bought a flimsy negligee, the women decide to stop at a coffee house before Maria needs to return to Mamba Imports for the cocktail party later that evening. They carry their drinks to an outside table so they can engage in some girl talk.

Maria begins the conversation with a question that's been on her mind.

"So Didi, how did you hook up with Jack?"

"Well, he kept coming in to watch me dance, and one night, when an over-served customer tried to climb up onstage, Jack came to my rescue. We started talking, and we've been together ever since. Don't tell anyone, but he just told me that he loves me!"

"Wow! From what I've heard about Jack, that's something. Are you sure he's not just stringing you along?"

"Maria, I have another secret for you, but first you must promise me that you won't say anything to anyone. Okay?"

"Okay, shoot."

"Jack wants to leave Florida, and he wants me to go with him! He has an interview lined up with the NYPD."

"Really? Wow, that's great! Maybe he *is* serious. I won't say anything about that, Didi, but you have to promise to give me a couple of lessons in pole-dancing before you leave."

Didi laughs. "Anytime, Maria, anytime."

Maria re-enters Mamba Imports while they're still setting up for the cocktail party. When she spies Sean LeDue directing the caterers, she gives him a flirty greeting.

"Ohh, Sean!"

Turning toward her voice, Sean is awestruck at the sight of his newest employee. His gaze begins at her six-inch heels, goes up her long legs, and stops at her breasts. With a smirk and a toss of her head, Maria responds to the ogling.

"Mr. LeDue, my eyes are up here, remember?"

Sean clears his throat. "Maria, you look fabulous!"

"Thank you, Mr. LeDue. Is this attire appropriate for a hostess at one of your parties?"

"It's spot-on, Maria, spot-on. Now why don't you go on over there to help Tracy? You may be working with her in the future, so you should get acquainted. She can show you what needs to be done with the caterers. Our guests will begin arriving soon, so I need to check with the bartender to make sure he's all set up. I should let you know that the guests include regulars from the social scene in Fort Lauderdale, along with three heavy-hitters who are coming into town just for the auction. Tonight you'll probably meet the mayor and some of the town commissioners, and sometime this evening I'll introduce you to our major client, the one with the 'special' needs. Wait for me in my office after you're done with the caterers. I want to make a grand entrance, escorting you into the party myself."

Later, Sean watches as a photographer for the local newspaper's social magazine takes photos of the socialites as they enter the building. When the heavy money arrives, he walks toward his office to get Maria, his prized showpiece for the evening.

Back at his condo, Jack begins to watch TV in order to pass the time before turning in for the night, but he quickly realizes that he's too lonely to sit at home by himself, so he decides to try to hook up with Didi again.

Normally, the drive to Didi's apartment takes about ten minutes, but Jack makes it there in five by disregarding all traffic laws. *Hell, what are they going to do, give me a ticket?* He takes up two parking spots as always, and walks through the courtyard to knock on her door. When Didi peers through the peephole, she is surprised to see Jack there.

Opening the door slightly, she asks, "Jack, what are you doing here?"

"I was feeling kind of lonely, so I thought I'd drop by. I was hoping I could stay for breakfast."

"Jack, I told you I was enjoying a girl's day today. I went shopping with Maria earlier, and now I have a couple of girls over from Shangri La."

"Aw, can I come in and play?"

Didi looks thoughtfully at Jack, and then says, "Wait a second, let me ask. I'll be right back."

Didi closes the door and walks inside the apartment to plead Jack's case. After a couple of minutes she returns and slowly opens the door.

"Jack, you're in luck. We wanted to play strip poker, but we were a hand short. Are you interested?"

"Thank God I have clean undies on! Deal me in!"

It may turn out to be a good night after all.

The "telephone company" van is parked outside the Mamba Imports warehouse again, taping everything that Maria is transmitting through the wire she has concealed beneath her skimpy dress. With her push-up bra working its magic, her breasts look as if they're going to escape at any moment.

Draped upon Sean's arm, Maria pauses as Sean surveys the main display room and whispers some last minute information.

"It's show time, Maria, and I will be introducing you to the three clients this auction has been arranged for. The first is Ivanovich Sharapov. He's an oil baron from the Ukraine, and an avid art collector and world-class poker player. After the party tonight, he'll be heading down to the casino in Hollywood for a high-stakes poker match. The second is Ho Chao Wang, an industrialist from Beijing, who is rumored to be one of the richest men in the world. He's here in Florida buying up foreclosures in our depressed housing market in order to flip them for huge profits, but he's always on the lookout for rare art objects. The third and most important client is Prince Abdul Farouch Salim from Yemen. He's our 'special' client, the one you'll be making the movie for, and the one you need to impress the most. Buying artworks is just a cover for his porn obsession. Besides these three, the room will also be full of local businessmen and politicos, and the local paper has sent a photographer to take pictures for their society pages."

"Okay, I understand. Let's get this show on the road."

Strategically placed among the crowd that is milling about the main display room are various paintings and sculptures that will be offered for sale at the auction. Some of the more valuable objects are paintings by Raphael and Caravaggio, and a sculpture by Donatello. But the item creating the largest buzz is a display of breastplate armor from ancient Rome with the name 'Pilate' engraved inside it, generally considered to be the breastplate armor worn by Pontius Pilate. Armed security guards are stationed everywhere around the room to protect the valuable objects that their private owners are putting up for auction.

As Maria and Sean enter the room, all attention turns in their direction. Sean escorts Maria to Sharapov and Wang, who are both admiring a sculpture by Donatello. He explains that Maria will be their hostess for the evening, and he lets them know that she will be at their service if they should need anything at all. Moving along, Sean guides Maria to the prince.

"Excuse me, Prince Salim, I would like you to meet Maria. She will be on screen for you later tonight. Do you approve of our latest acquisition?"

Maria takes the prince's arm into hers and gently pulls him close.

"I am your servant, sir. Please allow me to accommodate your every need."

"Maria, you are quite beautiful, and very alluring. I am sure your performance will be most enjoyable. However, I will be using my own 'participants,' if you will, for as sexy as you are, I can see that you are a little too 'mature' for my complete enjoyment. However, you will do nicely as a backdrop for the action that I require. I am most looking forward to witnessing your talents."

Attempting to salvage his pride, Sean interjects, "Prince Salim, Maria will be displaying her talents at the filming. You are welcome to watch the production as it unfolds. It will begin after tomorrow evening's auction, at about nine p.m."

"Mr. LeDue, I would not miss that chance. Thank you. You did remember the special need I requested?"

"Prince, your wish is my command, as always. It has been taken care of."

Catching Sean's attention, Maria smiles, "Sean, I'm going to mingle among your guests now, as a good hostess should." Then, turning toward the prince, she coos, "It was a pleasure to meet you, Prince Salim."

"The pleasure was all mine, my dear."

The prince, who is usually not very demonstrative in public, gives Maria a kiss on both cheeks before she departs from his company.

Sean is pleased.

Taking a moment to look over the crowd, Maria is surprised to see Commissioner Larry Daniels and his wife talking with the mayor of Fort Lauderdale. With a gleam in her eye, she whispers, *This is going to be good,* before sauntering over to them and exclaiming loudly, "Larry! I didn't expect to see *you* here!"

When she reaches the commissioner, she plants a wet kiss on his lips, then turns to the commissioner's wife and declares, "Incidentally, *ma'am*, I am NOT a tramp!"

In the ensuing commotion, she takes the mayor by the hand and leads him to the bar for a drink. Behind, them, Larry's wife throws her drink in her husband's face and walks out of the room with Larry following behind her, trying to explain away the preceding events.

After a glance at the theatrics she caused, Maria turns her charms on the mayor.

"Remember me, Mr. Mayor?"

Puzzled, the mayor studies her intently, then reacts in sudden surprise.

"Oh, my God! Ms. Assante? You look completely different out of uniform!"

“Please keep your voice down, Mr. Mayor. Yes, you handed me my diploma at the Academy. I'm working on the case that involves Sean LeDue."

"Then you're Jeffers' inside man, ah, woman. Brilliant! I must say, though, you don't look like a cop. My, oh my, not like a cop at all."

"Sir, if Captain Jeffers hasn't already talked to you, he will update you soon about everything that will be happening tomorrow regarding this case. Wish us luck, sir!"

Maria gives the mayor a kiss on the cheek, then abandons him at the bar to mingle with the other guests.

Still surprised by Maria's out-of-uniform charms, the mayor remains at the bar to watch her work the room for a while, then he finishes his drink and leaves the party.

After the mayor leaves, the cocktail party continues on for several more hours, but most of the guests don't know where to look first - at the art, or at Maria.

CHAPTER TWENTY-THREE

Jack awakens to Didi rattling dishes and pots in the kitchen, which sounds like bombs going off in his head. Too many shooters the night before have made today's hangover so bad that his tongue is asleep and his teeth itch, and no matter how hard he tries, he cannot make a fist.

Jack stumbles to the bathroom to relieve himself, then heads into the kitchen, where he sits down gingerly at the breakfast bar. Looking up at Didi, he squeaks, "Coffee!"

Glancing at her lover, Didi winces. "God, Jack. Close your eyes before you bleed to death." She pours a cup of coffee, which Jack sips slowly while trying to make a fist.

"What the hell did I do last night?"

Laughing, Didi replies, "Jack, you can't handle ladies' night, and you're not a very good poker player, either."

"Yeah, well, maybe I wanted to lose on purpose. Hey, got any aspirin? I'm dying here." Suddenly remembering what day it is, he groans, "Oh, wait, never mind. I gotta get home; I got a big day at work."

Wincing through the pain of his hangover, he quickly gulps down his coffee, then hurries into the bedroom to put on his shirt and pants and grab his gun. On his way out of the apartment, a sudden thought causes him to make a quick detour back into the kitchen, where he slaps Didi on the ass before he rushes out the door.

While Jack is still trying to make his way into work, Captain Jeffers is being greeted by the D.A. and Sergeant Wayne Jackson as he walks into the police station. The three men head into Jeffers' office, where they talk behind his closed door.

"Hello, Wayne. I see they managed to get you back here in one piece after your 'crash' this morning". With a smirk, Jeffers continues," I understand you're going to cooperate with our investigation and help us trap Sean LeDue. But before we continue, I have to ask, how'd you get yourself into this mess? Police work not exciting enough?"

"I know I got caught up in some heavy duty crap, Captain, and I'm sorry for letting down the Department and my family. I know I have to pay the price for what I did, but I want you to know that I'm willing to do whatever's necessary to get the sleaze ball who got me into this in the first place."

"You're an absolute disgrace, Jackson. I don't understand how you got involved, but since you're willing to help, I'll put aside my disgust for a while."

Turning to the D.A., Jeffers continues, "My operative inside Mamba tells me that LeDue is conducting an auction tonight at his main warehouse. Wayne will need to be at the warehouse during the auction, so Maria Assante will help him get into the building. You'll meet Maria today, Wayne. They're planning to shoot a porn movie about nine o'clock, after the auction ends. We need to have a team set up and in place to break the filming up as soon as Maria gives the signal."

"Wayne will be wired and ready to go as soon as you give the word," confirms the D.A.

Speaking up, Wayne declares boldly, "Guys, all you have to do is wire me, and I'll hand you LeDue. I'll get him to admit to what I know he did."

Enjoying a long sleep after a late night of entertaining high-powered art enthusiasts, Maria awakens slowly, stretches, and grabs the remote for her bedroom TV. She surfs the channels until she finds the local morning news show, then watches disinterestedly until she hears a reporter announcing the statement that was issued by the Fort Lauderdale Police earlier in the morning.

"...this morning, while transporting former Sergeant Wayne Jackson of the Fort Lauderdale Police to a more secure facility. Wayne Jackson is the accused murderer of Cynthia Walsh, Lisa Stevens, and Scott Simms. One of the tires of the van blew out, causing it to flip over on I-95. The transporting officer was knocked unconscious in the wreck, but Wayne Jackson was able to free himself from his shackles and has escaped. The accused murderer is classified as dangerous. If you see him or know of his whereabouts, please contact Fort Lauderdale Police by dialing 911. We have special officers on duty who will field your calls."

Maria smiles, then heads into the shower to gets herself ready for the evening's auction. On the way to Mamba Imports, she will stop at police headquarters to meet Wayne Jackson and to receive final instructions.

Jack finally makes it into work with a cup of coffee in one hand and a can of Coke in the other, the only things that help with his hangovers. When Captain Jeffers catches sight of the rundown state of his detective through his office window, he shouts out, "DEAD MAN WALKING! *Jack! In my office!*"

Entering the office with a frown, Jack finds Wayne Jackson and the D.A. sitting around Jeffers' desk.

"Damn, Jack!" Wayne exclaims. "You're gettin' a little old to be that hung over, aren't you?"

Jack takes a sip of his coffee, flashes half a peace sign at his former colleague, then takes a sip of soda. Squinting against the bright office light, he takes his sunglasses out of his shirt pocket and puts them on.

"Light's too bright in here. What's the plan, guys?"

"We're going in tonight. The D.A. will have Wayne wired and at Mamba around eight-thirty this evening. Maria will get him into the building, but it'll be up to Wayne to get LeDue to confess."

"So what makes you think you can get LeDue to man up, Wayne?"

"It's because I know that S.O.B. and how much he loves to gloat about all his schemes. Getting him to man up will be easy."

"Yeah, and what's in it for you? Why did you become a boy scout all of a sudden?" Jack sneers.

"LeDue is a dirt bag. He tried to frame me for Cindy's murder by planting one of my buttons at the scene, so I want his ass."

Captain Jeffers rises from his chair. "Listen, Jack, I hate to leave you two love birds here alone, but the D.A. and I have to fill the mayor in on what's going down tonight. Maria is due into the office this morning. If we're not back before she arrives, you need to introduce her to Wayne and fill her in on the plan. Now, you two play nice."

Jack and Wayne sit together in silence for what seems like hours, then Jack speaks up, unable to contain himself any longer.

"So Wayne, have you seen your kid since all this went down?"

"Nah, but I talked to his mother. It's better that he doesn't see me right now. After I help out on this case, maybe I'll earn some points with him."

The disgraced sergeant looks uncomfortably at Jack, then confesses, "Actually, he doesn't want to see me at all, but let's not talk about that anymore. Did you see the paper this morning? They have a bunch of photos of Commissioner Daniels getting kissed by some fox at that party last night. That guy is such an ass."

"That fox is a cop. That's Maria Assante."

Wayne's eyes widen in surprise, as his jaw hits the floor. "You're shitting me! A cop? She could be one of those lingerie models with the wings. Shit! She's wasting her talents here, man. Damn, if I had a partner who looked like that... Uh oh. Oh, shit!"

Both men turn to look out the office window as they hear the sound of whistles, hoots, and hollers from the squad room. With a knock on Jeffers' door, they wait expectantly while the door slowly opens and a gorgeous head pops into the room.

"I'm not interrupting anything, am I, guys?"

Maria Assante enters the office wearing a tight, zebra-print mini dress. When Jack whips off his sunglasses to get a better look, his hangover is instantly cured. Smiling at his new partner, he motions to Wayne. “Maria, meet Wayne Jackson."

Maria walks over to the two men, who are sitting together on the office sofa. She grabs each of them by the chin, a move she has made before, and pulls their heads upward. "My eyes are up here, guys."

Squirming, Jack sputters, "Hey! If you don’t want us to look at ‘em, cover ‘em up!” Pointing at Wayne, he says, “We need to talk, Maria. Wayne’s going to get LeDue to confess tonight, so he says. He doesn't have an invite to the auction, so you’re going to have to get him in sometime before the auction ends and the filming begins. He’ll be wearing a wire so we can get LeDue on murder and pornography, all in one shot."

"Okay. I can let you in through the front entrance, Wayne. There won’t be anyone at the door during the auction so you can go directly into LeDue's office. I assume you know where it is. I'll get him to come to you."

"I'll be there tonight as well, as part of the assault team,” announces Jack. “The captain wants to meet with all of us when he returns from the mayor's office. He’s there now, with the D.A."

"I hope this meeting won’t last long, because I have to be at Mamba's warehouse early this afternoon. There are several items that will be auctioned off, and it’ll probably take a couple of hours to move everything from the art gallery to the warehouse, and to get everything set up. The auction is scheduled to start about four o’clock and it should be over by nine. There will be about seven clients on hand for the bidding, along with several phone bidders. I'll be there to hostess at the auction and to ‘act’ in a porn film that will be shot after the auction. Wayne, you’re going to have to get Sean to confess to the murders before I call in SWAT and bust him for porn."

"No problem. I know Sean; he'll give it up. He’s an ego-driven asshole. But damn, girl! Too bad you can't make that movie; you've got the qualifications, all right! Yeah, yeah, I know your eyes are up there. I’m just window shopping."

Maria puts up a good front against male tendencies to treat women as sexual objects, but deep down, she loves the attention.

"Look, guys, this is only going to happen one time, so enjoy the show. But right now, I need some coffee; I haven't had my morning cup yet. You guys want some? My treat. I can get donuts, too."

"I'm still drinking mine; I'm okay," responds Jack.

Wayne pipes up, "I'll take it black with two sugars, and no donuts. But if you think you got harassed in here, Maria, wait till you parade around outside."

"Yeah, I know. Captain Jeffers introduced me around when I started this morning. I already heard all the whistles and catcalls."

The two men eye Maria intently as she walks out the door to get coffee for herself and Wayne, but when the whistles start again on the squad room floor, Jack pounces. Jumping up from his seat, he stands in the office doorway and shouts to his fellow officers, "Hey, HEY, HEY! Put your tongues back in your mouths! There's a police officer on the floor!"

Hearing Jack's remarks, Maria glances back at him and gives him a wink. Then she flashes everyone else the famous Florida state bird.

CHAPTER TWENTY-FOUR

"Sean, this is Lance. I didn't wake you, did I?"

"As a matter a fact, you did."

"Well, Boss, you need to wake up and turn on the TV! Wayne Jackson escaped!"

"WHAT?!"

Sean slams the phone down onto his nightstand and turns on the TV, surfing until he finds the local news channel. He doesn't have to wait long until the report he needs to hear comes on.

At that same moment, Captain Jeffers and the D.A. return from their meeting with the mayor to find Maria, Wayne, and Jack having their morning coffee in the captain's office.

The captain sits at his desk, then looks from one person to the other and smirks, "So, are all you daisies acquainted now?" And as he is always looking for an opportunity to pick on Jack, he sneers, "You're looking almost normal, Jack. Feeling better, are we?"

"Yeah, I'm aces," Jack responds snidely. "How's the mayor?"

"Still his ole, jovial self."

"Guess that means he's still an asshole."

"Be nice," counters the captain. "You don't want to give Maria the wrong impression of our beloved mayor, do you?"

"No wrong impression by me," declares Maria. "He's right; the guy's a politician, so that means he's an asshole. Look, Captain, I have to be at Mamba's headquarters early today, so can we get this briefing started? I need to get over there soon."

Shifting in his seat, Jack looks over at the captain for permission to speak, and when the captain nods his head, he begins.

"Okay, guys, here it is. The captain and I have come up with a plan that will shut down Mamba for good. You'll be wearing a special necklace tonight, Maria." Jack points to the D.A., who displays an innocent-looking necklace that he has retrieved from his pocket. "It has a camera and mike built into it so we can monitor you more closely, and when it's time for us to let you know the cavalry's in place, we can signal the necklace to vibrate. But Maria, you'll still need to let us know when to come in. You can whisper; the mike will pick up everything you say. Wayne will also be wired tonight, and it'll be his job to get LeDue to admit to the murders."

Glancing from Maria to Wayne, Jack continues to describe the plan.

"We'll have two SWAT teams ready. One will come in through the loading dock area, the other through the front entrance. LeDue will have armed guards on duty to protect the artwork and the artifacts, but we already talked to the security service he's using and they'll be prepared for the raid. Jeffers, do you have anything to add?"

"Yeah. Remember that there will be some high-profile local dignitaries at the auction, so we hope to get this all done *after* they leave. Oh, one more thing. There will be a foreign dignitary there, some prince who carries diplomatic immunity. He may be a pervert, but we won't be able to hold him for anything. So make sure the prince isn't harmed during the assault, and don't pull the trigger on the mission too soon; we don't want to have this escalate into an international incident. That's it, unless the D.A. has more to add."

The D.A. shakes his head no, so the captain continues. "Then I guess you can leave now, Maria. Don't forget your necklace."

Maria takes the necklace from the D.A., and weighing it in her hand, notes, "Wow, this thing is heavy!"

The D.A. replies, "Yeah, it was like putting twenty pounds of stuff into a ten pound bag."

Maria places the necklace around her neck, then exits the office.

When the door closes behind her, the D.A. turns to the former police sergeant. "Wayne, we'll wire you up just before we leave for the auction tonight, but right now, we need to take you back down to Lockup. You'll remain there until we're ready to go."

On the way to Mamba's headquarters, Maria stops at a local gun shop that caters to law enforcement personnel. She usually uses her purse to conceal a Ruger .380 semi-automatic pistol, which is just a little larger than the palm of her hand, but since she will be without her purse for most of the evening tonight, she needs an alternate way of carrying her weapon. The mini dress she's wearing is too tight and revealing to conceal a weapon under her arm or around her waist, so she considers a thigh holster, but the dress is short and won't conceal the gun on her upper thigh if she sits down. She needs a way to hold her weapon higher on her thigh. Noticing her dilemma, one of the salesmen suggests a compression holster. This type of holster is made of the same elastic material that is used in bandages for wrapping sprains and muscle strains and is designed for females to wear under their panties. Similar to a lingerie bikini bottom, it includes a pouch that can hold a small handgun over a woman's pubic area.

Maria tries the holster on, but soon realizes that the configuration of the pouch means that it will work best only under a skirt or slacks, where a weapon can be extracted from a beltline.

Without time to search for other options, she decides to purchase the compression holster. She knows that its main drawback means that she will have to pull up her dress in order to draw her weapon, but she chooses to ignore that looming inconvenience. Besides, her dress is so short that she will not have to hike it up very far anyway.

Feeling more confident, and surprisingly comfortable, now that her weapon is close by, Maria drives to Mamba's headquarters, ready for the showdown that will come later. When she arrives at the building, she notices that the police surveillance van is already in place down the block, but this time it's marked with the logo of a cleaning service company.

Fearing that Wayne Jackson may show up at his facility after his escape that morning, Sean LeDue calls his bodyguard into his office. Tony Galluda, an ex-navy seal and one-time ultimate cage fighter, is a formidable 6' 5", 275-pound wall of protection. Tony enters the office, just barely fitting through the door.

"Yes, Mr. LeDue?"

Holding out a photo of Wayne, Sean says, "Be on the lookout for this man. He's an ex-employee who just escaped from jail, and he might show up here tonight."

"Is this the guy who was on the news this morning?"

"One and the same."

"No problem, Mr. LeDue. I can take care of it."

"Be warned. He's an ex-cop, so he may be armed."

Tony responds by opening up his suit jacket to reveal a .45 caliber semi-automatic pistol. Smiling, he re-closes his jacket.

Pleased by what he has seen, Sean says, "That's good, very good. Place yourself in the auction room where I can see you."

Sean's secretary's voice comes over the intercom in the office.

"Mr. LeDue, Maria is here."

"Excellent. Send her in."

A few minutes later, Maria opens the door to make her entrance.

"Bought a new outfit... you like?"

"Ah, that's perfect! It has that wild animal touch! Maria, I want you to meet Tony. He's my personal protection for the evening. Remember what I told you about Wayne Jackson? Well, he escaped from police custody this morning, and I'm afraid he may show up here tonight."

"Oh, really? I woke up late today and didn't catch the news." Turning to Tony, she purrs, "Hi, Tony. My, oh my, you can protect *me* anytime."

Maria looks him over and tries to get a reaction, but Tony couldn't give a shit.

"Tony, this is Maria Assante. You two will be working together this evening. She's the hostess and special projects coordinator I told you about."

"Maria. Nice to meet you."

In a seductive tone, Maria continues, "Tony, you're going to be *my* special project for tonight. You need to loosen up a bit!" She gives him the slow once-over before returning her attention to Sean. "Mr. LeDue, with the auction starting at four, the clients will probably start arriving within the hour. I need to freshen up and check with Lance. See you boys later!"

After Maria leaves the office, Sean turns to Tony. "I can't wait to see her perform later tonight. Want to join in on the fun?"

"Sir, as good as that may be, I was hired to protect *you*. Another time and another place, and I'd be all over *that* like a fresh coat of paint."

"Boy, I'd sure like to put that on film! Listen, go on out and make yourself visible. The clients will be arriving soon, and you make a very good first impression."

At that same moment, Jack drives past the building. He parks down the block, walks casually up to the surveillance van, opens the back door, and climbs in.

"Anything new, guys?"

"Yeah. LeDue has a bodyguard on duty tonight, and he's armed. We called Jeffers to let him know."

"Okay, I'm gonna hang with you two until it all goes down. SWAT is staging at the empty hangar across the street. Jeffers will join them there with Wayne."

Within a short time, the bidders begin showing up for the auction. Along with the three international heavy-hitters, local professional athletes and socialites from Palm Beach begin streaming into the auction hall. Maria personally greets everyone who enters, and she plans to pay special attention to Prince Salim. As Jack and the surveillance team listen, Maria approaches the prince.

"Prince Salim! It's so nice to see you again! Are these your beautiful children?"

"No, no, my dear! These are my special companions. They will be working with you later tonight. As I mentioned, you are a very beautiful woman, but you are too aged for my liking."

Holding back her disgust, Maria gives each of the girls a hug.

"Hi, I'm Maria. It's very nice to meet you. I'll be with you all evening, and I'll be happy to assist with whatever you may need." Glancing at the prince, she declares, "Prince Salim, they seem to be so shy. What are their names?"

Presenting first one girl and then the other, the prince responds, "This is Liana, and this is Sofia. They are most precious to me."

"It's a pleasure to meet you. If you don't mind my asking, how old are each of you?"

Liana speaks for both girls. "I am fourteen and Sofia is fifteen."

"Thank you! You're sweet. Would you like me to give you a quick tour of the objects up for bid tonight? Of course, that will be only with your permission, sir."

"That will be fine, Maria. They seem to be in good hands."

Maria takes the hand of each girl and leads them into the gallery.

Back in the van, Jack and the surveillance team react to what they just heard through Maria's microphone.

"Holy crap! What a sleazeball! And the worst part is that he has diplomatic immunity! Call the D.A. and have him contact the State Department to see if we can take the kids away."

"Jack, the D.A. and Jeffers are with Wayne Jackson. They're on their way to the staging area across the street. SWAT is already there. Why don't you just ask them in person?"

"Good idea. I'll wait for them there."

Jack exits the van and crosses the street to meet with the SWAT teams while he waits for Captain Jeffers and the D.A.

CHAPTER TWENTY-FIVE

When LeDue addresses the bidders, Maria moves to the back of the auction hall.

"Before we present the prized piece of tonight's auction, the breastplate armor of Pontius Pilate, we have our final sculpture, which will make an excellent addition to any collection. The owner of this piece will remain anonymous, and our auctioneer will start the bidding at one million dollars. But remember, we still have one more piece after this one, so don't spend all your money now!"

As the bidding starts, Maria slips into the front lobby.

While the auction is taking place, Jack and several members of the SWAT teams diffuse the tension while they wait for the go signal by playing a few hands of poker.

Finally, over an hour late, Captain Jeffers, the D.A., and Sergeant Jackson join the team. Watching them enter the building, Jack takes a dig at his boss for arriving late.

"Captain! So glad you decided to join us. And I see that you brought a few friends with you!"

"Zip it, Jack. We got tied up with the mayor again."

"Okay, I got it, but listen, Boss, I need to talk to you. We know that the prince has diplomatic immunity, but that asshole is a pedophile! He's keeping two young teenage girls around for his pleasure, no doubt counting on his diplomatic status. Can the state department do anything about getting those girls away from him?"

"I'll have them check into it. If the girls aren't listed as part of his diplomatic office staff, we may be able to do something."

"Another thing, Captain. LeDue has an armed bodyguard, Tony Galluda."

Shocked, Jeffers retorts, "Isn't he a former cage fighter, and about the size of a truck?"

"That's the guy." Turning to Wayne, he sneers. "Are you scared, Wayne?"

"Up yours, Jack. The bigger they are..."

"Yeah, the farther you run."

Lieutenant Gomez, Commander of the SWAT teams, busts into the conversation.

"Listen, guys. We just got a call from Assante; time for Jackson to get busy. She's in the front lobby, waiting to let him in."

Jeffers jumps into action. "Okay, everyone, listen up! It's go time! Let's get this over with! Gomez, check with the van to see if they can hear Jackson."

Wayne speaks into his concealed microphone, listens for a minute, then turns to Jeffers and gives him a thumb up. With a wave of his hand, he leaves the hangar and heads across the street to Mamba Imports as one of the two SWAT teams readies to move near the loading dock at the back of the auction building, and the other one prepares for an assault through the front door.

Jeffers turns toward his men. "Remember, gentlemen, on Assante's signal!"

Maria is waiting in the lobby when Wayne opens the front door.

"LeDue is in the auction room with his bodyguard. After the last item is sold and everyone starts to leave, I'll arrange for him to go to his office. Go there now and wait. I have to go back inside."

Maria returns to the auction room while Wayne walks over to the lobby's reception desk and opens the center drawer, taking out the .38 Smith and Wesson revolver that is kept there for emergencies. He places it inside the waistband of his slacks, under his shirt, then walks into Sean's office. As Maria re-enters the auction room, she hears the auctioneer.

"We have seven hundred fifty thousand, do I hear eight? That's seven hundred fifty, seven hundred fifty. Yes? We have a phone bid of eight hundred thousand. That's eight hundred thousand. Do I hear eight hundred fifty? Eight hundred. Do I hear eight hundred fifty? Ladies and gentlemen, this is a piece of antiquity that is right out of the New Testament. Surely, it is worth at least one million. The bid is eight hundred. Do I hear eight hundred fifty?"

Ivanovich Sharapov motions Sean LeDue over with his hand and whispers into his ear. Sean calls out to the auctioneer.

"Mr. Sharapov would like to make a final bid of one million dollars!"

"We have a bid of one million dollars. Are there any other bids? One million. The last bid is one million dollars. Are there any more bids?" The auctioneer's gavel makes a sharp cracking sound. "Sold! For one million dollars!"

A large round of applause ends the night's auction as Sean LeDue approaches the microphone.

"I would like to take this opportunity to thank all of you for attending this evening's auction. We sincerely hope that each of you has enjoyed the festivities and that you will return for our next auction. In the morning, our office will contact each buyer and their agents to arrange for the transfer of their purchases. Prince Salim, Maria will now accompany you to the private viewing area so you can finalize your special purchase. Maria, please escort our honored guest and his entourage to meet with Lance Cutler."

Sean turns to Maria as she walks up to the dais and whispers in his ear. "There's a man waiting to see you in his office. He says he's an old friend."

LeDue frowns, then looks at Tony Galluda.

"Okay, go with the prince. I'll see who it is."

As he walks toward the door, Sean waves Tony over to join him.

Back at Sean's office, Wayne is sitting behind Sean's desk. He knows the auction is over, so he has the .38 cocked and ready. When the door opens, Tony walks in ahead of LeDue, and Wayne points the revolver at him.

"Okay, let's take this very slow. Come on in, both of you, and put your hands where I can see them."

After both men raise their hands into the air, he orders Sean to close the door, then stands up and walks out from behind the desk.

Unaccustomed to being out of control in his own office, Sean turns toward Wayne in anger. "What the hell are you doing here, Wayne, and what do you want from me?"

"Shut up, LeDue. I'll ask the questions. And you, big guy, draw your weapon out with your fingertips, very slowly."

Wayne watches carefully as Tony complies. "That's it. Now put it on the floor and kick it over to me."

As Tony's .45 semi-automatic Glock slides across the floor, Wayne states, "Good, very good," then he picks up the weapon and places it inside his waistband.

"Hey, Big Guy, why don't you go into Sean's private dressing room over there and close the door? And Sean, why don't you lock the door behind him?"

Irate at the suggestion, Tony blurts out, "Oh yeah? Just how do you think you're going to get me to go in there, *Big Guy*?"

"*Get* you to go in there? I've just been arrested for three murders; I'm already a dead man! One more murder won't get me any more jail time, so I have nothing to lose. Get your ass in that room, or you're dead."

Listening closely to all of this through Wayne's wire, Jeffers angrily confronts the D.A.

"How the hell did Jackson get a gun? You want me to end this now and send in SWAT?"

"No, we wait. We need to get LeDue."

Sean locks Tony Galluda in the dressing room, then turns back to Wayne, who demands, "Sit down, LeDue. Get comfortable."

Taking a seat in front of the desk, he waits for Wayne's next move.

"Tell me, LeDue, how'd you do it? How the hell did you frame me for all of this? Yeah, I killed Scott for you, but I didn't do the girls, not that Cindy didn't deserve it. Boy, what a bitch she turned out to be."

LeDue doesn't answer, preferring to stare at the floor, so Wayne tries again.

"Come on, Sean. I figure Laura got you some venom from that snake guy in the Everglades and you wasted Cindy with it. Scott and Cindy were in business for themselves, and I got my cut, so you had me get rid of Scott, and then you framed me for Cindy. But why Lisa? She was harmless. She wasn't involved at all."

"She was at the wrong place at the wrong time, you clueless bastard. I got Laura to take a button off one of your suits and I planted it at the beach to frame you. But Lisa just happened to walk into the apartment after I killed Cindy, so I had to get rid of Lisa, too. I used my insulin needles to inject both of them with the venom. Ha! I guess this is one time that being a diabetic came in handy! But damn, that venom is some good stuff! They died within minutes!"

Hearing the confession they were waiting for, Captain Jeffers tells the team, "That's it! We got him! Now we have to wait for Maria. Jack, put on a vest and get ready."

"You bet, Captain."

Maria watches uneasily as Lance prepares to start filming and Prince Salim preps the two young girls for their role in the movie. Suddenly, her necklace vibrates. That's her cue to begin the takedown.

Lance looks up from his camera and motions to Maria.

"Maria, this is Brad. The prince wants him to join you on the sofa with Scarlett. You can get him all worked up, then the prince's girls will come in and finish him off."

Maria walks in front of the sofa and stares into the camera.

"Lance, there aren't enough men here for me to work with, but I can fix that. Now's the time."

Hearing their cue, Jack and the first SWAT team head to the front door, while the second SWAT team makes their way down the hallway from the loading dock.

Maria pulls up her dress, draws her weapon, and shouts, "I'm Officer Assante, Fort Lauderdale Police! Nobody move!"

Within seconds, the rear SWAT team enters the sound stage, and with loud protests from the prince, takes everyone into custody, while Jack and the front SWAT team enter the lobby and neutralize the security guards.

Leaving several SWAT team members to watch the guards, Jack and the remaining team members make their way to LeDue's office.

"Wayne, we're coming in!"

An officer kicks open the door, enabling Lieutenant Gomez and his fellow officers to grab LeDue, who begins to shout, "Arrest that man! It's Wayne Jackson! He broke into my office!"

Wayne places the revolver on the desk and shows LeDue the transmitter he was wearing.

"You're toast, LeDue. You're on tape!" Looking at Jack, he continues, "His bodyguard is locked in the dressing room. The key is in LeDue's pocket."

Jack retrieves the key and leads Galluda out of the locked room.

As the SWAT team escorts Sean and his bodyguard out of the office, Jack remains behind with Wayne Jackson.

"Nice job, Wayne! But how'd you get a gun?"

"LeDue kept it at the front desk for protection. I wasn't going to come in here unarmed, with that monster bodyguard around."

"Where's the guard's gun?"

Instead of answering, Wayne slowly draws the guard's semi-automatic out from under his shirt. Surprised, Jack responds by raising his 9mm and taking aim.

"Put it down, Wayne."

"I'm not going to jail, Jack."

"Don't make me shoot you. Put it down."

"I'm not going to jail, but you won't have to shoot me."

With Jack yelling, "NO!" Wayne jams the gun in his mouth and blows the back of his head off.

Jack looks up as Lieutenant Gomez runs back into the office.

"WHAT HAPPENED? You okay?"

"Yeah. Wayne had the bodyguard's gun, and before I could stop him... *Damn!"*

Lieutenant Gomez looks at Wayne, and then at Jack. "Boy, he really made a mess of things, didn't he?"

As the second SWAT team begins to lead people out of the building, Prince Salim and his two young companions are escorted to a corner of the lobby. Protesting loudly, the prince declares, "You cannot hold me! I have immunity! I am a representative of Yemen!"

Hearing the prince's complaints, Maria walks over to him and speaks quietly.

"You're a pedophile and a pervert, and if I had my way, I'd cut your balls off."

As the prince spits out another protest, the D.A. and a representative from the State Department join the group.

"Officer Assante, we need to release Prince Salim immediately. Prince Salim, you need to leave now, before you receive some unwanted publicity."

Visibly relieved, the prince bows, "Thank you. Come with me, girls."

The State Department official puts out a hand to prevent the girls from leaving.

"Ah, no, these young ladies are not listed as part of your staff, Prince Salim. They do not have to go with you."

Turning toward the young girls, he gives them an option. "You don't have to go with him if you don't want to."

Sofia takes the prince's hand and looks around for her companion, but Liana is walking toward Maria. When the young girl reaches Maria, she grabs her hand and holds it tightly. "I do not want to go," she cries.

Hearing Liana, the prince looks over at her in disgust, then turns to leave with Sofia. But Maria cries out, "We can't let him leave with her! Sofia, stop!"

Restraining Maria, the D.A. states, "We can't do anything now, but we did let the Yemeni Embassy know what was going on. The Muslim clerics will take care of him when he returns home."

Captain Jeffers joins the group in the lobby as LeDue is escorted out of the building, followed by Jack. When the D.A. sees Jack, he looks around the room and asks, "Where's Jackson?"

"He's back in LeDue's office. He's dead."

Shocked, the D.A. asks, "What the hell happened?"

"He got the bodyguard's gun and offed himself before I could stop him. Oh, man! I feel real sorry for his poor kid!"

With a sigh, the D.A. looks back at Maria, who is still holding Liana's hand.

"Maria, let the girl go with the State Department. They'll set up a family for her to stay with here, while they try to find her family back in Yemen. By the way, don't leave with that necklace. We need it back."

Before Maria can move, Captain Jeffers grabs her elbow and turns her away from the group. He says quietly, "Be in my office in the morning. I want to talk to you about your career."

When Maria is free, Jack walks over and shakes her hand.

"Good job, rookie! There's an all-night diner on 84. How about some pancakes? My treat. I'll call Didi; she can meet us there."

"Sounds good, but I need to get out of this dress first. I have a change of clothes in the car. I can be with you in five minutes."

"No, no, no! A change of clothes? You can't take that dress off! You look fabulous!"

"Thanks, Jack, but the next time I wear this dress, I'll be looking to get laid, and it sure won't be you, not now, not ever. I'll be back in a couple of minutes."

Shaking his head, Jack turns to Lieutenant Gomez, who was listening to the exchange. “Damn, she’s wasting her talents as a cop!”

“Jack, I’d give a month’s salary to take a peek under that dress.”

“Yeah, stand in line. Listen, get your guys and join us at that diner on 84.”

“Sounds good. See you later.”

Gomez rounds up his team members while Jack calls Didi.

“Hey, Hon! Maria and I and some of the guys are going out for pancakes. Are you hungry? Good. I’ll pick you up in ten minutes, and we’ll head to that all-night diner on 84. Yeah, me, too. Yeah, we got him good.”

Jack, Didi and Maria sit in one booth while Lieutenant Gomez and his crew fill in the booths around them. Jack has already told the manager that he would be paying for all the cops’ meals, and the manager said he would cut him a break on the tab to show his appreciation for the guys in blue. After everyone orders, a giant BS session ensues until the orders are served.

Jack, still wondering why Maria is a cop, asks, “So Maria, what are your career plans?”

“Well, I originally intended to put in some time wearing a uniform, but what I really want is to join the FBI. Jeffers says he has some information about that, so we’ll see. How about you, Jack? Is this your life’s work?”

“This is all I know, but it ain’t going to be all down here. I got an interview with NYPD. With luck, I’ll go north.”

“Wow! Good luck, Jack.” With a wink at Didi, she asks, “Did he invite you to go with him?”

Winking back, Didi replies, “Yeah, he can’t get rid of me that easily!”

Overhearing the conversation, Lieutenant Gomez declares, “So what is this, Jack? You’re leaving us for the big city? Jeffers is really going to be pissed off. He’ll be losing two detectives at the same time.”

"Screw Jeffers; he's one of the reasons I'm leaving. Don't say anything to him, though. I want to tell him myself."

"We'll leave that to you. Give 'em hell in the Big Apple! But Jack, you're a Florida boy. How you gonna survive the winter in the frozen north?"

"A little cold weather won't kill me; I *hate* the heat! Besides, I got Didi to keep me warm!"

"Yeah, but who's gonna keep *her* warm?"

Jack smiles and flashes Gomez the Florida state bird.

CHAPTER TWENTY-SIX

Jack's interview with Deputy Inspector Rawlings goes well, so beginning next month he'll be the newest homicide detective at the New York Police Department's First Precinct.

Didi is very happy about the move to New York. She had been thinking about moving and about getting out of the stripper business to do something more nine to five, so Jack's desire to leave South Florida is perfect for her. With all the money she was able to save from her stripper job, she wants to open a lingerie boutique on the Upper East Side.

Didi plans to travel to New York before Jack gets there in order to rent an apartment and find a business location for herself. In this economy, Didi knows it will be a gamble to open a new business, but if it fails, she knows she can always jump back on the pole.

Until next month, though, Jack still has a job to do in Fort Lauderdale.

It's another typical August morning. Only nine o'clock, and the temperature is already eighty-four degrees. Detective Jack Stenhouse is fast asleep, but he's suddenly awakened by his ringing telephone.

Sleepily, he picks up the phone and growls, "This is Stenhouse, and it better be good."

"STENHOUSE! This is Jeffers! I know you only got two more weeks here, but you still need to do your job! You comin' in soon, or what?"

"Hold your water, I'll be right there. Gotta do my three S's."

Jack hangs up the phone and turns to Didi, lying naked in his bed, and yeah, all he can think of is the front bumper of a '58 Caddy.

He slaps her on the ass to wake her up, then reaches down to the floor to get some cash out of his pants pocket. Tossing it on the bed, he says, “Here, take a cab home. I’ll come down to the Shangri La after work and take you out for dinner.”

Jack heads to the bathroom while Didi rolls over and goes back to sleep. Within thirty minutes, he jumps into his ‘68 Road Runner, gives a quick “beep, beep” of the horn and squeals out of the parking lot. On his way to work, he turns on the radio and listens to the morning news as thunder rolls in from offshore storms at the beach.

Ten minutes later, Jack walks into Captain Jeffers’ office to find Maria Assante there, waiting for him with their impatient boss.

“So glad you could come in to work this morning, Jack,” Jeffers needles. “No coffee, no Coke today?”

Jack sits down on the sofa and gives Maria a wink, then turns to his boss. “Captain, was it your idea to give Wayne a police burial? Gee, I almost wanted to tear up when I heard it on the radio this morning. What did you tell his son?”

“Yeah, I know, but it was so sad to see the poor kid; the bastard really screwed things up. I should have worn boots when we told him about his father, though; it was getting really deep in there. The mayor told us to say that his father had a brain hemorrhage.”

“Wasn’t really a lie, was it?”

“Yeah, okay, that’s enough for now; let’s get back to police business. You’ll be happy to know that LeDue has been charged with two counts of murder one. He’s trying to plea bargain down to murder two or manslaughter so he won’t get the death penalty, but either way, he’s going to be gone for a long time. I also want to let you know what I found out about Prince Salim, but it’s not good news. Unfortunately, when he returned to Yemen he faced no disciplinary action even though he was basically trafficking in slavery, because women in Yemen and in most Arab countries are considered to be second class citizens. A new, twelve-year-old girl soon joined

Sofia in keeping the prince 'company', so I guess power and money work well to shield the scums of the earth."

Maria moans, "Oh, Sofia; that poor baby! I'm glad that at least one of them is out of his clutches!"

"Yes, we did manage to save one of them. And Jack, the other reason I called you here is because I want to let you know about Maria's new job before you leave the department. She's going on uniformed patrol and will be featured in a new reality TV show called *Female Cops On and Off Duty*."

"TV? Really? That's great, Maria! You'll be a smash hit!"

"Thanks! Hey, Jack, maybe I can get them to film Didi teaching me how to pole-dance before she leaves for New York. What do you think?"

"Yeah, from your lips to God's ears."

While they are laughing, Captain Jeffers' phone rings.

"This is Jeffers. Yes, good morning, sir. What? Holy crap! Sorry, Mr. Mayor. Are you serious? Yeah, all right, I'll put Jack on it."

As he hangs up the phone, he declares, "Jack, I hate to break this up, but that was the mayor. Commissioner Larry Daniels was found dead by the housekeeping staff of a motel near Commercial and Powerline with his genitals cut off and stuffed into his mouth. Apparently, the staff knew who he was, and they called the mayor's office instead of 911 to try to keep things quiet. Man! This job is getting tougher and tougher. The mayor wants you to work on this case before you leave."

"Happy times are over, guys!"

As Jack leaves the office to start on his last case in the Sunshine State, he can't help but smirk. *Well, that just proves Daniels was a dick head!*

Jumping into his car, he gives two quick beeps of the horn and heads east.

The month before Jack's formal starting date at the First Precinct, Didi made several trips to New York and found a cute apartment, and also a great spot for her lingerie boutique. She's happy that those tasks have been taken care of because she knows that after they make their final move to the city, Jack will be busy with work, and she will be occupied by her new business.

With a new apartment and a new job in a new city, it appears that everything is coming together for Jack. But appearances are not always reality.

Jack's new home will soon supply more action than he thought he wanted.

SATURNALIAN AFFECT

CHAPTER ONE

Detective Jack Stenhouse sits in front of Deputy Inspector Gene Rawlings' office, waiting to meet with his boss on the first day of his new job as a homicide detective for New York City Police Department's First Precinct. As he waits, he recalls how pleasantly surprised he was by how cool the weather was this morning. Being a Florida boy, he is not used to the low temperatures at this time of year; he would usually begin to sweat as soon as he stepped out of the house.

Jack and his girlfriend, Deidra "Didi" Lee, a former stripper with breasts to match her nickname, recently moved from South Florida to New York's Lower East Side after Jack accepted a job with the New York Police Department. The newly-engaged couple shares a loft apartment on Suffolk Street, which includes an underground parking spot that's perfect for Jack's second love, his beloved '68 Hemi Road Runner.

Jack is hoping that his relationship with Didi will be the one that lasts. With more than one disastrous marriage under his belt and many other failed relationships, he's doing everything he can to make this one work, and so far it seems he's succeeding.

Didi is very happy. She's enjoying life with her man in a new city and is thrilled to be finally realizing her dream of owning a lingerie boutique, which she aptly named Deidra's. At the great location she found on Sixth Street and Avenue B, she specializes in selling exotic dancer costumes, dresses, and sexy sleepwear, and also offers pole-dancing lessons for fun and fitness in a small studio at the back of the store.

Deputy Inspector Rawlings walks into the building with his morning coffee and waves Jack into his office, closing the door behind them. Rawlings, a twenty-year veteran of the NYPD, worked his way up from uniformed street cop to head of the First Precinct. One of the smallest New York precincts area-wise, the First spans Lower Manhattan Island from the Hudson River to the East River. It covers mostly business districts, including the new Trade Tower area and City Hall.

Jack sits in front of D.I. Rawlings and waits for his instructions.

"Welcome to the First, Jack. You passed your physical, and your marks on the target range were quite impressive. I'll introduce you to your fellow detectives in a little while, but first, I want you to review two unsolved files. I always have my new detectives go over old cases before I give them any new assignments. You'll be working with Detectives Javier DeSoto and Allison Giancarlo on these cases, and Allison will be your mentor until I think you're ready for solo duty. I'll give you one month to investigate these two homicides before setting you free. Any questions?"

Trying to look and stay positive, Jack quickly responds, "No, sir, but the sooner I can get together with my tutor, the sooner I can leave her."

"Good, I'll bring both detectives in to meet you."

When Rawlings walks out to the squad room to find DeSoto and Giancarlo, Jack finds himself alone, so he begins to review the files of the two unsolved homicides from the previous year. He quickly notes that while neither file indicates any clues, the two crimes occurred fairly close to each other, one on December 17 and the other on December 23.

Andrea Edwards Singletary is trying to hurry; her job as press secretary to Rod Johnsville, New York City's mayor and an old college friend, requires her to be at work early. She knows that her car and driver will be waiting for her downstairs within the hour, so she's rushing through her morning shower.

Andrea was given the press secretary position by Rod after her recent bitter divorce from Governor Edwards. Rod felt sorry for her, so he offered her the position to keep her busy, and to take her mind off her problems.

As she steps out of the shower, she is startled by the sound of someone in her apartment. With a towel wrapped around her, she cautiously walks out of the bedroom.

"You again!" she shouts. "I told you I didn't want you around anymore. How'd you get in here?"

"Oh, Rea. You know I have a key. I'm here to protect you. Nothing will harm you while I'm around. I'm just letting you know that I'll be here for you when you need me the most."

"Look, I thought you were going to stop stalking me last year, for good!"

"For good? Ha! I am here for good, but it's good-bye for now. I'll be seeing you soon, just when you need me the most."

Andrea watches him leave, then makes sure the door is locked. As if nothing has happened, she returns to the bathroom to finish getting ready for another day at City Hall.

Deep down, she really wants him to stick around, however. He makes her feel safe.

CHAPTER TWO

Toshiba Johnson and Tammy Wilkens were two of New York's many street-walking working girls. The case files on their deaths are what Jack is reviewing. The two women were found last December within a week of each other, Toshiba on the seventeenth, and Tammy on the twenty-third.

Toshiba was found at dawn, positioned on a bench at the Vietnam Veterans Plaza, her lifeless eyes staring at the East River. Tammy was found at dusk, also positioned on a bench, but she was staring at the Hudson River, in Robert F. Wagner, Jr. Park. The coroner's office determined that both women died from carbon monoxide poisoning, which indicates that they were killed somewhere else and then placed where they were ultimately found. Nothing in the records of either file points to a motive or lists any witnesses. Neither was anything found on either area's surveillance cameras. It seems that the perpetrator or perpetrators may have known where the cameras were located and took precautions.

There are a couple of similarities between the two crimes, however. Jack notes that both victims were prostitutes and that each of them was found staring out at the water, one staring east, and the other staring west. As Jack makes some notes, he is interrupted by the D.I.

"Jack this is your mentor, Detective Allison Giancarlo."

Jack stands to greet his colleague, whom he immediately notices is pretty easy on the eyes.

Allison Giancarlo, an eighteen-year veteran of the NYPD, is married and in her mid-forties. She lives in a three-bedroom cape in West Hempstead, Long Island with her husband, a Nassau County fireman, and her two high school-aged sons.

Allison extends her hand in greeting.

"Welcome aboard, Jack. I'm the one who'll be showing you the ropes."

"Nice to meet you, Allison."

After the greetings, Rawlings says, "Allison, the ball's in your court. I have a meeting now, so I'll leave you to it." With a nod, he turns to Jack. "If there are any questions that Allison can't answer, Jack, you probably shouldn't have asked them."

The Deputy Inspector leaves the two detectives alone in his office while he hurries to his meeting with Police Chief Williams and the mayor.

As the two detectives size each other up, Jack breaks the awkward silence.

With a wry smile, he starts the conversation. "So what's a nice girl like you doing in a place like this?"

Allison grins, "Hey, I'm not that nice, Jack. I've been doing this for eighteen years; I followed in my father's footsteps. And you? Why the hell did you leave South Florida for South Manhattan?"

Shaking his head Jack retorts, "Too damn hot, for too damn long. Besides, Fort Lauderdale is too quiet. I was hoping to round up more bad guys up here."

"Yeah, well, we don't get victims killed by snake venom up here. Come on, I'll show you around the office, and then we can grab an early lunch."

D.I. Rawlings and Police Chief Williams have been sitting in Mayor Johnsville's office for a while, waiting for the mayor. When he finally walks in, he is not alone. Andrea Singletary, his press secretary, is by his side.

"Sorry, guys, I'm running late this morning, so let's get down to business." He sits behind his huge oak desk and stares at the two men, while Andrea stands next to him. "I called this meeting to brief you about an important visitor to the city and to discuss all the pomp and circumstance that will surround his visit.

"Benjamin Dyan, the mayor of Jerusalem, will be here in two weeks. I'll be giving him the key to the city at a press conference, and after that he'll be staying at Gracie Mansion for the weekend. Mr. Dyan will arrive at JFK Airport, then take a helicopter directly to the City Hall complex. We'll hold the press conference after I greet him at City Hall, then we'll both board a helicopter to Gracie Mansion. I've been advised to forgo the use of motorcades around the city to make it easier to protect the mayor against outside threats. We want to ensure that his visit is a safe one."

Turning to his press secretary, Mayor Johnsville asks, "Andrea, please pass out the report on Dyan's visit."

As Andrea walks around to the deputy inspector and the police chief, the mayor continues, "Later this morning, I'll be meeting with Inspector Ramirez of the Nineteenth Precinct to discuss the security issues around Mayor Dyan's stay at Gracie Mansion, but Rawlings, you'll be responsible for security at City Hall. Of course, Israeli security agents will also be with the mayor at all times. And to keep you in the loop, Andrea will be holding a press conference at noon today to inform the great people of New York about Mr. Dyan's visit. Gentlemen, I have every confidence in your abilities to run your departments, but I must emphasize the importance of everyone remaining at the height of vigilance while the mayor is in town. I don't have to tell you that Mr. Dyan has enemies, and I don't want any incidents in my city. Review your reports and send me your action plans. I'll meet with both of you again on Monday, and we'll include Ramirez at that meeting. Now, if there aren't any questions, I need to excuse myself to conduct other city business."

Looking thoughtful, D.I. Rawlings asks, "Mayor Johnsville, I do have one question. Do you know if there are any current, credible threats against Mayor Dyan?"

"As far as I know, Gene, there are no current threats, but that don't mean diddly."

"Yeah, I know, but we can use it as a baseline. Thank you, Mr. Mayor."

"No, thank you, Gene. Your teams and the Chief's teams are the ones in harm's way. I'm just the one in the way."

CHAPTER THREE

After a quick tour of the police station, Allison invites Jack to accompany her as she walks a few blocks toward Walker's, a favorite of the detectives of the First.

Upon entering the establishment, they take seats at the bar and order burgers and cokes.

"So, Allison, Rawlings gave me two unsolved murders to review from last year before I can go out on my own, and both of them involve hookers. One was found on the East Side and the other on the West Side, within a few days of each other. Do you know anything about those cases?"

"No, not much, just that the two hookers were found at different parks and that they both died of carbon monoxide poisoning. There were no clues left at either scene--no evidence at all. No one saw anything, and there was nothing on the surveillance cameras to be concerned with. We think they pissed off their pimps. Oh, if I remember correctly, one of them had an arrest record. I think it was Toshiba."

"Do you think I can get the surveillance videos from the cameras at the parks? I don't know, something about those cases just doesn't sit right with me."

The bartender interrupts with two cheeseburgers and seasoned fries. As they take their first bites both detectives abruptly turn their attention toward the television over the bar, which is displaying a news conference from City Hall. Jack comments, "Who's the looker at the mike? I've seen her before."

"That's the mayor's press secretary, Andrea Singletary. She was married to our former governor."

Wiping the ketchup off his chin that dripped out of the bun, Jack asks, "Kyle, right? Didn't he off himself?"

Allison, taking a sip of her soda, replies after she finishes, "Yeah, he got busted for being on the Big Apple Madam's client list. Apparently, he was on the Madam's dole while he was still a D.A. here in Manhattan, and he protected her prostitution ring in exchange for certain on-the-job favors. After it all went down, he resigned from office and Andrea filed for divorce. Once the divorce was final, which was rather quickly, he ate a 9mm."

"Well, Andrea seems to have fared pretty well."

"You think so?" Allison shook her head. "When Andrea was growing up, her dad was an abusive alcoholic. Supposedly, he beat her mother up just for giggles and grins. When he died of liver failure, her mother started turning tricks to keep food on the table, which eventually led to drugs, making her a heroin addict, as well as a hooker. Even though she managed to put Andrea through college, she never got off the drugs, and then, right after the governor blew his brains out, she OD'd. Well, when her mother died so soon after the governor killed himself, Andrea flipped out, and she had a nervous breakdown. She ended up at Pilgrim Hospital for five months. Luckily for her, Mayor Johnsville is an old friend of hers from college and he appointed her as his press secretary last winter, after she released herself from the hospital."

"Wow, she looks okay now."

He then returned to the subject at hand. "So anyway, any chance on those tapes?"

"Tapes should be no problem; we have them archived. I'll get them after we down our burgers."

"Okay, great. That'll give me something to do for a while. Besides, from what Andrea just said, we're all going to be busy in a couple of weeks."

"Yeah, more political bullshit. Welcome to New York."

As they eat their burgers, Detective Javier DeSoto walks up to Allison with his pastrami sandwich and sits down next to them.

"Hi, Allison. I was at the booth in the corner and decided to come over to join you." Nodding at Jack, he asks, "So, are you the Jack from Florida? It's a little different up here, huh?"

"Yeah, I have to wear a suit and a tie; no Hawaiian shirts anymore. But the good thing is, no heat!"

Interrupting the exchange, Allison introduces their colleague.

“Jack, this is Detective DeSoto. He’s going to be working with us.”

DeSoto continues as if Allison never spoke.

“Hey, you think it’s not hot here? Just wait till next summer! And how is a Florida boy going to put up with fifteen inches of snow? Man, welcome to New York!"

CHAPTER FOUR

Back at the First, Jack follows Allison to the Archives Department, where she retrieves the two video recordings that Jack wants to review. He brings both surveillance tapes into a media room and sets up two monitors and two tape players so he can study each tape simultaneously. Knowing that the process could take days, he begins reviewing each tape methodically, hoping that he can pick out something at each location that will provide a lead in solving the murders.

On the Lower East Side, everything is going well at Didi's boutique. She has been busy with customers every day, and she even has enough people signed up for one of her pole-dancing classes.

As she assists a young woman with a lingerie purchase, the front doorbell chimes and another customer walks into the store. Didi glances at the new arrival, then does a double-take, exclaiming, "Maria! Maria Assante! OMG, what the hell are you doing here?"

"Well, I told you I wanted you to teach me to pole-dance!"

"Oh, my gosh! I'm so happy to see a familiar face! Let me take care of this customer, and then I'll be right with you."

As soon as Didi wraps up her sale, she rushes over to give Maria a welcome hug. Maria, a rookie cop, worked with Jack on his last case in Florida. After a brief stint as an actress, she was noticed by the FBI and recruited as a field agent. Maria and Didi had become friends after meeting each other at a dinner with Jack.

"Maria, what are you doing in New York?" Didi asks.

"I'm on OJT, on the job training, with the FBI. Did some snooping around to find you, and here I am."

“Really? What happened to your reality show about police women?” The last thing Didi had heard about Maria before she and Jack moved was that she was chosen to appear in a reality TV show about female cops.

“Yeah, that didn’t work out. I did two episodes and then went over to the FBI. Too much T and A for my taste, and the show moved from Florida to Southern California, so it’s just as well.”

“Oh, well. I hope you had a few laughs on the set while you were there. Hey, Maria, I’d invite you to lunch, but I can’t leave the store. I haven’t hired any clerks yet, but if business keeps up like this, soon I won’t be able to handle it all alone, and I’ll need an assistant. How about dinner tonight with Jack?”

“Sounds good. But don’t tell Jack; I want to surprise him. Seven okay for you?”

“That’ll work. Jack usually picks me up at six, when I close up. Chinese take-out okay with you?”

After they exchange addresses and phone numbers, Maria signs up for pole-dancing lessons. Smiling slyly, she says, “You know, Didi, you were supposed to teach me to pole-dance in Florida, so when you skipped out on me, I just had to follow you up here to get my lessons!” With a wave at her friend, she exits the store. “See you tonight!”

For several hours, Jack has been staring at two screens. With four more hours of surveillance tapes to go through, he is beginning to feel like a member of one of those paranormal reality TV teams, who view hours of recorded video while searching for ghosts.

So far, nothing has caught his attention, so he stops the videos and reads through the two written case files once again. Nothing jumps out at him there, either. There seems to be no common denominator to these cases, except that both of the women were prostitutes.

Glancing at his wristwatch, he notices that it’s now after five o’clock. Knowing that he needs to head over to the East Side of Manhattan to pick up Didi, he pulls the videotapes out of the players so that tomorrow he can pick up at the point where he left off today.

Before leaving the station for the evening, he stops at Deputy Inspector Rawlings' office, to fill him in on what he has been working on so far.

The D. I.'s office looks like a giant glass fish bowl. Even though the office's large glass windows don't provide the Inspector with any privacy, they do enable him to watch over the activities of the entire squad room in front of him.

When Jack knocks on the door, Rawlings waves him into his office.

"How did your first day go?"

"So far, those files you're having me review are giving me nothing. No clues, no forensics, no information at all. The only thing we know is that they were both prostitutes."

"Stenhouse, that's why they aren't solved yet. Keep reviewing them and treat them like new cases. Remember, you got two weeks. Keep me posted."

"You got it. Good night, sir."

"See you tomorrow, Jack."

Jack leaves the office and jumps in his Road Runner, heading east. He has one stop to make before he picks up Didi.

CHAPTER FIVE

Detective DeSoto has every intention of leaving the station right behind Jack, but he is stopped by the incessant ringing of his desk telephone. An anonymous caller on the line is reporting a dead body at the World Trade Center construction site and is insisting that the dead body shot someone.

Being single and unmarried, DeSoto is not actually in a rush to go home to an empty apartment, so he decides to investigate the tip. However, before heading over to the crime scene, he stops at Rawlings' office to let him know about the call.

When he arrives at the scene, he parks his car just outside of the Trade Tower site's construction fence, and walks quickly toward a flashing display of red and blue lights. DeSoto approaches the uniformed sergeant in charge of the cordoned-off crime scene to get a report on the incident.

"Hey, Joe. What's with the dead shooter?"

"How's it goin', Javier? We got a bad one here. One of the first responding officers approached the body and didn't notice that it was booby-trapped. The body was placed on a sheet of plywood, and apparently a tube-charged round of ordnance was set off when he stepped on the board, shooting him in the back of his upper left thigh. The EMT's are preparing him right now for transport to Downtown Hospital."

"So they rigged up a couple of bullets to go off if someone snooped around, and he was shot in the ass?"

"Yeah. I lifted the board and saw three more charges stuck into the ground. They look to be .45 caliber rounds. When you step on the board, the rounds are pushed down onto a pin, and they ignite. The bomb squad is here to disarm the charges, and to conduct a search for any more of them."

"Any evidence on the body to show how the guy died?"

"He was shot in the back of the head, execution-style. I guess the shooter rigged that booby trap to kill or injure some cops for collateral damage along with his kill. Oh, and are you ready for this? We ID'd the victim, and it's Jimmie 'Little Ducks' Catalano!"

"Hot damn! He was a soldier for the Sorrento family!"

"Yeah, and that was a typical Chinese booby trap. There's been some trouble lately between the Italian and the Chinese mafias because Chinatown is growing and Little Italy is shrinking. The Sorrento family has been protecting its turf, so this looks like it was retaliation. I guess there's gonna be a mob war."

"Good! Maybe they'll kill each other off."

Jack is at a small jewelry shop on East 2nd Street. With no parking available, he double-parked outside the store with the blue strobe light flashing on his dashboard. He should be okay if a patrol car comes by, but if a meter maid spots it, he'll get a ticket.

"Evening, Mr. Steinman. Is it ready?" Jack hands over a sales receipt.

"Yes, Mr. Stenhouse, let me show you. It is very beautiful, if I say so myself."

Ben Steinman, the owner of the shop, walks into the back of the store and returns with a one-carat emerald-cut diamond engagement ring in yellow gold. Jack has been saving up for months for this, and knows that Didi will be shocked. He pays the balance due and whistles as he heads out of the store.

Within a few minutes, he has parked a few doors down from Didi's boutique and has walked up to the front door, only to find it locked. He knocks loudly to get Didi's attention, and waits for her to let him in.

"Hi, Jack. I was just finalizing my deposit for the night!"

"You have a deposit on your first day?"

"Yeah! Ain't that great?" Didi gives Jack a French kiss that nearly takes his breath away. "Business is great, and my dancing class is full!"

"That is so wonderful, Babe! Let's go out to dinner to celebrate."

If this were any other evening, Didi would be happy to go out to dinner, but now she needs to think fast because of the surprise dinner with Maria.

"Oh, Jack, that sounds wonderful, but it was very busy today, and I'm tired. Can we just stay in and get some Chinese?"

"Oh, no! I really wanted to take you out to celebrate. You know, first day at work, business success? We can go to a Chinese place."

"You're going to force me to tell you my secret, aren't you?"

"Secret? I was snipped, so you can't be pregnant... or are you?"

Laughing, Didi says, "No, Jack! We're having a guest for dinner tonight."

"Whew! Anyone I know?"

"Yeah, but let me at least keep that secret, okay?"

"Fine, takeout it is, but tomorrow we go out and celebrate."

"Deal."

Jack grabs Didi's butt and follows her around trying to give her a kiss while she gathers up her deposit and closes up the shop.

CHAPTER SIX

Andrea Singletary is sitting in her office after a long day, staring into space, when Mayor Rod Johnsville knocks on her door and walks in.

"Andrea, I'm finalizing the vacation schedules for the rest of the year. Are you still planning to take two weeks off for Christmas?"

Andrea seems to be in a trance, like a deer staring into headlights, and does not respond. Rod walks over and places his hand on her shoulder, giving her a slight nudge.

"Earth to Andrea. Hello, are you there?"

With a cold, faraway stare, Andrea slowly turns her head and seems to peer into the mayor's soul.

"Why, yes. I will be busy that week. I will need that time for myself." She turns back around and stares out of her window as if the mayor wasn't even there.

"Okay... then, ah, I guess I'll see you tomorrow. Is everything okay, Andrea?"

After a pregnant pause, Andrea suddenly stands up and turns toward the puzzled mayor. "I'm sorry, Rod, I was just daydreaming. It's been a long day, and I'm very tired. Yes, I would like two weeks off. I think Christmas is on a Sunday this year. It will give me some extra time in Aspen."

Puzzled by this odd exchange, the mayor nevertheless decides to shrug it off.

"Andrea, get a good night's sleep. See you in the morning."

With a nod of her head, Andrea watches as Rod walks out of her office. After he's gone, she turns back to the window with a smile on her face, like the cat that ate the canary.

Jack's and Didi's apartment is in a converted factory, and the only access to their unit is through an old freight elevator with doors that open vertically, not horizontally, onto a narrow hallway. The style of the 1200 square foot, two-bedroom, two-bath loft apartment, is industrial chic. Exposed pipes and fire sprinklers cover the fifteen-foot high ceiling, and the only rooms with floor to ceiling walls are the two bathrooms. The rest of the living area, including the two bedrooms, the living and dining area and kitchen, are separated by what can best be described as office-type cubicle walls. The partitions that enclose each of those areas are movable so that room arrangements can be changed at any time.

While Didi takes a quick shower, Jack hears the freight elevator door open in the hallway. Curious to see who their mystery dinner guest is, he walks over to the door and pulls it open, just as Maria is getting ready to knock. With a look of surprise, he takes in the sight of skinny jeans, black six-inch heels, and a white turtleneck sweater trying to keep a pair of breasts from escaping. As he ogles, a hand reaches out and grabs him under the chin, slowly lifting his head.

"You just don't learn do you? My eyes are up here."

Jack gasps, then grins widely.

"Maria! You haven't changed a bit! What the hell are you doing here?" Giving her a quick hug, he guides her into the apartment and closes the door behind her.

"I'm on OJT with the FBI. It wasn't hard to find you guys, so I signed up for pole-dancing classes today and got my teacher to invite me to dinner! How's the NYPD, Jack?"

"So far, so good. The D.I. down at the First has me reviewing two old cases to get my feet wet, so I haven't gotten involved with New York City at its finest yet. But hell, look at you – FBI! You hit your goal! How do you like it? TV wasn't good enough for you? Listen, I'm getting a beer, want one?

"Wow, how many questions do you want me to answer at once? Beer's fine, TV sucks, and it's great to be an FBI agent."

Jack returns from the kitchen with two Buds, and rejoins Maria in the living room. As he hands her a cold one, he hears a voice coming from the bedroom.

"Get me one, too! I'll be right out."

When Jack heads back into the kitchen, Didi walks into the living room.

"Hi, Maria! I guess you found the place all right. Let me give you the nickel tour. Hey, Hon, set up dinner, will ya?"

"Sure, no problem, Di."

Jack sets up three orders of sweet 'n sour pork, shrimp fried rice, and egg rolls as Didi shows Maria around the apartment. While setting up the food, he starts thinking about the best way to propose to Didi and about how much he hopes he will get the right answer. As Maria and Didi walk into the dining area, Jack looks up, and then his mind wanders to Didi's dance studio, with Didi and Maria on a pole.

Seeing two gorgeous women before him and hoping that one of them will soon be his fiancée, he feels like the luckiest man on the face of the earth.

Andrea enters her apartment on the Upper East Side of Manhattan, overlooking Central Park. She drops her purse on the kitchen counter, then enters the master bath, where she notices a message on the mirror, written in lipstick: DO NOT WORRY, REA. I WILL BE BACK TO PROTECT YOU, JUST LIKE I HAVE BEFORE. SEE YOU SOON.

With a cold, distant stare, she reads the message and smiles, then takes a leisurely shower and turns in for the night.

CHAPTER SEVEN

The next day, Jack is back at work, still tediously reviewing each frame of last December's surveillance tapes from the two parks. With a can of Coke and a bag of Cheetos for lunch, he continues to run the two tapes side by side.

Suddenly, he sees something that looks familiar and stops the playback. A man in a white baseball cap and sunglasses is walking past a park bench at Memorial Park on the East Side. Looking carefully at the image on the screen, he realizes that he has seen this man before, on the tape from the other park. Jack reverses the tape from Robert F. Wagner, Jr. Park on Manhattan's West Side until he finds the scene he wants, and there he is. The same man from Memorial Park is sitting on the park bench at Wagner Park where Tammy Wilkens' body was found.

At that moment, Allison walks in to check on the progress of the precinct's newcomer.

"Any luck, Jack?"

"As a matter of fact, yeah. Take a look at the guy sitting on the park bench. You were involved in this case. Do you remember him?"

Allison looks at the man and says, "No, not at all."

"Well, this bozo was at both parks. On the other tape, he's just walking through the park, but here, he's sitting on the same bench where we found one of the victims. Unfortunately, the only photos we have were taken from the back, but I'd like to have this one blown up. Can Forensics do that for me?"

"Sure, let me get one of the nerds down here so you can show him what you want. What are you gonna do after you get your blowup?"

"As my mentor, that's where you come in."

At Didi's boutique, business is booming. Sex sells, even though the store has only been open for a few days and the economy is in the toilet. She already needs help running the store, so she wants to discuss the situation with Jack over dinner tonight. In order to sweeten the pot, she decides to wear an outfit that he won't forget.

Finally free of staring at flickering screens, Jack takes a moment to get a cup of coffee while Allison heads to Forensics to place a request for help with the surveillance tapes. On the way to the coffee station, he runs into Detective DeSoto.

"Hey, Javier! I hear you got a dead body shooting people!"

"Yeah, looks like we got a gang war going on between China and Italy, and they're dumping the bodies in the First. They just found a Chinese gangster in the Hudson River with his balls cut off. I'm going over to Hester Street now to meet with a couple of guys from the Fifth Precinct. We need to talk to an informant down there."

"Didn't the Mafia in Sicily castrate the French infiltrators over there?"

"Yeah, what goes around hey, you still doing busywork for the D.I.?"

"Yeah. Bullshit is what bullshit does. Good hunting, Javier."

"You too, Jack."

Coffee in hand, Jack heads back to the media station where the two video tapes are set up. Sipping the hot coffee slowly, he settles down to wait for Allison. Just as he is taking his last sip, she walks in with the geek from Forensics.

"Jack, this is Gus, our video guru."

Jack shakes Gus's hand, then gestures toward the screen. "Hi, Gus. I hope you can help. I need this shot blown up to see if we can get a better look at the guy on the bench."

"You want some 8 x10's and some wallets?"

"Geez, everyone's a comedian. How long before I get my shot?"

"Oh, let's say twenty minutes. Is that okay?"

"Yeah. See you at three o'clock."

Gus takes the tape and exits the media room, leaving the two detectives alone.

"Hey, Allison. Where do the working girls hang out in this area?"

"Don't laugh... they're mostly at Broadway and Beaver Street."

Jack laughs so hard that coffee comes out of his nose.

"Damn! You had to tell me that while I was drinking? Beaver Street? Really? If you wrote that in a novel, they'd say you were lying!"

"No lie, man. Why do you want to know?"

"I want to show off the photo; maybe someone will remember something. As you're my mentor, you'll need to join me."

"Well, let's hope Gus can get us something good to show off."

CHAPTER EIGHT

Javier pulls into an alley off Hester Street for his meeting with the two detectives from the Fifth Precinct. They have already parked in the alley and are waiting for him.

"So guys, what do we have?"

Lieutenant John Saldone, head of the Organized Crime Unit, does the talking.

"We got a low-level soldier inside the Sorrento family meeting us here today. Vince Simonetti has been tipping us off about this latest conflict, but he's late. He should have been here by now."

The three cops walk deeper into the alley, past a dumpster and some cardboard boxes stacked to the side. Javier kicks a box out of his way, then jumps back a few steps.

"Hey guys, is this Vince?"

The two detectives walk over to where Javier is staring, and Saldone clears away another box.

"Shit! That's him!" Pulling out his cell phone, he calls the discovery into the station.

Vince was shot in the back of the head, and his tongue was cut out.

When Lieutenant Saldone finishes his phone call, Javier says, "Thanks for the tour of Little Italy, guys. You got anything else for me?"

"Yeah, maybe. We got someone else inside, under deep cover. It's gonna take a couple days to get in touch with him and set up a meeting, though. We'll probably have to arrange for a raid so we can 'arrest' his ass to keep his cover. I'll set it up and call you. Listen, if you want to wait until the uniforms show up, the food around here is to die for, no pun intended."

"Sounds good, man. If you're buyin', I'm eatin'."

The trio stands around making small talk while they wait for a patrol car to respond to their call. When the car pulls up, they hand the crime scene over to them, then drive their cars out of the alley to get some eggplant parmigiana.

Good at what he does, Gus returns to the media room in no time at all with an 8 x 10 print of Jack's mystery man. He hands the photo to Jack, who begins to study it in detail. After a few minutes, Jack's eyes widen as he notices something.

"Hey, look at this. There's a mark on the back of this guy's neck. Can you blow up this area without losing resolution?"

"It's kinda grainy, but come on, let's see what my computer can do."

Jack follows Gus back to his station, where the image is still on his screen. Like a fine artist, he begins to do his thing with his keyboard and mouse, manipulating and enlarging the image as best he can.

"The software is going to try to fill in any missing pixels now, so we need to wait until it's finished." After a few minutes, he prints out another photo. "Hey, we got something here! It looks like a cross or something."

Jack stares at the neck of the stranger, but he does not see a cross. What he sees is something else entirely.

"That looks like a symbol of something, astrology maybe."

Turning back to his computer, Gus Googles "astrological symbols", then blurts out, "Saturn! That's the symbol for Saturn!"

Thanking Gus with a clap on his shoulder, Jack takes both photos and heads directly to D.I. Rawlings office, where Detective Giancarlo is talking with their boss.

"We were just talking about you, Jack. Allison says you might have found something."

"Yes, sir. I checked the surveillance tapes from both of the parks where those hookers were found, and I found the same guy at both parks." Handing the two photos to Rawlings, Jack says, "Here, take a look at this. He has something on the back of his neck. Looks like a tattoo."

"Yeah, I see it. Detective, do you know what that image is?"

"It's the astrological symbol for Saturn. Sir, I'd like to go down to Beaver Street with Allison to talk to some of the working girls down there. Maybe one of them saw this guy."

"That won't be necessary, Jack. Vice is doing a sweep of the First due to the Jerusalem mayor's visit. We'll be cleaning up the streets tomorrow night, from the Hudson to the East River. You and Allison can join them."

Allison rolls her eyes. "Inspector, he's a big boy. I think he can handle himself now."

"Maybe so, but these were your cases and you should have already found 'Saturn Man.' So, you two have fun on the night shift tomorrow." He looks at his watch. "Now I have another meeting with the mayor about the Jerusalem thing. I'll be around tomorrow evening when you come in so I can brief you and the guys from Vice about the raid. See you tomorrow."

As the two detectives walk away from the D.I.'s office, Allison turns to Jack with a frown on her face. "Thanks a lot, Jack! You had to go and find this mystery man, and now I'm going to miss my husband's birthday party."

Flashing half a peace sign, she leaves Jack staring at her retreating back.

Shaking his head, he dismisses Allison's outburst, and gazes down at the photo of his mystery man, mumbling, "Why Saturn? What *are* you up to?"

CHAPTER NINE

On his way to pick up Didi, Jack turns his thoughts to the woman he hopes will become his fiancée. When he pulls up to the boutique, Didi is locking up the store, and when she sees his car, she runs to the Road Runner, holding her night deposit and the outfit she picked up for tonight's dinner. After a quick trip to the bank, the couple is at their loft, heading up the elevator together.

"Jack, I need to shower first, then get ready for dinner. I'm looking forward to some good Chinese food tonight."

"Sounds great, Di. I'll join you in there."

"Hold on, stud, you can shower in the guest bathroom. I want my outfit tonight to be a surprise." Didi pushes Jack out of the bedroom and heads into her shower while Jack gathers up his clothes and goes into the guest bathroom.

With the temperature in the high 60's, it's a surprisingly warm September evening for New Yorkers, but still quite chilly for transplanted Floridians, so Jack decides to wear a tan sports coat over black Dockers and a black knit tee shirt. However, his outfit is not complete until he adds a Glock .40 caliber to his waistband, and an untraceable 9mm automatic to an ankle holster on his right leg.

After he is finished dressing, he meanders out into the living room to make himself comfortable while he waits for Didi's big reveal for the evening. He has long ago resigned himself to the fact that he is usually finished dressing well before his sweetheart.

When Didi finally walks out of the bedroom, Jack's jaw drops to the floor. She's wearing a white, skin-tight, crocheted mini-dress with a deep V-neck front. The entire dress is only seventeen inches long, and with no bra, her double D's are pointing out the way like the bumper of a '58 Caddy.

Wanting to impress Jack, she chooses not to wear an overcoat to dinner and intends to grin and bear the chilly evening temperature while showing off her 'assets'.

"Di! Good God almighty! I'm the luckiest man on the face of the earth."

"So I guess you like?" Twirling around so that he gets the full effect, she asks, "You ready to go?"

"Just a second. I can't stand up right now."

Didi's long dark hair falls over her shoulders as she bends in front of Jack and gently places her hand under his chin, pulling him up off the sofa.

"I really don't mind, Jack, but my eyes are up here. Let's go now, though. I'm hungry."

"So am I, but not for Chinese."

As the couple walks down the hallway, Jack shakes his head in disbelief when he notices that Didi's dress has a sheer lining and that he can clearly see that his gorgeous girlfriend is wearing a white thong under that skimpy outfit.

Dinner this evening will be in New York's Chinatown, so when the Road Runner exits the building's parking garage, Jack points it toward Delancey Street and heads toward the Bowery. Then he drives south to Canal Street and parks at a garage on Elizabeth Street. From there, the couple walks the rest of the way to the Oriental Garden Restaurant, with Didi turning heads the entire way.

After they are seated at their table, Jack smiles and says, "As I've said before, Didi, I don't understand why everyone stares at me every time I go out with you."

Returning Jack's smile, Didi runs her hand up Jack's thigh and murmurs, "Must be your good looks, Jack. But I'll be back in a minute; I have to powder my nose. Don't go anywhere, you hear?"

When Didi leaves her seat, Jack watches her shake her stuff as she saunters off to the ladies' room. The waiter must have also seen Didi, because when he arrives at the table, he tells Jack that he is a very lucky man.

Jack orders a split of champagne and a pot of tea, and tells the waiter to return after a short while for their food order. Meanwhile, he places the box containing the engagement ring under Didi's napkin and folds the napkin around it.

As the waiter returns with the champagne, Didi is also approaching the table, so the waiter lingers and holds the chair out for her. As she sits the waiter pours the bubbly. Didi lifts her napkin, causing the ring box to fall onto her plate.

"What the hell is this, Jack?"

Raising his glass of champagne, he says, "Di, I never thought I would say this again, or ever feel this way again. I love you."

After a momentary pause, Didi asks, "Jack, what are you saying?"

As beads of sweat start to appear on Jack's forehead, he takes a gulp of champagne, looks into her eyes, and asks, "Didi, will you marry me?"

Momentarily shocked, Didi opens the box, stares at the ring and looks intently at Jack. As tears well up in her eyes, she smiles broadly while grabbing her napkin to dab at her eyes.

"Of course I'll marry you, Jack! But you couldn't wait until the evening was over? My makeup must be a mess now!"

Taking the ring, Jack puts it on her finger. "No one is staring at your face, Babe, not in that dress."

Didi leans over and gives Jack a French kiss that takes his breath away.

"Later tonight, I'm going to rock your world, but right now, I have to go back to the ladies' room to fix my face."

CHAPTER TEN

Luckily for Jack, he is scheduled to work the night shift with Detective Giancarlo the next day, which allows him to sleep in this morning. He needs the extra sleep after a busy night with Didi.

Didi was able to get up early, though, and took a cab to her boutique because she didn't want to wake her fiancé. Business at the boutique is booming, and since she can no longer do all the work alone, she has set up a few interviews today for a sales clerk to help out at the store.

When Jack finally wakes up, he begins to re-hash the two cold cases, hoping that he can make some headway on them so Rawlings will release him for regular duty sooner than later. At least that is what he is thinking as he showers and completes the first two S's of his daily routine. As soon as he shaves, he intends to head to the boutique to surprise Didi with lunch.

At the Giancarlo house, Allison's husband is home from work today, having taken the day off for his birthday. They decided to hold an early party this afternoon, before Allison has to go to work.

But neither Allison nor Jack knows that D.I. Rawlings has decided that they won't be trolling for trollops with the Vice Squad tonight after all. Instead, they will remain at the station to interview them as they are brought in. Vice is expecting to bring in about fifty working girls, so the interviews are expected to take all night.

As Jack walks into the boutique with the two pastrami sandwiches and two cream sodas that he picked up at Katz's Deli, he immediately notices an unfamiliar face behind the counter.

"Hi. Who are you? Where's Didi?"

"She's in the back, setting up the studio for tonight's class. My name is Sonya. I started working after my interview this morning. And you are?"

"I'm Jack, her fiancé. I thought I'd surprise her with lunch."

"Aww, that's nice of you; I'll let her know you're here. Congratulations, by the way. The ring is beautiful."

When Sonya leaves the counter to find Didi, Jack revels in the happy feeling of calling Didi his fiancée, so when Didi comes running to the front and gives him a big kiss, he is on cloud nine.

"Miss me already?" she asks.

"That's why I'm here! I brought your favorites from Katz's Deli."

"Oh, how you spoil me, Jack! Come on, we can go into my office. I want to see if Sonya can handle the front for a while, anyway."

Jack waves at Sonya while they head for Didi's office at the back of the store. As soon as they enter the office, Didi rushes to clear off her desk so they can have a place to eat.

"So tell me about Sonya."

"That was funny, Jack. Sonya is a customer who has been in the store many times since we opened. She bought some dresses and lingerie for her husband. Well, to please her husband. She worked the pole to pay tuition while she was in college and ended up marrying a lawyer, so now she doesn't need to work anymore. She was bored at home and saw the 'help wanted' sign in the window, so here she is. In addition to the assistance she's going to give me with work, I don't like being in the store alone, so she'll keep me company."

"Well, I'm happy that worked out well for you! Do you want me to do a background check on her, just in case?"

"I don't think I need one, but it couldn't hurt–thanks. To change the subject, when do you want to get married?"

In mid-gulp of his soda, Jack nearly chokes as liquid runs out of his nose. Enjoying the moment, Didi asks innocently, "What's the matter, Jack? Did I hit a nerve?"

Shaking his head as he cleans himself off, Jack quickly responds, "No, Babe, just caught me by surprise. How about this spring? Does that give you enough time to do the bride thing?"

"Bride thing? Jack, I have no family, and neither do you. There's no need for a 'bride thing.' I was thinking that we could do a weekend in Vegas, and bam, we're married."

"No church wedding, no reception, no shower? No bachelor party?"

"Why do you need a bachelor party, Jack? I can dance the pole for you anytime."

"Yeah, you're right, but what about you? Don't you want the traditional thing? I thought all women dreamed of a wedding gown, the church, and all the other BS."

"It would be nice, Jack, but you've been there before, and, well, I'm not church-worthy."

"Look, everyone is church-worthy, even me, although it's been forever since I've been in a church. I'm not getting any younger, you know, and I've come to the realization that I'm not immortal. Why don't we think about this for a while? By the way, your new assistant is hot! She's perfect for this shop!"

"Jack! While we're talking about getting married, you tell me another woman is hot? That doesn't sound very church-like."

"Hey, I said I'm not immortal, I didn't say I'm dead!"

"I know. You sure weren't dead last night." Giving Jack a wink, Didi takes another bite of her pastrami sandwich.

Then, almost as an afterthought, she adds, "And you know what? I would like to get married in a church."

CHAPTER ELEVEN

"My sources at the First Precinct of the New York City Police Department have told me that there is renewed interest in two murder cases from last year. They believe there may be a cover-up involving these murders. Could we have a serial killer roaming the streets of New York? I will keep you posted as I dig further into this story. This is Peter Sloan, your investigative reporter on the job for WPIX TV."

Jack arrived at work a little early this morning. He wants to go online to check out churches in the area. Although he was baptized and confirmed as a Catholic, Jack's late stepmom was Episcopalian, so as he grew up he attended those services intermittently until he went to college, when he stopped practicing altogether. Locating the website of Our Lady of Victory Church on the Lower East Side, he writes down all the information he needs, intending to check out the church this weekend. Just as he places the scrap of paper containing the church information into his wallet, Rawlings walks out of his office and beckons him to join him.

"Jack, there's been a change for this evening. You and Detective Giancarlo will stay here and interview the ladies as they're brought in. Vice will have three teams out, so we can expect that somewhere between twenty to fifty ladies will be rounded up. That should keep you and Allison busy for a few hours. Oh, by the way, did you hear the news flash on WPIX this morning from that asshole Sloan?"

"No. Who is Sloan?"

"A guy on local TV who calls himself a reporter. He says he has a tip on two murder cases that we're investigating that could be the work of a serial killer, and he says we're covering it up. You haven't talked to any reporters, have you?"

"Hell, no. Why would I?"

"I don't know; there's a leak somewhere. Try to stay quiet on this."

"Ten-four, sir. If I do find something out, can I reopen those cases and continue my investigation?"

"I'll see. If you get a hit on your photo, it's all yours. However, you'll have to fit those cases in with any new ones you'll be assigned to, because if you do get a hit, I'll release you from your training and probation period. Good luck, Jack."

Jack leaves Rawlings' office to check on that strange tattoo. He's hoping that it will show up in other cases, or on additional perpetrators.

Didi's day is going well. Ten women have signed up for her pole-dancing class this evening, including Marie Assante and Sonya, her new employee.

Didi is looking forward to seeing Maria at the class tonight, so she can show off her engagement ring and ask her to be maid of honor. However, she is worried about going home alone, since Jack won't be able to pick her up, and she hopes that Maria will agree to share a cab with her.

When Detective Giancarlo arrives at the station, she checks in with Rawlings and receives her new schedule for the night. Then she joins Jack at his desk while he reviews records of past felons to see if the Saturn tattoo shows up. It will be a few hours before the Vice teams start coming in, so he uses the time to dig through old files. It's going to be a long night.

Detective DeSoto walks by as Jack pours a cup of coffee for Allison.

"Hey, Javier, you working late tonight, too?"

"Yeah, gotta meeting up at the Fifth. They pulled an operative in from deep cover. He's supposed to have info on the Italian-Chinese war we have going on." Turning to Allison, he asks, "I thought it was your hubby's birthday today. What are you doing here?"

Sighing heavily, she responds, "This is Rawlings' idea. Jack picked up a clue on those two hookers who were murdered last winter and got me involved, since they were my cases. Vice is cleaning up the city tonight for the mayor because of our visitor from Jerusalem, so we're going to interview the working girls when they come in to see if they know anything about the murders."

"Well, have fun, guys. I gotta go see a man about a horse."

After DeSoto leaves, Allison turns to her shadow. "Jack, why do some guys say they have to go see a man about a horse when they have to take a leak?"

"It's an old cowboy thing. Because the outhouses were outside, behind the saloons, instead of saying that they had to go and take a piss, they would say the horse thing. Look, I hope you don't blame me for missing the birthday party."

"I did at first, but we had a party at home this afternoon. Besides, it was Rawlings' idea. You get any hits from the mug shots on that weird tattoo?"

"No, not a lick. Hope the girls know something."

CHAPTER TWELVE

Andrea Singletary is anticipating the beginning of a very enjoyable evening. A special exhibit of Greek and Roman mythology, a particular interest of hers in college, is opening tonight at the Museum of Natural History. The museum is not far from her apartment so she decides to walk there instead of waiting for a cab, but just as she gets ready to leave, her phone rings.

"Hello?"

"Rhea, just checking in to make sure you're okay. I'll be coming back to see you sooner than I expected. I will probably hang around for a couple of months before I have to leave again in December. That doesn't bother you, does it? Ciao."

Andrea stares at the phone, takes a deep sigh, and hatches an idea that will keep him around for a while.

The pole-dancing class at the boutique went well, and Maria and Sonya stay behind to help Didi close up the store.

While they are cleaning up, Maria asks, "Didi, why don't you and Sonya share a cab with me so we don't leave the boutique alone?"

"Oh, that's okay, Maria," responds Sonya. "My husband is coming to pick me up any minute now. You two can go on ahead."

"Nonsense, we'll wait until he shows up, then we'll all leave at the same time. Didi, do you have any cold drinks?"

"Yes, I have some cold bottled water in the mini fridge. Hey, Sonya, is that your husband walking up to the door?"

"Yes, that's him! I guess I'll leave now; no water for me, thanks. See you tomorrow, Didi."

Sonya opens the door for her husband and introduces him to Didi and Maria before they leave the store. After the door closes on them, the two remaining women gather up their things and also leave the store.

Outside on the sidewalk, Maria hails a cab, and within a few minutes, the women are climbing into the back seat of one of New York's omnipresent yellow taxis. After giving directions to the driver, Maria turns her attention toward Didi and exclaims, "I can't believe that Jack actually proposed! He doesn't seem like the marrying type."

"No, he doesn't, but I think he feels that he's getting old and vulnerable. And get this! He said he wants a church wedding!"

"A *church* wedding? If he walks into a church, it'll be hit by lightning!" As the ladies share a laugh, the cab begins its trek through the dark, neon-lit streets of Manhattan.

The first vice team has returned from Beaver Street with the six ladies they managed to round up. Allison interviews three of them and Jack interviews the other three, but none of the women have any information on the mystery man from the videos, or on his unusual tattoo.

After escorting the last of the six ladies to the lockup where they'll spend the night, Jack gets two cokes and chips from the vending machine and shares them with Allison.

"Do you think we're gonna get any information tonight?"

"I don't know, Jack. Probably not, but who knows?" She changes the subject. "Anyway, how long have you been doing police work?"

"Too damn long; over fifteen years now. Still like it, though, but it's getting harder every day. I just like catching bad guys."

"Me, too, but sometimes it gets a little old. You take five bad guys off the street, and six bad guys take their place. My dad did this all his life, but he said it was like pissing up a rope."

Laughing, Jack responds, "That's perfect! Your dad was a smart man." Jack turns abruptly at the sudden sound of raised voices. "Oops, looks like the next group just came in."

"I'll go over and see how many we have," says Allison.

"Oh, good. I got that horse thing to do before we start in again."

When they return to their desks, they divide up the seven new arrivals between them, with Jack taking the first four. On the second interview, he begins to make progress.

"Evening. I'm Detective Stenhouse." Skimming through the woman's file, he comments, "I see that you've been here before, Sandy. How are you doing tonight?"

"Look, I'm fine! Can we just get this over with so I can post bail and get back to work? I'm losing money here!"

"Hey, calm down, or I'll slow down and keep you here for hours. Did you know Toshiba Johnson or Tammy Wilkens?"

"I know Tammy, she works the West Side." Sandy does a double-take. "Wait, what do you mean 'did'?"

"You haven't seen her in a while, have you?"

"Not since last winter. Why?"

"Well, she was murdered. Take a look at this photo and tell me if you remember seeing this guy before."

Sandy glances at the photo and responds immediately. "Yeah! I remember seeing this guy last winter. Who can forget that weird tattoo?"

"Good. Where did you see him?"

"He drove by the Battery and picked up a couple of girls for a party. I remember that tattoo. Funny, but I never saw those girls again."

Jack's eyes open wide. "Do you remember what he was driving?"

"Yeah, a white van. Ford, Chevy one of those."

"Do you remember which ladies he picked up?"

"Just working girls. We know each other as coworkers, not friends."

"You knew Tammy though?"

"Yeah, we had the same pimp, until he was shot."

"Okay. I need you to look at some photos to see if you can identify the two women."

"Yeah, and what's in it for me? I'm not doing this for nothing. Want some trade?"

Jack is repelled by that statement from Sandy, who appears to be on the older end of the scale.

"As good as that may be, no thanks, but we may be able to get you released after you look at some photos. Follow that officer over there, and he'll get you some books to look through."

After Sandy leaves with the officer, Jack calls Allison away from her interview.

"I got a hit on the photo, but it's not all good news."

"What do you mean?"

"The bad news is that it looks like we may have more killings to deal with. Our tattooed stranger picked up some hookers last winter near the Battery and they never returned to work. But the good news is that he was driving a white van."

"Oh, that's just great, Jack, a white van in Manhattan. Good luck tracking that one down!"

CHAPTER THIRTEEN

"Hello, New York! As I previously reported, our Finest down at the First are taking another look at two murders from last year, and I can now report that they have recently identified a man with a strange tattoo on the back of his neck as a person of interest in those crimes. When I questioned Andrea Singletary, our beloved Mayor's press secretary, about the renewed interest in the murders, she had no comment. This is Peter Sloan with WPIX, always on the job to keep you informed."

Days turn into weeks, and while some things change, others remain the same. The mayor of Jerusalem comes and goes, but the Italians and the Chinese are still killing each other off. However, for the time being they have stopped dumping bodies in the First Precinct, so Detective DeSoto has moved on to better things.

Jack is still working on the two unsolved murders, but he hasn't been able to gather any information beyond what he found out from the hooker who was brought in by the Vice Squad.

Didi's business is still doing well, and as the holiday season approaches, her boutique is busier than ever with satisfied customers.

However, even though most New Yorkers are looking forward to Santa's arrival and the big parade at the end of the month, not everything will be jolly in the big city.

On a cold Monday morning, Detective Giancarlo walks past Jack's desk as he settles in with a cup of coffee and a Coke.

"Jack! Close your eyes before you bleed to death! You look like something the cat dragged in."

"Hey, try to keep it down, will ya? I celebrated a little too much last night. Didi's boutique is doing great, so we did a little partying." He closes his eyes and groans. "Crap! Even my hair hurts."

At that moment, Rawlings calls Jack and Allison into his office.

"We got a body down at the ferry terminal on the East Side. It's of a young female, and she was found sitting on a bench, facing the sunrise."

"Sir, that sounds like the way they found the two bodies from last year."

"Yeah, but this one has no arms, and whoever put her there, left a note. Uniforms are down there now; I want you and Giancarlo all over this like white on rice. Sloan is going to have a field day."

The two detectives rush out of the office with Jack shouting that they can take his car. When he fires up the beast, the '68 Hemi Roadrunner roars to life while he gives two quick beeps of the horn.

As they approach the East River, they can see the crime scene bathed in a field of blue lights. After parking the Roadrunner as close as they can, they head towards the first officer they see.

"Hey, how ya doin'? Detectives Stenhouse and Giancarlo here. What do we have?"

The cop, however, is distracted by Jack's car. "Nice ride! You need some twenty-two inchers on that beast."

"Naw, keepin' it old school."

"Too bad. Well, I found her sittin' on the dock, starin' at the river. No one noticed her, until one of the ferry passengers passed by and saw that she has no arms. No blood, though; the body seems to have been cleaned up. There's a note pinned to her blouse. I didn't touch it."

"Good," says Allison. "Get a statement from the one who found her, while Detective Stenhouse and I check out the victim."

Before approaching the body, each of them pulls on a pair of the rubber gloves they keep in their pockets for just such occasions. Allison bends down and reads the note.

"It's our guy! He signed the note with that funky symbol."

"Great, what does it say?"

"Sunlight breaks through leafless limbs."

"Don't you mean no limbs? I guess this joker is back again, but why, after a whole year?"

"Maybe he never left. We just don't know if there were other victims; not too many people report missing street hookers. Well, Detective, you left Florida for more action, didn't you? Welcome to the bigs!"

"Yeah, I know, but a psycho serial killer?"

"Hey, we don't know it's a serial killer. Let's not jump to any conclusions, okay?"

While they wait for the M.E. to arrive, Allison introduces Jack to a few of the other cops, which prompts a spirited swapping of on-the-job war stories and good-natured ribbing. A lively conversation ensues until a commotion near the street interrupts the discussion.

Looking toward the source of the noise, the officers are dismayed to see Peter Sloan jumping out of a WPIX remote video truck and heading directly toward the dock. They hold their collective breaths until they are satisfied that he has been stopped by the uniformed patrolman who is cordoning off the area.

"Hey, I'm with WPIX! You can't stop me from going over there!" Peter tries to push his way past the officer, but the officer holds him in a tight iron grip.

"Look, I don't give a goddamn if you're the governor. You are *not* entering this crime scene. Back off, or I'll cuff ya."

"Hey, hey, hey!" shouts Jack, quickly walking over to the men in order to calm flaring tempers.

Addressing the patrolman, he quips, "Let's not treat our buddies in the press with disrespect, Officer."

Turning to the reporter, he says, "Hello, there, Mr. Sloan. I'm Detective Stenhouse. How may I help you?"

"Hello, Detective. My sources tell me that you found another victim of the serial killer who's been stalking the hookers in our fair town for the past year. Is that true?"

"I cannot comment on an ongoing investigation, Mr. Sloan."

"Oh, come now, Detective. Don't try to snow a snowman. What's the skinny?"

"Look, you'll be the first to know when, and if, any of the details can be released, but for now, there are no details. This is just another crime scene. So I am politely asking you to back away, because if you don't, I'll have to unleash that officer over there on you. Capeesh?"

"Yeah, I capeesh, Stenhouse. I CAPEESH."

Sloan backs away, but he and his cameraman set up their equipment nearby to begin his broadcast.

"This is your investigative reporter, Peter Sloan, on the scene at the ferry terminal on the East River. Another body has been found, and it seems that it may be the work of a serial killer who is stalking the Big Apple. Once again, the police have no comment, hiding behind the restrictions of an ongoing investigation. What's going on, Mayor? What's the story? This is Peter Sloan, on the job for WPIX."

CHAPTER FOURTEEN

Dr. Klein has the latest victim split open on the autopsy table like a frog in a high school science lab. Jack and Allison watch as Klein removes the internal organs and checks each of them over.

"So Doc, any insight on the death?"

"Well, if you look at the color of her lips, it was probably oxygen deprivation by carbon monoxide exposure. After that, her arms were removed by a large, sharp object. I would guess it was a quick amputation by a large axe. You can see a sharp edge here, on the top of these bones."

As he points to a cut three inches down from each shoulder, Allison bends down to take a closer look while Jack walks away from the table.

"What's the matter, Jack? Not feeling well?"

"Look, Ally, my head is still pounding from this morning, and this ain't helping." Feeling a little green, he tells Klein, "Doc, give us a call down at the First when you're done, okay?" Heading for the door, he says "Let's go, Allison. We have to run the victim's photo through our records to see if we can identify 'Venus De Milo.' Take care, Doc."

The twenty-minute ride back to the precinct gives Jack and Allison some time to discuss this disturbing development.

"Looks like you may be right, Jack. We may have a serial killer on our hands."

"Yeah. Let's check out the surveillance cameras from the dock area to see if our mystery man, or a white van, appears. I'm afraid there may be more prostitutes who have been missing since last winter but never showed up dead. And just wait; Peter Sloan is going to be a real pain in the ass about all this."

"You're right on both counts. I'll check with the adjoining precincts to see if anyone reported a missing person who happened to be a hooker. I know no one reported any missing persons in the First."

"Just wait till we drop the bomb about a serial killer on Rawlings! And what about Sloan? How do you think he's getting his info? I think we need to get the FBI involved in this one, and I know just the person to contact."

When Jack pulls up to the precinct, the cops outside the building gawk at his Roadrunner and give him thumbs up. He returns the gesture and follows Allison inside to touch base with Rawlings.

At the boutique, business continues to boom against all odds as word spreads about the new business in the neighborhood. Didi's pole-dancing class is also becoming very popular, and when the class becomes too large to handle, Sonya volunteers to teach a second one.

One busy afternoon, a longhaired redhead walks into the store, prompting Didi to look up from the counter and wonder, *where have I seen her before?*

"Welcome to Diedra's!" Sonya says to the new arrival. "How may I help you today?"

Looking around the shop, the customer replies, "Hi. A friend of mine recommended that I check out your pole-dancing class, but she didn't tell me that you also sell lingerie and clothing!"

"Well, let me introduce you to Didi, the owner. She can tell you about the classes and our line of clothes." With a wave of her hand, Sonya motions Didi over to speak to the customer.

"Hi, I'm Didi. I hear that you'd like to caress the pole."

"Yes, my name is Andrea..."

Cutting her short, Didi exclaims, "Andrea? Now I know where I've seen you before! You're the mayor's press secretary, right?"

CHAPTER FIFTEEN

As soon as D.I. Rawlings gets off the phone, Jack and Allison burst into his office. Seeing the expressions on his detectives' faces, he braces himself before asking, "Okay, what do we have?"

They glance at each other as if deciding who should give their boss the bad news, with Allison losing the bet.

"You know those two cases you gave Jack to review?" she asks. "Well, it looks like their killer is back. There was a note pinned to the body at the ferry terminal with the same symbol as our mystery man's tattoo. And if you remember, one of the hookers we interviewed during that cleanup of downtown remembered seeing that same guy. Jack and I believe there are more victims that we haven't found yet. But it gets worse. This one has no arms."

"Geez! What did the note say?"

"Sunlight breaks through leafless limbs. We think it refers to the sunrise. The body was positioned to face east, overlooking the river."

Rawlings takes a minute to process this information, then states, "Look, I want you two to get together with the Terrorist Command Center. You told me before that you think this guy's driving a white van; well, the city set up a grid of over two thousand cameras to monitor downtown because of 9-11, so there must be something useful on at least one of them. The Command Center can help you with the videos. Also check for missing teenager reports with the neighboring precincts. Our young lady may have a concerned parent who's looking for her. Guys, we need to stop this animal before the mayor gets involved. Lord knows I don't need *that* aggravation on top of everything else! Was there any ID on this new victim?"

"No ID, sir."

"Jack is calling her Venus De Milo."

Frowning, he snaps, "Don't let that get out! Get a name on her and hit the streets to see if any of the other working girls saw anything. The mayor has too many eyes and ears. Let's try to keep a lid on this for as long as we can. I'll call Commissioner McQuade to give him a heads up. Jack! Venus De Milo? That's cold!"

"Sorry, sir, but can I ask you something? Who is this Peter Sloan guy? He showed up at the crime scene and seems to have inside info."

"He's a whiz kid who's trying to make a name for himself..." As a thought comes to mind he pauses, then quickly adds, "Whoa, wait a minute... What do you mean, 'inside info?' "

"He talked about receiving information from 'sources' about a serial killer who's been stalking the city for the past year."

Opening his eyes wide in surprise, Rawlings exclaims, "Dammit, we have a mole!" With a sigh and a shake of his head, he continues, "I'll look into it. Thanks, Jack."

Outside the D.I.'s office, the detectives divide responsibilities. Giancarlo offers to confer with the Command Center about surveillance videos while Jack reviews mug shots to try to identify Venus De Milo.

On the way to Booking, Jack gets a coke and a bag of chips out of the vending machine, then stops at his desk to call Didi.

He knows he's going to be home late tonight.

Slowly and methodically, Jack is combing through the seemingly endless mug shots of known hookers that are filed in the police department's computer system. But while this system is a breeze to operate in comparison to South Florida's cumbersome binders of mug shots, the sheer volume of photos has him hoping that Allison will return quickly, so she can assist him with the task.

However, at this moment, Allison is being slowed down in her quest for surveillance camera information by typical bureaucratic nonsense. She is stopped at the front desk of the Command Center near City Hall by a Sergeant Cummings, an older man in his fifties, who is so out of shape that his uniform makes him look like a blue bowling ball with short legs and tiny arms.

"Can I help you?" he asks.

Flashing her badge, Allison replies, "I'm Detective Giancarlo from the First. I need to review surveillance tapes of the downtown area on the East Side, near the ferry terminal."

"Well, you need written authorization from the head of your precinct, and that has to be reviewed and approved before you can come in here."

"Look, Sergeant. I don't have time for this. New York may be faced with a...." She cuts herself short. "Look. I'm investigating a murder, and I need to see tapes of the areas adjoining the ferry terminal."

"Sorry, Detective. Not without the proper paperwork."

"Okay, who's your boss? Get him here right now, or else."

Reaching out, she grabs Cummings by his manhood and takes a firm hold, convincing the sergeant to pick up the phone and call his superior.

Sweating like a pig and trying to talk through the pain, the Sergeant hurries his call.

"Hello? This is Commander Lansing."

"Commander, ugh, this is Cummings at the front desk. I have a Detective Giancarlo here from the First. She wants access."

"Tell her to go and get it."

"Commander... You need to come down here, sir. She's not going to go away."

"Shit... I'll be right there."

"He's coming down. You wanna ease off a little?"

Allison releases her grip and steps back while Cummings takes a deep breath and wipes the sweat off his brow.

While she waits, Allison gives Rawlings a call to inform him of the access problem. His response is, "Don't worry, I'll fix it."

When Commander Lansing walks into the lobby, he has an attitude that his shit don't stink. Addressing Sergeant Cummings, he asks, "Is this Giancarlo?"

"Yes, sir."

Turning to Allison, he scowls. "Look, Detective, I don't give a rat's ass *why* you're here. Without authorization, you're not getting anywhere. Understand?"

Before she can respond, Lansing's cell phone rings. Stepping a few feet away, he answers the call. "This is Lansing... Yes, sir!... No, no problem... Yes, right away."

Returning to Detective Giancarlo, he is noticeably calmer.

"Welcome to Terrorist Central, Detective. Follow me."

After reviewing mug shots all afternoon, Jack is relieved when he finally finds what he's been looking for. Lana Jenkins, a nineteen-year-old busted for drugs and prostitution in the Fifth Precinct, matches the photo of his Venus De Milo. As he updates his reports with Lana's name, he receives a call on his cell phone.

"Jack speaking."

"Jack, its Giancarlo. We got a hit from one of the security cameras. There was a white van near the ferry dock early this morning. We can't get a license number, though. There seems to be a cover over the license plate to block cameras from recording an image. However, we were able to get a quick shot of the driver, even though the van's windows are tinted. The only thing is, he was wearing a baseball cap and sunglasses."

"Well, at least we got something! I guess our mystery man isn't quite the mystery he once was. Look, I got an ID on the newest victim, and she was only nineteen years old. Still haven't heard from the other precincts about any young girls reported missing and not found, so I guess I'll call it a day. See you tomorrow. Take care, Allison."

"Yeah, you too."

Jack had already told Didi that he would be home late this evening, so now that he has a little extra time, he decides to make use of it by visiting Our Lady of Victory Church. When he pulls up in front, he places the blue light on his dashboard in order to avoid a parking ticket, then sits in his car for a minute to gather up his courage.

When he finally steps out onto the sidewalk, he mumbles, "I hope I don't get struck by lightning!"

As Jack slowly walks down the center aisle of the church, the scents of wood and beeswax fill the air, along with the echo of his footsteps. He has an appointment with the pastor, Father Lucarelli, but there doesn't seem to be anyone else there, beside himself.

Taking a seat in a pew three rows back from the altar, he gazes at the Crucifix hanging high above it, transfixed by what the image represents.

Within a few minutes, Father Lucarelli walks out of the sacristy, the small room where the priest changes into his priestly vestments and prepares himself for Mass. He looks at the man sitting alone in the church to try to determine his purpose for being there, then clears his throat loudly. At the sound, Jack stands to greet the approaching priest with an outstretched hand.

"Father Lucarelli? I'm Jack Stenhouse."

"Nice to meet you, Jack. There usually isn't anyone here until our evening Mass at 7:30, so I assumed it was you. When you called, you said you had a question about marriage?"

"Yes, Father. Is there anywhere we can talk in private?"

"Well, since there's no one else here but you, me, and Jesus, why don't we remain right here? I'm sure Jesus is most interested in what you have to say."

"Okay, then, here's my story. I was baptized as a Catholic and attended religious instruction until my Confirmation. Not long after that, my mom passed away suddenly, and my father married an Episcopalian woman. I attended my stepmother's church until I went away to college, but I haven't been to church since then, except when my father and stepmom passed away. I've been married and divorced more than once, but I was never married in a church. I'm a homicide detective, and I deal with the results of evildoers every day of my life, which has probably strained my past relationships. But now, as I'm getting older, I'm starting to realize that I'm not immortal, and since I've become engaged to a wonderful woman, I want to start our marriage out the right way. So Father, I'm here to find out what I need to do to get it onto the right track."

"Hmm, the prodigal son!" Father Lucarelli quipped. "It's good that you've come home! I'll want to speak with you and your fiancée, so please make an appointment at the Rectory. What's her name, Jack?"

"Diedra, Father."

"Is she Catholic, and has she been married before?"

"Yes, and no."

"Okay, good. I'm looking forward to speaking with you and Diedra, but since you've both been away from the Church for over twenty years, you'll need to return to good standing with Jesus Christ by going to Confession. Since we're alone right now, Jack, this is as perfect a time as any!"

As a look of panic comes over Jack's face, he stammers, "Right now, right here, in front of you? I haven't done this since I was a kid, Father!"

"There's nothing to worry about. I'll help you, but if you feel more comfortable in the confessional, then follow me."

With Father Lucarelli's arm around him, Jack is led into the confessional at the back of the church.

This is going to take a while.

CHAPTER SIXTEEN

As Didi prepares to close up shop after the end of the pole-dancing class, Andrea Singletary, the mayor's press secretary, lags behind and helps her clean up the studio.

"Didi, this was my first class, and I had a wonderful time. I didn't realize that it would be such a workout, though!"

"Thanks. That's why I started this class, to keep us ladies fit and sexy. Oh, by the way, I've been admiring your earrings. Are they Egyptian?"

"Yes. I studied ancient mythology in college--Egyptian, Greek and Roman. These are the Eye of Horus. They symbolize protection and good health. You like?"

"Yeah, they're great."

"Well, here, you can have them." Andrea removes the earrings and hands them to Didi.

"Oh, no, I can't take your earrings!"

"I insist. They're not expensive, and I can get another pair any time. Besides, I like people who like mythology."

Gathering her belongings, Andrea waves goodbye and walks out the door, leaving Didi holding the earrings.

Surprised by the unexpected gift, Didi smiles, then realizes that it's getting late and that Jack has still not called. She doesn't like going home alone, so she calls his cell phone to see where he is.

"Hi, Jack. Are you coming to the store or should I take a cab home?"

"I'm right outside, Babe. Let me in. I got a couple of pastrami sandwiches and beers for dinner."

Very relieved that she is no longer alone, Didi quickly puts on her new earrings before she runs to the front of the store to let Jack in.

Jack notices the new earrings as he gives Didi a kiss.

"Where'd ya get the new earrings?"

"Oh, one of my students gave them to me. Do you like them?"

"Yeah, they look kinda mystical. Egyptian?"

"Andrea said they're the Eyes of Horus, whoever the hell he is."

"Cool, but why did she give them to you?"

"I don't know. She was wearing them tonight, and when I said I liked them, she just gave them to me. She said she studied mythology in college. I guess she wants to get others interested in that stuff."

"Okay, whatever. Let's eat before the sandwiches get cold and the beer gets warm."

Jack follows Didi into the dance studio, where they sit opposite each other on a pair of folding chairs and start eating their dinner. Between bites, Jack brings up a sensitive subject.

"Um, I stopped by the church today and spoke to the priest about getting married there."

"What?! You really did it?" Didi laughs in surprise. "Lord, Jack, did lightning strike?"

"No, but I was ready to duck. The priest said it would be okay, but he wants to talk to us first, and we would have to join the church. Are you okay with that?"

"If he's still willing to marry us after we talk with him, I guess I'm okay with it."

"Great! Well, he already knows all about me. I went to Confession today."

Didi was in the middle of taking a gulp of beer when Jack dropped that bomb on her, and her reaction to the news caused the beer to gush out of her nose. Coughing and wiping up the mess at the same time, she gasps, "Argh, cuh ca! Jack, you couldn't wait until I finished my beer?!! *You went to CONFESSION*?! Damn, you really *are* serious about this!"

"Yup, I want to get everything right, and this is what you want, isn't it? Besides, I'm not immortal, and dealing with all the evil in our society on a daily basis is wearing me down. I figure that if I re-join the Church, maybe it will give me a little help from upstairs, and marrying you in the Church to boot, well, it's all aces. Anyway, this new case I'm working on is getting worse every day. The city has a serial killer on the prowl, and I think he got started a year ago. So maybe I could use a little help with this one."

Still wiping her face, Didi leans over and gives Jack a warm and loving hug to thank him for respecting her wishes about their wedding.

"When do you want to go back to the church?"

"I set up a meeting tomorrow night at 8:30, after the evening Mass. I should be able to pick you up at the regular time, so we'll eat dinner first, then go to the meeting afterwards, okay?"

Didi looks into Jack's eyes and smiles. "You're going to make a lady out of me any way you can, aren't you?"

She takes a large bite of her sandwich while shaking her head in wonder.

"Tomorrow is going to be very interesting, very interesting indeed! Now, tell me about this killer."

After the cabbie drops her off at her apartment building, Andrea stops in the lobby to get her mail, then goes directly up to her floor. Once inside her apartment, she drops the mail on the kitchen table, then walks into the bedroom to get ready for bed. She has not been sleeping well lately and is hoping that the pole-dancing classes will help her to relax.

Before getting under the covers, she walks back into the kitchen to warm up some milk, hoping that it will also help her to sleep. In the morning, she plans to ask the mayor for a leave of absence, to gain some time to clear her head from the nightmares that have been plaguing her.

She hopes the nightmares won't return tonight.

CHAPTER SEVENTEEN

Enjoying a moment of downtime, Jack is sitting at his desk drinking a cup of coffee when Rawlings calls him into his office.

"Jack, as soon as Giancarlo comes in, I need you two to go down to Battery Park. A body washed up on shore this morning with another note. I already sent the CSI team and the M.E. to check it out."

"Oh, great. It looks like this is going to get uglier."

"Yeah. I've asked the FBI to take on this case, and they're sending down an agent. You'll meet each other at the park this morning."

"I sure hope Sloan doesn't show up."

Just as Jack returns to his desk, he spots Allison walking over to her own desk.

"Hey, Giancarlo! We're busy this morning. Got a floater down at the Battery. Let's go."

Within ten minutes, they are at the shore of the New York Harbor, watching as an unmarked black sedan pulls up behind their vehicle. When the driver exits the sedan, she waves at the detectives, then quickly joins a broadly-smiling Detective Stenhouse.

"Maria! I guess we're working together again!"

"Mornin' Jack! It's just like old times!"

"Yeah, you can't get rid of me so easily!" Gesturing to Allison, Jack continues, "Maria, this is Detective Giancarlo. We're working together on this case. Got a floater here, but we don't know much more. We just got here."

"Okay, let's check it out, then."

The trio walks over to where the crime scene investigation team and the M.E. are huddled together. Putting on a pair of rubber gloves, Jack unpins the note from the young woman's sleeve.

"Looks like he signed this one."

He hands the note into the gloved hands of Detective Giancarlo, who reads it to Maria Assante, the

FBI agent assigned to the case: *Winter's gray will take its toll on the unsuspecting few. --- CRONOS*

"Anyone have any ideas about what this could mean?"

After a brief silence, Maria offers her opinion.

"I think Cronos was a Greek god, or maybe a Roman one, and that funny looking symbol at the bottom stands for Saturn."

The medical examiner adds, "Yes, I think you're right. Saturn was also known as Cronos. He castrated his father, Uranus, and took his place as ruler of the universe. And by the way, this body is half frozen. From what I can observe, it looks like the damage to her skin was caused by freezer burn. I would say that she has probably been frozen for a while, maybe as long as a year."

Detective Giancarlo confers with Jack and Maria.

"This is the same sicko from last year. He must have stashed some bodies somewhere and is now releasing them slowly, like a twisted time capsule." Glancing down at the water's edge, she says, "The water level here is high, so the tide came in last night. The body could have been dumped anywhere out in the harbor to allow it to float toward the shore. I guess this guy has a boat *and* a van."

Jack interrupts, "He must have a warehouse somewhere in south Manhattan, probably near the shoreline. Why don't you two go back to the morgue for the autopsy? I'll return to the office to fill in Rawlings. We're going to need more help if we're going to stop this maniac."

At the sound of a car door slamming, all heads turn and someone complains loudly, "Oh, great! Look who just pulled up! It's *Sloan*!"

At the sight of the WPIX van, audible moans erupt from the officers on the scene, causing many of them to walk as far away as possible while Peter Sloan jumps out of the van with his cameraman in tow and runs over to Jack with a microphone in his outstretched hand.

When he reaches Jack, he whispers, "We're live."

"This is Peter Sloan, your investigative reporter, on the scene where another victim of the serial killer who is terrorizing our great city was found. Detective Stenhouse, is there anything you would like to say about the latest victim?"

"I have no comment at this time. You need to back away from this crime scene."

"Detective, is it true that the killer left another note?"

"Again, I have no comment. Now, if you would please excuse me, I have the city's business to attend to."

As Stenhouse walks away, he leaves Sloan and his cameraman out to dry like yesterday's laundry. But Peter Sloan is relentless.

"Again, the police have no comment. Looks like we have a problem, New York. The criminal I am going to call the 'Poetic Killer,' has struck again. Always on the job for you, this is Peter Sloan, WPIX."

Andrea is sitting at her desk, but she is exhausted. She had another night full of nightmares and very little sleep. When the mayor walks into her office, she is drinking a double espresso, trying to wake up.

"Holy crap, Andrea, you look like something the cat dragged in! Are you feeling all right?"

"No, I haven't been getting much sleep lately. Look, Rod, I know this is short notice, since Thanksgiving is next week, and a couple of weeks after that, I was scheduled to take a vacation, but I really need to take a leave of absence now to fix myself up. If I don't get some quality sleep soon, I may have another breakdown. I don't think I've recovered from those two deaths occurring so close to each other. I need to get away, to get a change of scenery or something, before I explode."

"Sure, I guess that's okay. Your assistant can cover for you. Holiday time is kinda slow around City Hall, anyway. Fill her in on what's coming up and go home at lunch. Take all the time you need."

Andrea rises from her chair and gives Rod a hug. They have been friends for a while, and Rod has always hoped that it would go much further. He wants to kiss her, but not in her current condition, and not in the office.

CHAPTER EIGHTEEN

"So what bad news do you have for me today, Jack?" asks Deputy Inspector Gene Rawlings.

"This morning's victim is definitely a product of the killer of last year's hookers. However, this one is not a recent casualty; she was frozen for a while before being dumped. The M.E. guessed she was frozen for about a year. There was also another note, and it has the same type of warning as the first one from the Venus de Milo victim: *Winter's gray will take its toll on the unsuspecting few."*

"Hmm. I thought that line from the first note sounded familiar, like a poem I read in college that had something to do with winter, so I Googled it last night and found it. It's on my laptop; the author is anonymous. Take a look at it, Jack." Rawlings spins the laptop around so Jack can read the verse:

Sunlight breaks through leafless limbs
silhouetting sky.
Jack's breath numbs the diamond dew
as South the birds do fly.
Winter's gray will take its toll
on the unsuspecting few.
As sunlight ebbs from lifeless limbs
and Jack's breath numbs the dew.

"I'm convinced this 'Poetic Killer' is going to strike again, so I'm putting together a task force with the neighboring precincts and the FBI. The Bureau is going to supply one of their profilers to help us try to understand him."

"Boss, you're starting to think just like Peter Sloan! But damn, it does seem as though those last two sentences are telling us who he's going to hit, and when he's going to strike again!"

"Yeah, I know. The Department's media coordinator is going to make a statement this morning, and a circus atmosphere is already starting to build up around this thing. But that poem is what inspired me to call him the 'Poetic Killer'. Take a look at the morning paper."

The D.I. Googles the newspaper's web page on his laptop, then shows the headline to Jack: *Poetic Killer Foretells a Gruesome Winter*.

"They know about the notes? How did they find out about them, Chief?"

"Someone at the crime scenes must have passed them around. Listen, Thanksgiving is next week, and winter officially starts in less than four weeks. It was winter when this all began last year, and it stopped when winter was over. This year, it started before winter, so we really need a break in this case; it's going to be a bad one. When the media coordinator issues his statement today, he's going to ask for anonymous tips on our tip line from anyone who has seen a white van with a driver who fits our perp's description, and you know how these things go—we're going to get hundreds of tips. Look, I've been keeping you under my wings until I could see that you're ready to go, and now's the time. You're officially on your own now, but I need you to continue to keep in touch with your squad leader, Lieutenant Conrad. He'll be at your team meeting today, and the FBI profiler will be here this morning."

"Thanks, Chief. I won't disappoint you."

Andrea is on her way home with a splitting headache. Ever since her divorce and breakdown, the year-end holidays have been difficult, so she is hoping that a relaxing getaway this year will do the trick. In the morning, she plans to head up to a little cottage along the Hudson River that she was awarded in the divorce settlement, instead of going to Aspen, her usual vacation spot.

CHAPTER NINETEEN

Jack drums his fingers on the table in the empty conference room as his stomach grumbles. He's waiting for Allison and Maria to return from the morgue, and for the detectives from the Fifth and the Nineteenth Precincts, as well as the FBI profiler, to arrive for a strategy meeting. Everyone should be there within the hour, but Jack is hungry. He glances at his Armitron, which reads almost two o'clock. Again, no lunch.

He walks out of the room and heads toward the vending machine, where he gets a bottle of Coke and tries to buy some Dorito's, but they're sold out. When he eyes a bag of salted peanuts, he smiles as he remembers a snack trick from when he was a kid.

Retrieving the peanuts from the machine, he opens the bag and gently pours the nuts into his open bottle of Coke. He knows that when the salt mixes with the soda, it will cause a mini-volcano to form and force the Coke out of the top of the bottle. So in anticipation of this reaction, he places his mouth over the top of the soda bottle to catch the exploding soda, but that move only works for about a second, as Coke quickly begins to squirt out of his nose and mouth, spilling onto the floor.

Choking, and with his sinuses on fire, he runs into the men's room for paper towels, and is on his hands and knees cleaning up the mess when Maria and Allison appear in the hallway. Stopping short, they take in the amusing scene, asking in unison, "Moonlighting, Jack?"

Not happy about being caught in an undignified position, Jack immediately flashes them the Florida state bird.

"Had a little accident, okay? So what did you learn from the doctor of the dead?"

While Maria responds to Jack's question, Allison bends down to help him clean the floor.

"We didn't learn very much because Jane Doe appears to have been frozen for a while. There won't be any new information about her death until after she's completely thawed out. There doesn't seem to be any blunt force trauma, though."

Allison steps away to throw out the wet paper towels, leaving Jack with Maria.

"By the way, Maria, your FBI office is sending down a profiler and we're assembling a team here, composed of us and the Fifth and Nineteenth Precincts. Everyone should be here within the hour, so you'd better take a quick break now, before we get started. We'll be in Conference Room Two."

Andrea lies down on her bed in the dark, with the blinds and curtains closed up tight. She has taken some Imitrex and has placed a cold compress on her head. As she drifts off to sleep, she dreams of Roman gods and mythological events, with flashes of Zeus, lightning bolts, death, and destruction.

In the offices of WPIX TV, Peter Sloan is sitting at his desk typing while his phone rings incessantly. Reaching over a pile of papers, he finally picks it up and declares brusquely, "This is Sloan. Make it fast; my time is money!"

An unfamiliar voice proclaims, "Mr. Sloan, you like talking about me, don't you?"

"Who are you?"

"You know who I am, Mr. Sloan. I'm the Poetic Killer."

Thinking fast, Sloan responds, "How do I know who you are? You could be anyone who wants a little publicity."

"Bodies will be floating, Mr. Sloan...hehehehehe."

After a soft click, there is silence on the other end of the line.

"Hello, hello? You still there? Hello?"

Awakening suddenly in a cold sweat, Andrea gets up to take a shower. When she enters the bathroom, she sees a message left in lipstick on her shower door: DO NOT WORRY, MY LOVE. I AM RIGHT BY YOUR SIDE. CALL ME IF YOU NEED ME.

With her headache now miraculously gone, she smiles as she removes her undergarments and steps into the shower. As the cold water hits her face and torso, she remains there motionless, like the statue of Diana in the ancient city of Pompeii under a cold rain.

While waiting for the rest of the team to arrive at the First Precinct, Jack thinks back on his decision to leave Florida. He wanted to get more action, and now it seems that he got it. As the old saying goes, you need to watch what you ask for.

Maria Assante and Detective Allison Giancarlo are the first to arrive in the conference room, and they are quickly followed by Lieutenant Conrad. When Detective Timmons from the Fifth and Detective Luis from the Nineteenth arrive, everyone introduces themselves, and Giancarlo starts the meeting.

"Okay, everyone. We have news on Jane Doe, our latest victim. She's a hooker from your neck of the woods, Luis. Her name is Candi Jones, twenty-one years old. Her mother reported her missing last December. Jack, fill us in on what we have so far."

Jack walks over to a white board at the front of the room, but just as he is about to begin, the FBI profiler enters and introduces himself.

Andrea is looking forward to her getaway on the Hudson. She has already finished packing and has placed her suitcase near the door. As she looks around the apartment, she remembers that she has an open bottle of Lambrusco in the fridge, and in wild desperation, like a heroin addict needing a fix, she retrieves her liquid bounty like an English pirate celebrating the raping of a French cargo ship three to four hundred years ago. There are only one or two servings left in the bottle, so she forgoes a glass and takes her bounty into the living room, where she puts on some Sinatra, reclines on the sofa, and brings the bottle to her lips like a long lost lover. Taking a deep swallow, she closes her eyes and drifts off into a twilight state, not asleep, but not awake, either. When the phone rings, she picks up the receiver and listens through the fog.

"Rhea, I'm coming over. I have something to show you."

Hanging up the phone, she drops the empty bottle on the floor, and laughs.

With FBI Agent Lew Donnelly sitting next to Maria Assante, the two FBI representatives are taking over one end of the table. Jack passes around the mug shot of Lana Jenkins, the Venus de Milo victim, the stills of the killer taken from the surveillance camera, and some photos of the latest victim. Then he begins his briefing, beginning with the two case files from last year.

"As you can see, it appears that our killer has returned. So far, all of the victims have been prostitutes and were found either on the East Side or the West Side of the city. One of them has been mutilated, with her arms missing. The last two bodies also had notes attached. I believe this person that the press is calling the Poetic Killer is trying to tell us that he wants to be stopped. It appears that he is letting us know what is going to happen through his notes."

Jack looks over at the FBI profiler. "Agent Donnelly, do you have any thoughts about the case? I know it may be premature for you at this time, but anything could help at this point."

Donnelly had been skimming through the original cases files and photos of the suspect and victims while Jack was speaking, but he takes another quick glance through them before offering his opinion.

"It appears that our suspect is influenced by Greek and Roman mythology. He has a tattoo of the symbol for the planet Saturn on the back of his neck, which is the name of the Roman god who was also known as Cronos in the Greek. As you know, Cronos is the name that is used in the notes. The first two murders that we know of occurred in December of last year during the time of Saturnalia, the ancient Roman festival that was named after the Roman god, Saturn. As to Cronos, the Greek version of this god, mythology states that he devoured his children because he thought they would kill him. That myth is illustrated pretty graphically in a painting by the Spanish artist Francisco Goya, which depicts a victim with no arms. I fear that the suspect in this case has an urge to kill and devour that is now overtaking him and is driving him to start a new killing spree before Saturnalia begins again this year. I also believe that it is very likely that 'Cronos' has established a base of operation somewhere in the city, a place where he's keeping his 'children', and that the notes he is leaving may either be a cry for help, or his way of boasting about what he's doing. Let's hope that there aren't any more victims who have been 'devoured,' if you will."

When the agent finishes speaking, everyone contemplates the worst in an atmosphere of complete silence, until the sudden ringing of Jack's cell phone startles them out of their reveries.

CHAPTER TWENTY

Jack stares wordlessly at his ringing cell phone, but when Didi's work number pops up on the screen, he answers it quickly.

"Hey, Di. This isn't a good time. I'll call you right back." Ending the call, he continues the meeting.

"Sorry, guys. I should have shut the damn thing off. Look, we need to see if there are any abandoned warehouses in the areas where the victims were found, and if a white van has been seen near those places. Timmons and Luis, I'll leave that to you. Giancarlo, check to see if we have any 'working girls' in lockup. Maybe we can get a lead on the white van from our friends on the street. Okay, that's it. Let's get going, everyone. We have a lot of work to do and not a lot of time to do it."

Before the meeting can be formally adjourned, all heads turn toward the door as D.I. Rawlings rushes into the room.

"Jack, I just received a phone call from Peter Sloan."

"Oh, yeah? What did that asshole want, Boss?"

"Our serial killer called him today and said there will be more bodies floating around here soon. Sloan said he'd contact us if he gets another call."

Turning toward the others in the room, Rawlings orders, "Keep vigilant, everyone. This is going to get uglier."

Sighing deeply, Jack states, "Well, guys, the shit just keeps hitting the fan. We'll meet again here tomorrow morning."

As the room empties, Agent Donnelly takes Jack aside. "Assante and I are going to review the last autopsy again. I think we got a bad one on our hands here, Jack. I'll keep Lieutenant Conrad briefed on all the latest developments so he can update the D.I. and the mayor as things move forward." He turns toward the door. "See you tomorrow, Jack."

Suddenly alone in the conference room, Jack mumbles to himself as he stares at the white board.

"Well, I wanted more action, and boy, did I get it."

Shaking his head, he dials Didi's number.

"Hi, Babe, what's shakin'? Sorry about cutting you off, but I was in a meeting."

"Oh, I just called to remind you about that meeting at the church tonight."

"Wow, I nearly forgot about that. Okay, I'm on my way; I'll see you in about twenty minutes." Ending the call, Jack gathers his files, intending to work on them at home later tonight.

As he walks down the hallway toward the building's exit, he is stopped by Lieutenant Conrad.

"I'm glad I found you before you left, Jack. Peter Sloan just told us that our killer called him and promised more killings."

"Yeah, I heard; Rawlings filled us in. Shit, between the media and the mayor, we're going to be in deep kimchee."

"Yeah. Sloan said he'd keep us in the loop, but he wants our 'cooperation' in return."

"That's just great. Rawlings told us that Sloan would let us know what was going on, but he forgot to mention the 'cooperation' crap."

As he makes his way through the parking lot to his beloved Road Runner, Jack tries to put the details of the case out of his mind, at least until after his meeting at church. Reaching the car, he buckles up, gives a quick "BEEP, BEEP" of the horn, and hauls ass over to Didi's.

Didi is alone in the boutique, having just locked the door behind Sonya. As she closes up the register, she listens anxiously for Jack's arrival.

Meanwhile, Jack has just parked the Road Runner down the block and is walking briskly toward the boutique, while keeping a close eye on a couple of young street punks who are hanging out near the storefront.

As Jack approaches, the two punks begin to walk toward him in a menacing manner, prompting him to lower his head and mutter, "Oh, crap."

Waiting until the punks are close, he casually opens his sports jacket to show off his Glock. "Walk away, guys, or you'll have a very bad evening."

Spotting the firearm, they stop short and wisely decide to turn around and slowly walk in the opposite direction, until one of them suddenly stops and lifts his basketball jersey to give Jack a look at his .38.

Jack watches the youth closely, and when he sees the kid begin to pull the gun out of his waistband, he pulls out his .45 and warns, "Don't do it, asshole."

When the kid doesn't stop, it becomes the last thing he does. Jack fires, placing a .40 caliber slug in the center of the punk's chest, exploding his heart and throwing him back about three feet. He is dead before he hits the ground.

The second punk remains frozen in place, staring at his friend in shock while he pisses himself.

Hearing the gunshot from inside the boutique, Didi runs outside to find Jack standing over the body of a young boy.

"Call 911, Babe, call 911!" Jack yells as he warily watches the other kid, who is standing in the same place, quite wet.

"Put your hands over your head and clasp your fingers together. Don't move, got it?"

The kid not only complies, but sits down on the ground to wait quietly for the consequences of his friend's actions.

As the sound of sirens becomes louder, Jack looks over at Didi.

"Damn, I don't think this kid was much older than thirteen, maybe fourteen."

The dead youth is sprawled on the sidewalk, still clutching the .38, and his buddy is now crying uncontrollably.

Still a little foggy after finishing off her bottle of wine several hours ago, Andrea can't remember much of what happened back in her apartment. Imitrex and wine don't mix well, so she doesn't remember that her mystery man, Cronos, stopped by.

As her mind slowly comes back into focus, she realizes that she's no longer at home. Taking in her surroundings, she finds herself cold and without light in a large, open warehouse, not knowing exactly where she is, or how she got there. As her brain tries to decipher her condition, a familiar voice surrounds her like a warm blanket.

"Rhea, welcome to my world. I hope you are doing well during this festive season."

Cronos gives Andrea the nickel tour of his home, which she finds out is an abandoned meat-processing facility in the shadow of the Manhattan Bridge, deep on the East Side. There's not much to see though; the building is just a large, empty space, with walk-in freezers at the back, and a couple of rooms on the second floor. Outside, there is a white van parked alongside a trailer that is cradling a Boston Whaler sport fishing boat.

"I just put a hitch on the van, Rhea. It may be a little cold, but let's take the boat out for a ride."

"You turned this place into a home? Where do you sleep?"

"Up those stairs. I turned some old offices into a living area; I'll show them to you later."

Grabbing her hand, he urges, "Come with me."

Jack is talking with the uniforms who responded to Didi's 911 call while he watches the EMTs check the victim. After working on the young boy for a while, one of the EMTs rises and approaches the group.

"He's done; there's nothing more we can do. Better call the M.E."

At that moment, Lieutenant Conrad pulls up and walks over to the group of cops, demanding loudly, "What the hell happened here?"

"Boss," Jack volunteers, "I was walking up the street, when these two punks started walking toward me in a threatening manner. I showed them my gun and told them to walk away. One did, and one didn't. This kid pulled his firearm, and I shot him; the other kid saw it all. Damn, they can't be older than thirteen."

Sighing loudly and holding out his hand, Conrad says, "I need to take your gun, Stenhouse. After we investigate, you'll get it back. I don't think there will be any problems, though. The dumb ass is still holding his gun."

Conrad takes a pair of latex gloves out of his pocket and removes the gun from the dead boy's hand. Then he walks over to the boy's friend, who is still crying.

"What's your name, son?"

"Dwayne. Dwayne Thomas. We just wanted to scare him. Dontrell is a little crazy."

"Dontrell is your friend there?"

"Yeah. When that guy told us to walk away, Dontrell said, 'Nobody tells me what to do,' and turned around. Before I could stop him, he got shot." Dwayne rocks back and forth saying, "It's all my fault! I should have stopped him!"

Conrad pats Dwayne on the shoulder, then walks over to one of the uniformed cops.

"Get a statement from that boy and see if we can get in touch with his parents."

Eyeing Jack, he continues, "I need you back at the station to fill out paperwork. This looks like a clean shoot; no worries here."

"NO WORRIES? DAMN, I just killed a thirteen-year old kid, Boss."

"I know. Listen, if you want to take a couple of days off, you can."

Staring at the ground, Jack tries to compose himself. "No, I'll be okay. We still need to catch that killer, remember?" Turning away from the crowd, Jack puts his arm around Didi and walks her inside the boutique.

"Jack, are you okay?"

"I'm fine, Babe. It's not the first time I shot anyone, but, DAMN! He was just a kid! Look, let's grab some dinner and then go see that priest. I gotta go back to the precinct later, so we need to get going."

"Okay, Jack, but I'll be here anytime you need to ease your tension."

As they leave the boutique, they notice that there is no crowd gathering around the scene, no reporters, no TV. It's just another day in the Big Apple.

CHAPTER TWENTY-ONE

Father Lucarelli is walking up to the church as Jack and Didi pull up in front of Our Lady of Victory.

"Hey, Di, there's the priest we have to talk to."

"Wow, he's kinda cute....for a priest."

"What? Cool down, okay? We need to get his approval, and by the way, I want to thank you for dressing conservatively tonight. I know it's hard to hide your assets."

Cronos guides the boat near the shore of the East River. Moving to the stern, he unwraps the frozen body of a young girl and drops it off the side and into the water. The tide is going in, so eventually it will hit the shore.

Cronos smiles, and says, "Another one for my Rhea. All will be well."

Andrea is silent. She has nothing to say.

Jack and Didi follow Father Lucarelli into the church and then into a small office just adjacent to the sacristy. The priest takes a seat behind his desk while Jack and Didi occupy the two chairs in front.

Looking from Jack to Didi, the priest cannot help but notice Didi's exotic charm.

Addressing them both, he says, "Good evening! I'm happy that both of you could make it tonight. Jack, you have chosen a very lovely bride."

Turning his attention to Didi, he asks, "Diedra, what brings you back to the Church?"

"Well, Father, the Church was part of my life when I was a young girl, but I left it behind when I grew up. However, as I'm getting older now, I'm beginning to long for the good ole days."

"Ah, I hear that a lot. So, tell me. What have you done with your life until now?"

"Oh, I was afraid you would ask me that. Okay, here goes. I, um, put myself through college by becoming an exotic dancer, and to my surprise, I became good at it. The money was great, so I kept it up."

Jack lowers his head in empathy for Didi's feelings.

"I met Jack a few years ago, and we moved in together. When he invited me to move to New York with him, I decided that it was my chance to get out of the dancing business, and with the money I saved up, I opened a boutique not too far from here. I always wanted to get married in a church, and after Jack proposed, he set up this meeting. I hope you let us back, Father; we've been away for a long time."

"My dear, God *always* welcomes his children home, and He is thrilled to have you back. Your stories are like the story of the prodigal son. Actually, in this case, you're the prodigal children. But as I told Jack, you will need to go to Confession, and then both of you have to sign up to attend a Pre-Cana course with other engaged couples before your wedding. The Pre-Cana course will prepare you both for married life. When are you planning to get married?"

Didi looks meaningfully at Jack while Jack looks back at her blankly. After a few seconds of uncomfortable silence, Jack takes the hint and replies, "This spring, Father. May or June."

"Well, the church is booked for weddings until July. Is that going to be an issue?"

Didi quickly responds. "No, Father, not at all. July is fine."

"Good." Handing some forms to Jack, he continues, "Here are the parish registration forms. You can begin to fill them out while Didi and I go into the church."

Nodding to Didi, he adds, "Come, my dear. I can hear your confession now, and remember, I expect to see the both of you at Mass this Sunday!"

Didi gives Jack a wink as she follows Father Lucarelli out of his office, prompting Jack to mumble softly, “Oh, to be a fly on the wall out there!”

CHAPTER TWENTY-TWO

Before returning to the First Precinct to submit his report of the shooting, Jack drives Didi to their apartment. He idles the Road Runner in front of the building to give her a quick kiss goodbye, but before leaving the car, Didi bats her eyes and says, “Hurry home, Jack. I have a surprise for you.”

Swallowing quickly, he replies, “I’ll be back as fast as I can, but remember, you just went to Confession.”

Didi smacks him on the arm, which causes Jack to laugh out loud. Waving to his fiancée, he gives two quick beeps of the horn, then screams off to work.

When Didi enters the apartment, she turns on the TV to pass the time, and catches a breaking news report.

“....the NYPD has further released this grainy photo of a person they consider to be of special interest in the Poetic Killer case. They are asking anyone who has seen a man with this unusual tattoo on the back of his neck to call the tip line. Your call will be anonymous...”

Didi stares at the photo, wondering where she has seen that tattoo before.

Nicole Colletti, a paralegal who lives near the Manhattan Bridge, likes to jog in the early evenings on the bike path along the FDR drive. As she passes the Brooklyn Bridge, she notices something floating in the water. When she stops to take a closer look, she gasps in horror, and immediately takes out her cell phone to call 911. When the operator answers, she reports a body drifting between the pilings under the Fulton Fish Market.

Jack is at his desk completing the report about the shooting when Deputy Inspector Rawlings walks over to him.

"I heard about the shooting earlier this evening, Jack. This is just routine, but I have to relieve you of duty. Your gun was sent out for ballistics testing, and there will be a departmental review of the incident. You should be back at work within forty-eight hours. I'm sorry, but this is standard operating procedure."

"But Rawlings, what about the case I'm working on?"

"The team will do just fine without you. Take a couple of days off; that's standard procedure for a shooting."

Jack knows this is standard stuff; he went through it in Fort Lauderdale many years ago.

"Okay, but I'm still working this case. If there are any updates, I want to be in on them."

"Giancarlo will take the lead while you're out, but you can take work home if you want. I'll have her update you if there's anything new. Now, go home and enjoy your two days off."

Jack hands in his report on the shooting, then makes a copy of the case file to take home with him. He wants to review it again away from the office, to see if there is anything he may have missed.

On his way out of the building, Jack waves to the sergeant on duty at the front desk, unaware that the phone call the sergeant is about to answer is one that he should be available to take.

"First Precinct, Sergeant Hanson."

After a brief pause on the other end of the line, a voice says, "Winter's gray will take its toll on the unsuspecting few." After another pause, the caller hangs up.

Knowing that Jack has left the station, Hanson immediately dials Detective Giancarlo.

CHAPTER TWENTY-THREE

Detective Giancarlo pulls in front of the Fulton Fish Market just behind Agent Maria Assante from the FBI. As they greet each other in the parking area, a NYPD river patrol boat dumps two divers into the water to retrieve the body floating under the market.

"Hi, Maria. On my way over here, I got a call from the desk sergeant down at the First. He just got a call from someone who recited a line from our killer's poem. He said, 'Winter's gray will take its toll on the unsuspecting few.' "

"Great, and now here we are." Giancarlo and Assante approach the two uniformed units on the scene.

"What do we have here, guys?"

Nodding at Nicole Colletti, who is standing with a police officer, he replies, "That young woman over there reported a body in the water."

"Maria, I'll go and talk to our witness. Check the body after they recover it, okay?"

While Allison walks over to speak with Nicole, Maria watches the dive team pull the body out of the water.

"Hi, I'm Detective Giancarlo. You're Nicole, right? Can you tell me what happened?"

"Yeah, it was gross; I never saw a dead body that wasn't in a coffin. Anyway, I like running along the river, and I go jogging every other night after work. Jogging usually has a calming effect on me, but not tonight." After a bit of nervous laughter, she continues. "As I was approaching the market, I caught something floating in the water out of the corner of my eye, and when I turned to see what it was, WHAM! – a body appeared! It looked like a woman."

"Why do you say a woman?"

"Oh, by the clothes. A halter top and mini skirt."

"Did you see anything suspicious on the river or in the surrounding area, a van, or maybe a boat?"

"No, nothing. Not even a seagull."

"Well, here's my business card. You can call me anytime if you remember anything else. Thank you."

"Can I go now?"

"Sure, and thanks again. I'll have one of the uniformed units drive you home."

Allison takes Nicole to one of the patrol cars and asks the officer to drive her home. Then she walks over to Agent Assante.

"So what did they find?"

"Looks like another victim. You can tell by the eyes that she was frozen and not all thawed out yet, either. Where's Jack? I thought he would be here."

"Jack is on administrative leave for forty-eight hours. He was involved in a shooting earlier today."

"Really? Is he okay?"

"Yeah, but the kid he shot is dead. The stupid ass pulled a gun on Jack."

"How old was the kid?"

"Early teens. They grow up too fast on the street. Let's wait here for the M.E. to show up. Then, we'll go down to the First. I'll give Jack a call in the morning."

After a few minutes, a TV news van pulls up with Peter Sloan sitting in the front seat.

"Oh, shit! Maria, look who just pulled up! How the hell does he know where to go all the time?"

"Damn! I'd like to tell him where to go, but we have to cooperate with him, remember?"

Taking the lead, Allison walks up to the news reporter.

"Mr. Sloan, I'm Detective Giancarlo. How can I help you?"

"Detective, I'm here unofficially tonight. The killer called me again and told me to check out the East River. When I headed out, I heard on my scanner that something was going down at the Fish Market. Is it another body?"

"Yeah. We're waiting for the M.E."

"Look, I may be obnoxious at times, but that's just theatrics, you know, ratings stuff. I'll help you as much I can, as long as I can get exclusive updates."

"Like doing business with the devil? Mr. Sloan, whatever D.I. Rawlings agrees to, you will have, but you will have to go through his office, capeesh?"

"Yeah, I got it, Detective. I capeesh."

It's about eleven o'clock when Jack finally arrives back at his apartment. He throws his badge on the table in the hallway and un-holsters his personal Kel Tec 9mm from his ankle, placing it next to his badge. They may have taken his service pistol, but he's never without his personal firearm as backup.

"Oh, Jack!!" a singsong voice calls from the bedroom.

When Jack turns toward the voice, he finds Didi standing in the doorway in a bright red teddy that covers, well, nothing.

"I told you I had a surprise for you."

Smiling widely, Jack takes her by the hand, and takes her to bed.

Lying on a daybed in the loft at Cronos's warehouse, Andrea finally begins to drift off into a deep sleep. She dreams of being in the clouds, and then being locked in a white room. In her dream, she pounds on the door, but cannot escape. As she drifts deeper into sleep, she thinks she hears Cronos laughing somewhere in the background.

CHAPTER TWENTY-FOUR

The phone rings and rings and rings. In a haze, Jack finally answers it.

"Yeah? This better be good."

"Jack, it's Giancarlo. We got another body and another message from the killer."

"Wuh, what?"

"Jack, wake up! Our killer struck again!"

Rubbing his eyes, he asks, "The uh, message, was it more of that poem?"

"Yeah. 'Winter's gray will take its toll on the unsuspecting few'."

Jack is now wide awake.

"Allison, when does that festival of Saturnalia begin?"

"Next week."

"The body--where was it?"

"Floating under the Fulton Fish Market on the East River."

"Fresh or frozen?"

"Frozen."

After a moment of silent thought, Jack continues, "There has to be a warehouse of some type on the East River. Anything on that yet?"

"Negative, but will keep you posted."

"Okay. Rawlings has me out till Monday at least. Any word on my shooting yet?"

"Rumor says it was justified, and no further action will be taken. The boy was an orphan. His father is unknown, and his mother is in jail for trafficking."

"How about the other boy?"

"Wrong place, wrong time; they let him go. His parents said they'll take care of it. I think he was scared shitless."

"Well, pissless, anyway. Thanks, Giancarlo."

Detective Giancarlo is in the makeshift situation room with Agent Maria Assante from the FBI, reviewing the Poetic Killer case with the rest of the team.

"Okay, people, we have another victim. Miss Karlena Robinson, nineteen years old, a working girl from the Lower East Side. Her mom reported her missing around Christmas last year. No body parts missing, but she was frozen. The M.E. thinks she was in deep freeze for about a year. Because of the message we got at the precinct, we believe she's another victim of our tattooed killer. Any updates, any news? Come on, we need a break here."

Detective Luis pipes up. "We've come up with a list of empty warehouses on the East Side. With the economy in the toilet, there are ten units to look at, and we think we can do two a day. Timmons has started the process of getting search warrants, so we'll be set to start on Monday. It's hell trying to get a judge on a Saturday, and a Sunday would be impossible."

Assante responds, "The festival of Saturnalia starts Monday, so we need to be more vigilant out there. I'm going undercover as a street walker; maybe we can spot this guy in action. I'll hang out near the park to see if I can spot him, and I'll have a backup team with me from the Bureau. Agent Donnelly, any thoughts?"

"I don't think this guy's going to do anything until Monday. That's when he'll kick in again; it's the start of that festival. Remember that Saturnalia was an ancient Roman festival in honor of the god Saturn, who was called Cronos by the Greeks. He ate the children he had by his sister, Rhea, because he was afraid they would kill him and take over his throne. The festival was also a time of wild revelry. I think the killer has been baiting us all this time. He thinks he's superior and in control, and that he won't get caught. Saturnalia is the key."

Cronos stands over Andrea, who is fast asleep. He looks at her lovingly, then bends down and whispers in her ear, "Sleep well, my love, sleep deep. The festival starts Monday, and I will be busy, for you must be saved, you must be protected." Kissing her cheek softly, he turns and leaves the room.

The warehouse is quiet now, except for Cronos' harrowing laugh as he washes down his boat and van outside the building.

CHAPTER TWENTY-FIVE

Stepping out of the shower, Jack grabs a towel and wraps it around himself before heading to the kitchen to start breakfast. He intends to spend the day at the boutique, going over the case files while keeping Didi company, in case any other street punks want to make trouble.

Speaking loudly so that Didi hears him, he asks, "How do you want your eggs? Sunny side up, or over easy?"

It's a typical Saturday afternoon, and Sonya and Didi are handling their customers with cheerfulness and efficiency. The boutique is busy, as Christmas is just around the corner. Men are shopping for their women, and women are shopping for their men. Jack has staked out a place in the back office, where he is trying to find something, anything, new amid the paperwork relating to the Poetic Killer.

It is cold in New York; winter has finally kicked in and a storm has been forecasted to hit the area by early Sunday. Jack is not upset, as the storm will give him an excuse not to go to church. Road Runners don't have much traction in the snow, and there is no way in hell that he will put snow tires on his baby.

Allison and Maria are planning to enjoy the weekend with their families. Allison is planning some quiet time at home, and Maria intends to be her visiting brother's tour guide, come rain, sleet, snow, or whatever.

Each member of the team knows that Monday is the start of the festival of Saturnalia, and that means that everyone will be busy. Jack will be back in the office, and Assante will be hooking--well, posing as a hooker, anyway. Warehouses will be searched, and Cronos....

It is 10 p.m. on Sunday night. The winter storm started about six hours ago as a mixture of sleet and freezing rain. The main storm cell came up from the D.C. area, but it combined with a low off the coast of Cape Hatteras. This deadly combination is expected to produce a snowfall over New York in excess of ten inches.

The storm does not deter Cronos. Before he leaves the warehouse in search of the first sacrifice of Saturn's festival, he makes a phone call.

"This is Sloan."

"Hello, Peter. This is your favorite poet. Meet me tonight at St. Mark's Place. It will change your life." Cronos hangs up quickly so the call can't be traced.

When the call ends, Peter considers calling Jack Stenhouse about the meeting place, but instead decides to face the killer on his own, hoping to get the scoop on a great first-person story.

With the news that the Poetic Killer is loose in New York and preying on hookers in a white van, Cronos is having a hard time getting a "Party Girl" to join him. It has just started to snow, but it will probably come down heavier as the night goes on.

Cronos parks his van in an alley on Second Avenue and walks around the corner to St. Mark's Place. He is heading toward the last remaining automat in the city because he knows that the working girls like to hang out at the fast food restaurant on cold nights.

Pleased to see that his vigilance may be rewarded this night after all, he eagerly approaches the two pros who are standing in front of the restaurant. One of them can't be older than eighteen, and the other is probably in her thirties, but both look twenty years older than they actually are.

"You gals looking to party and get out of the cold?"

Each of them takes a moment to size him up. A composite sketch of the Poetic Killer was released by the police, but his identification will not happen tonight. Cronos is wearing a large overcoat with a ski mask and ski goggles. The older hooker is wary.

"Why the hell are you out tonight?"

"I could ask the same of you. Obviously, you need money. I got money, and I'm also very horny."

Cronos puts his arm around the younger one. "I got money for the both of ya, but I'll give it all to you, honey. Let's go."

The young girl shrugs her shoulders and walks away with Cronos while the older hooker turns around and enters the automat.

"My car is parked around the corner in an alley. We can party there."

As they approach the alley, the temperature drops and it begins to snow a little harder. Suddenly, the hooker spies Cronos' van, and stops short.

"Wait, you got a van? You're not that killer, are ya?"

"Would a killer be out on a night like this?"

As Cronos slides opens the side door of the vehicle, he reaches into his pocket and grabs a taser. When the young girl climbs in, he zaps her on the back of the neck, causing her to convulse and drop to the floor, unconscious. Cronos quickly pushes her into the van, climbs in after her, and closes the door. With duct tape in hand, he covers her mouth and binds her hands and feet. After making sure the hooker is secured, he jumps out the back door, locks it, and enters the driver's door. Turning the ignition key, he starts up the van, but keeps it parked in the alley while he waits for Peter.

Cronos has done a lot of work on the van. He has sealed off the rear compartment from the driver's area with a sheet of Plexiglas and has rigged an old hot-rodder's exhaust cutoff valve into a system for venting the vehicle's exhaust gases into the rear compartment.

The killer waits patiently, expecting Sloan any minute now.

When Peter exits his cab on Second Avenue, he doesn't see anyone around, so he starts walking toward the automat. When Cronos sees him from the alley, he rushes out and hails his target.

"Mr. Sloan, Mr. Sloan! Come with me! I have something to share with you."

At the sound of his name, Peter turns and walks toward Cronos. When they meet, Cronos takes firm hold of Peter's hand and guides him into the alley. When they reach the van, Cronos stops and takes a bow. Peter freezes in his tracks at this odd behavior and does not know what to do.

"Come on, Mr. Sloan, this will be your finest hour. Just slide the door open."

Hesitant at first, Sloan makes a decision. He reaches over to grab the handle and slide the door open, but before he can react to the body that is bound and lying on the floor in front of him, he is tasered from behind and pushed into the back of the van.

Cronos quickly slides the door closed, walks around to the driver's side, climbs in, and heads to the warehouse, laughing hysterically. His latest victims will be dead within the hour.

CHAPTER TWENTY-SIX

On Monday morning, Jack wakes up early and walks over to the window, only to stare out at a sea of white. The storm, which didn't arrive until late Sunday afternoon, started out as rain, then turned into freezing rain, and then snow, preventing Jack and Didi from attending church.

"Son of a...it's still f 'n snowin'!"

Placing a call to the First, he gets Conrad on the phone.

"Hey, Boss, this is Stenhouse. I'm going to be late; I'm snowed in."

"Not a problem. Just make your way over to Houston; I'll have a uniformed unit pick you up there in an hour."

"Okay, thanks." Jack curses under his breath and slams the phone down.

As he walks toward the bathroom to do his three S's, he stops to give Didi a shake.

"No work today, Babe. You're snowed in."

Didi jumps out of bed, and runs toward the window.

"Holy shit! I better give Sonya a call and tell her to stay home today."

Before she can make it over to the phone, it starts ringing.

"Hello? Oh, hi, Sonya, I was just about to call you. No, don't worry, we're closed today. See you tomorrow... maybe. Keep warm!"

Still in her teddy, Didi runs to the closet to put on a robe, then sprints to the thermostat in the front hallway to turn up the heat. As a former Floridian, she is not used to the cold.

While she makes coffee, Jack is in the bedroom, trying to dress warmly enough to hoof it a couple of blocks to catch his ride to work. From the rear of his closet, he retrieves a pair of ostrich-skin Tony Lamas that he purchased in Florida at Griff's.

Grateful that he has a pair of boots to use in the snow, he pulls them on and carefully tucks in his Kel Tec, then heads to the kitchen for a cup of hot coffee.

He is looking forward to getting his Glock back, but he is happy that he still has his 9mm.

Seven hours earlier, Cronos returned to the warehouse, careful not to awaken Andrea from her deep sleep. He crept up to his office in ninja-like silence, and upon entering his inner sanctum, gently closed the door behind him and turned on the light. As he stood before his wall of photos, he smiled as he admired all the women he has protected Rhea from.

After tearing himself away from his prize wall, he searched through his desk, looking for his Polaroid camera. He still uses an old instant camera because he needs to be very careful when he takes his trophy shots. He can't send film out for processing, and he doesn't have a digital camera or a cell phone with a camera. He knows that film for the antique is nearly impossible to find, but he only has one more photo to display on the wall.

Finally locating the camera, Cronos quickly returned to the van to immortalize his last victim on his wall of triumph. He had to take the photo in a hurry because the snow was starting to accumulate on the ground and he still had to type out a message for everyone to see.

When he rushed back into his office, he pinned the newest photo to his trophy wall and then sat down at his desk to type out his last note. After inserting paper into an old IBM Selectric, the ball pecked out his message: *Winter's gray will take its toll on the unsuspecting few, as sunlight ebbs from lifeless limbs.*

In a rush, Cronos pulled the paper out of the typewriting relic and headed back out to the van to pin the message on his victim. With that accomplished, he dragged Sloan out of the van and stuffed him into the large freezer unit in the back of the warehouse, where another frozen body lay waiting. Then he climbed back into the van to pose his last victim before the snow made it impossible to drive.

His destination is a park bench overlooking the Hudson River in Lower Manhattan. He has scoped out this bench as the one he wants to use since it is not in the line of sight of any of the park's security cameras.

Now bundled in his pea coat and boots, Jack gives Didi a kiss and heads out into the "frozen tundra." Jack has a two-and-a-half block walk to meet the police cruiser. As he exits his building and turns north, he walks right into a thirty mph headwind with blowing snow, an almost white-out condition. Jack squints and tucks his hands in his pockets as he trudges through eight inches of snow, but his Tony Lamas are keeping his feet warm and dry. With his trek half completed, he begins to walk a little faster when he sees flashing blue lights through the swirling clouds of snow.

As a Florida boy, this is no fun for him at all. Through chattering teeth, he mumbles, "Damn, if it gets any colder, I'm gonna have to yell, 'Snake!' so I can take a piss."

When he reaches the cruiser, he literally jumps into it, causing the officer behind the wheel to laugh hysterically.

As Jack settles himself into the back seat, the officer turns to him with a smirk. "Welcome to New York, Sunny Boy!"

Flashing half a peace sign, he retorts, "Just drive, okay? And put the f'kng heat on!"

With a warm robe wrapped around her, Didi is sipping coffee while watching the morning news about the storm. Fascinated by the coverage, she almost doesn't hear the phone when it starts ringing.

"Hello, this is Didi!"

"Good morning, Ms. Lee, this is Father Lucarelli. I didn't wake you, did I?"

"Oh, no, Father. To what do I owe this call?"

"Well, I thought you might like to help out my youth group. I know that you have a business that's located within my parish, and I hope you would allow my boys to shovel the sidewalk for you. They need the work, and we need the money. It's a small donation of $15.00. Will you help?"

"Father, you price yourself too low. It will be my pleasure to help your group. Stop by the boutique tomorrow and I'll give you the cash."

"Bless you, Ms. Lee, and say hello to Jack for me. I hope to see you in church this Sunday."

"Thank you, Father. I hope to see you, too."

CHAPTER TWENTY-SEVEN

While Jack is on his way to work at the First Precinct, Cronos is standing in the blowing snow next to the seawall behind the warehouse.

As he stares down at the East River and watches the ice floes heading out to the Atlantic, he cries out, "This is perfect! I still have one more trophy from last time."

Turning around, he runs inside to get the young girl that he has been keeping in the freezer. After dragging her out into the blizzard, he dumps her over the wall and into the frigid water. He is hoping that his human popsicle will blend in with the ice and flow out to sea.

When he can no longer see the body, he goes back inside and begins to prepare breakfast for himself and Andrea. He doesn't realize that, although Peter Sloan is bound and gagged and still unconscious, he is still clinging to life inside the freezer.

Happy to finally be inside the warmth of the building, Jack takes off his pea coat and throws it over the back of his chair, then walks into his boss's office.

As he enters, Lieutenant Conrad and Detective Giancarlo look up and ask simultaneously, "Is this your first blizzard, Jack?"

"Yeah, and it's colder than a well digger's.......knee. I guess it's going to be quiet around here today."

"Yeah, Luis and Assante will be delayed until tomorrow and half the shift didn't show up today," Conrad tells him, "but put on your mukluks, there's another victim. A young woman was found on a bench overlooking the Hudson. She was covered in snow, so she must have been there all night. And your buddy left another note. I borrowed one of those armored 4bi's that SWAT purchased from Homeland Security, so you can use that to get down there. She's on the Esplanade, off First Place." He smirks at the two detectives. "Have fun playing in the snow, kids."

Reaching into his desk, he adds, "Jack, this is yours," as he hands Jack his Glock.

Cronos cannot seem to make breakfast successfully this morning. With his mind wandering back to his trophy room, he ruins the eggs that he is cooking on the portable electric burners in his makeshift kitchen while the toast burns in the toaster.

In anger, he throws the burned eggs, pan and all, up against the wall, not caring if his lovely Rhea awakens.

Saturnalia is now upon him, and he must protect his love and find more victims. Storming into his trophy room, he complains, "This damn weather! No one will be out, and if they aren't out, I can't get there! DAMN IT ALL TO HELL!"

In a place far away, Andrea hears his cries, and tries to escape from her deep sleep. She knows something is wrong, but she feels as if she is trapped and locked away in a tall tower.

Desperately, she calls out for Cronos.

At the Esplanade, Jack and Allison exit the armored Mine-Resistant Ambush Protected vehicle known as the MRAP. The snowfall is beginning to taper off, but ten inches have accumulated so far, and there are drifts as high as two feet.

A snowplow is parked on First Place, along with a police cruiser. Jack and Detective Giancarlo trudge through the snow to meet the men who are standing near the vehicles.

"Mornin'. I'm Detective Stenhouse, and this is Detective Giancarlo. Who found the body?"

The uniformed officer responds. "Kevin Simmons, here, found it. He's a sanitation driver and was plowing the street when he thought he saw a person sitting on the bench. He stopped to check it out; those are his footprints in the snow over there. He confirmed what he thought he saw, then called 911 with his cell phone. When I arrived, he was still near the bench. I noticed that there was a piece of paper attached to the front of the body, so I assumed it was another victim, and I called the First."

Because of the cold weather, Detective Giancarlo is already wearing gloves, so she carefully brushes the snow off the note paper and confirms what everyone is thinking.

"Yeah, it's another line from that poem. We're going to need the crime scene techs and the M.E. With this weather, it's gonna be awhile before they get here, though."

"You know, Allison, I don't get it. My street ain't plowed, but they squeezed a plow down here to the Battery to clean this park! That's just nuts," declares Jack.

While the detectives try to round up some officers to come down to the crime scene, an NYPD marine patrol boat spots a body floating down the East River near Brooklyn Bridge Park.

CHAPTER TWENTY-EIGHT

It has finally stopped snowing, and Cronos has calmed down.

Fully awake now, Andrea has convinced Cronos to get some sleep, so when he accompanies Andrea to her bedroom, she lies down with him and they both fall asleep, together in their alternate realities, and oblivious to the world around them.

Jack and Detective Giancarlo are sitting in the MRAP to escape from the cold. Although it has stopped snowing, a steady, blowing wind makes the wind chill factor below zero. They are hoping that the M.E. and the CSI team will release the body soon.

"Allison, how the hell do you get used to this cold? I am f'n freezing!"

"Hey, I've lived here all my life, but you don't get used to it, IT'S *COLD*!" Smiling, she adds, "We tolerate it, or we move to Florida."

Just then, a call comes in over the radio, and Jack answers it.

"This is Stenhouse."

"Jack, this is Assante. Marine patrol found the frozen body of a young woman in the East River. I mean, frozen solid. She's probably another victim. They're bringing her in at Wall Street Pier 11. I'm heading there now."

"Okay, I'll tell Allison. One of us will meet you there."

He ends the call and turns to his partner. "Allison, that was Assante. We got another victim. The aqua cops found her floating down the East River. As soon as the M.E. is done here, I'll follow the body back to the morgue, so you can hitch a ride with the M.E to meet Assante. She'll be at Wall Street Pier 11. We can all meet later at the morgue."

The detectives exit the vehicle to give the Medical Examiner the news that his day's work is just beginning.

While Allison arranges her ride with the M.E., Jack walks back to the MRAP. He fires up the beast and waits, ready to follow the body back to the morgue.

When she arrives at Wall Street Pier 11, Allison looks around for Agent Assante, and finds her standing on the pier. Together with the M.E., they wait for the marine patrol officers to lift the body out of the boat.

At the same time, on the other side of town, Jack watches as the other body is lifted onto a table in the morgue.

The storm has left the city covered in white. Like a vision out of a fairy tale, it is beautiful and silent.

With the sun dancing off frozen crystals in a prism of colors, two sides of the city are exposed. One side is beauty, and the other side is death.

Andrea is asleep again, and Cronos is outside the warehouse, trolling for victims.

CHAPTER TWENTY-NINE

An officer from Forensics hands Jack a folder on the young lady lying on the autopsy table.

"We ID'd her, Jack. She's a runaway from New Jersey with a record for soliciting. We contacted her mother, but she doesn't want to be bothered."

"Sheesh. Nice mom."

"Yeah, well, what a waste."

The officer leaves Jack with the life history of his newest Jane Doe. As he reads the file, he finds out that the young girl's name is April Lansing, and that she was nineteen years old. She ran away from her home in Ridgewood, New Jersey three years ago, and has been in Manhattan ever since, hooking to support her heroin addiction.

Turning to the doctor prepping the body, he says, "You can go ahead. She has no family...well, no family that gives a shit. Her name is April, and she was only nineteen."

"Nineteen? She looks about thirty. From the marks on her arms, she was deep in addiction."

"Yeah, she's been busted before. Says here she worked the St. Mark's Place area. Isn't the automat still there?"

"Yeah, working girls like to hang out there. It's a cheap meal and a safe haven for them. Look, Detective, if I find anything unusual, I'll let you know. Right now, it looks like she died just like the others."

"Okay, here's my number. Call me with any news at all. I'm heading over to the automat."

Maria and Allison stand over the M.E. as he inspects the floater.

"It looks like this one has been frozen for quite a while; her eyes are pretty well clouded over. Looks like it could be the same M.O. as the previous victims; frozen for at least a year or so. She looks to be in her early twenties, but we won't get much more info than that until we thaw out the body. We'll transport her to the morgue now, and prep her for autopsy in about twenty-four to thirty-six hours."

Detective Giancarlo thumbs Jack's number into her cell phone.

"Stenhouse, this is Giancarlo. Assante and I are heading over to the morgue; looks like we got another victim. Our floater needs to thaw out before we can get any more info."

"Good. You can watch the autopsy on the snow queen. I got a lead I'm checking out at the automat at St. Mark's. I'll see you two later."

Ending the call, he climbs into the MRAP and heads over to the St. Mark's area with a uniformed officer riding shotgun.

Now that the snow has finally stopped falling, the sun has come out and is illuminating the canvas of white that is covering the city. Surprisingly, the temperature is expected to reach into the low forties during the day today, and by tomorrow, the low fifties.

Unless New York gets more snow, the potentially white Christmas will instead become a grey, slushy mess.

Jack heads northeast on roads that are pretty much deserted for a Monday morning, even though most of the major arteries have been cleared of snow. Some of the secondary streets are still unplowed, but they will be cleared by day's end.

Driving down West Street, he turns east on Houston, then crosses Manhattan to Second Avenue, where he turns north to St. Mark's Place. One problem, though. St. Mark's Place has not been plowed.

When Andrea awakens from her second nap, Cronos is nowhere to be found. While looking for him, she pokes her head into every room in the warehouse, except the room that is locked – Cronos' office hideaway.

Realizing that she is alone, she decides to go home, but takes her time getting dressed. When she is ready, she leaves the warehouse and begins walking down the middle of Montgomery Street, because the sidewalks have not yet been shoveled. When she reaches Madison Street, she is able to hail a lone cab to take her to the Upper East Side, where she lives.

Her mind is now completely focused on a hot shower and a change of clothes.

Unconcerned about the snow piled up in the street, Jack turns the armored vehicle down St. Mark's Place. The unplowed street is no match for this leviathan.

Because the automat is open twenty-four hours, the sidewalk in front of the restaurant is shoveled and clear. When he pulls up to what he thinks is the curb, he notices a couple of people inside the restaurant and mumbles to the uniformed cop in the passenger seat. "Working girls. Probably stayed there all night."

CHAPTER THIRTY

After a forty-minute cab ride through deserted city streets, Andrea arrives back at her apartment building. She pays the cabbie, then stops to pick up her mail in the lobby before taking the elevator up to her apartment.

After entering her unit, she locks the door behind her and immediately prepares to take a well-deserved shower. While the steam from the hot water fills the bathroom, she disrobes, then steps inside the shower stall to allow the hot water to engulf her body while her mind drifts to Cronos and Mount Olympus.

As a busboy cleans off tables in the automat, Jack flashes his badge and introduces himself.

"Mornin'. I'm Detective Stenhouse. Is the manager in?"

"I'm the manager, and the only one here right now. Damn weather's going to make me close soon. What do you need?"

Displaying a photo of the latest victim, Jack asks, "Have you seen her here before?"

Before responding, the manager takes a long look.

"Yeah, I think she was here last night. I've been here all night long, and I think I saw her last night with those 'ladies' who are sitting at that table over there." He nods at two working girls who are drinking coffee in a corner booth.

With a quick "thank you" to the manager, Jack turns his attention toward the women, who notice his interest and quickly head for the door.

Calling out to them, he flashes his badge and announces, "Hold on, ladies! I'm Detective Stenhouse, and we need to talk!"

Unhappy that they've been stopped by a cop, the older of the two addresses him indignantly.

"Hey, Officer! We're just having coffee. Is that illegal now?"

As Jack becomes aware that both women aren't half bad looking, especially the older one, his mind goes to a place he doesn't want to visit. With effort, he shakes off his feelings and continues.

"Look, girls, no hassle, we just need to talk." Displaying the latest victim's photo, he asks, "Do either of you know April here?"

The older one responds, "Yeah, I was with her last night."

"Really? She was found dead this morning. Is there anything you'd like to tell me about that?"

"Oh, crap! It must have been that creepy guy!" With a glance at her companion, she resumes, "Look, this is off the record, all right? No hassle?"

"I'm not with Vice, so no sweat."

"Okay. This creepy guy stopped us last night while it was snowing and wanted to party. We were just about to head inside the automat when he walked up from Second wearing a full face ski mask and goggles. He creeped me out, but not April. She left with him."

"He was on foot? You didn't see a car or a van?"

"No, I backed off and asked him why he was out in this weather. He said he was horny and put his arms around April. They walked toward Second and turned the corner."

"Can you describe him?"

"Nothing unusual. He was about my height, I guess. Maybe five-five, five-six. I couldn't see his face, but he did have small feet. I always look at the feet."

"Okay. Is there anything you can tell me about April?"

"No, not much. She's been around here about six months and worked alone to support her drugs."

Taking out his billfold, Jack hands the hooker ten dollars.

"Here, take this. Thanks for your time; go get something to eat."

The woman takes the money and puts her arm around Jack, propositioning him suggestively.

"Hey, handsome, for ten bucks, I could treat you right!"

Pausing to redirect his thoughts, Jack makes a determined effort to shake off his feelings once more.

"Sorry, girls. Gotta check out Second Street to see if I can find out where that guy parked his van. Don't go anywhere, though. This nice officer here will take your statements, and we'll probably need you to talk to a sketch artist so we can get a composite of that creep."

Heading out of the automat, Jack hears groans from the hookers.

With the sun shining brightly off the snow, Jack takes out a pair of sunglasses to protect his eyes from the glare and walks down the street. As he rounds the corner, he notices an alley about fifty feet away, which hasn't been plowed. Entering the alley carefully, he scans the area and immediately notices ghost prints of tire tracks in the scant amount of snow that fell there, along with an oil stain where the snow did not stick to the ground.

Retracing his own footsteps out of the alley, he runs back to the MRAP and drives it over to block the alleyway's entrance, while calling the precinct to request assistance from the crime scene unit.

CHAPTER THIRTY-ONE

When Andrea steps out of her shower, she notices a note written in condensation on the mirror. She had not heard anyone enter the bathroom, but is not alarmed. She reads, "RHEA, I AM WAITING FOR YOU IN THE LIVING ROOM. I HOPE YOU DIDN'T FORGET OUR DATE. —CRONOS."

Smiling, she towels herself off, and prepares for a day out.

Assante and Giancarlo are watching the autopsy of April Lansing, while the body of the frozen floater who is yet to be identified is lying on a special table designed to thaw human flesh.

The women have been patiently waiting for the M.E. to comment on his findings, but as he continues to remain silent, Maria finally asks, "Find anything interesting, Doc?"

"No, same as the other ones. There's a small burn mark on the back of the neck, though, probably from a taser, and the condition of the arms says April was a drug addict. See the blue color of the lips and fingernails? I suspect oxygen deprivation. When I get the blood work back, I bet it'll show that carbon monoxide poisoning was the actual cause of death. No new clues; same as the other victims."

"Great. Two more victims and no leads," grumbles Giancarlo. "The mayor is gonna be pissed."

A police sketch artist has arrived at the alley with the boys from CSI. Wasting no time, Jack drives him over to the automat and introduces him to the hookers, instructing them to try to remember every detail of the suspect so the officer can create a realistic composite sketch.

Leaving the artist with the women, he motions to the uniformed officer to join him, and drives to the morgue to meet with Assante and Giancarlo.

Even though it is turning into a fine December day, with bright sun and royal-blue skies overhead, the task force has lost one day of investigation due to the previous day's weather. At the command center, Detective Luis is reviewing a list of ten warehouses, trying to narrow them down to the ones located on or near the East River. When he finishes his eliminations, only two of them still fit the criteria, and the owner of one of the properties seems familiar. He enters that address into the city's property appraisal database and... BINGO! He gets a hit and gives Jack a call.

Andrea and Cronos have left on their date. She has no idea where they are going, except that their day out will start with a late lunch at a local restaurant. They hail a taxi in front of her building and direct the cabbie to head west around Central Park.

After the snowstorm, the park looks beautiful, like a scene from Currier and Ives. It's covered in white, with only a few brave souls frolicking in the snow.

Jack pulls the armored vehicle up to the city morgue and jumps down out of the driver's seat, as his fellow officer does the same on the passenger side. Turning to his companion, he says, "I'll drop you back off at the First after I make a quick stop inside."

While he heads to the morgue to talk to Assante and Giancarlo, his passenger goes to see a man about a horse.

Before Jack enters the morgue, his cellphone rings.

CHAPTER THIRTY-TWO

"Stenhouse here."

"Jack, this is Luis. I've been narrowing down the warehouses our killer might use, and..."

"Spill it, Luis."

"Well, there's a vacant warehouse right on the river that used to be a meat distribution center. It's been closed for three years, but the original owner was our late Governor Edwards, who was a major real estate developer. After his divorce, this property was put into a trust, and when he offed himself, it went to his ex-wife."

"Doesn't she work for the mayor?"

"Yeah. I called the business next door to this warehouse, Simcona Imports. The manager there said a caretaker lives at this supposedly closed business, and get this – he drives a white van!"

"Holy shit! Are you at the First?"

"Yeah."

"Get a hold of Rawlings; I'll be there in fifteen minutes. We gotta go see the mayor and talk to his press secretary."

Hanging up the call, Jack rushes into the lab and runs straight into Assante and Giancarlo.

"Hey, I'm glad I found you two! Detective Luis got a lead on a warehouse, so I'm headin' over to the First. Stay here with the doc, and I'll catch you up with the details later."

Turning quickly, he runs back to his vehicle, where he finds the uniformed officer waiting for him.

At the First Precinct, Detective Luis has just entered D.I. Rawlings' office.

"Sir, we got a break on our killer, but you're not going to like this. Our lead goes straight to the mayor's office."

"WHAT?"

"Yeah, I think the warehouse used by our boy is owned by Andrea Singletary, Mayor Edwards' press secretary, and a guy at the business next door spotted a white van at that building. We need to speak with Ms. Singletary, so when Jack returns, we're going down to City Hall. You'll probably need to call the mayor to let him know we're coming down there, since he's been all over you like white on rice about catching this guy."

"Okay, I'll call him right now, and I'll get Lieutenant Conrad to join you."

Rawlings picks up the phone as Detective Luis leaves the office to locate Conrad.

"Mr. Mayor, this is Rawlings. Are you sitting down?"

Andrea is sitting at the bar in The Oak Room at The Plaza Hotel, enjoying her martini. Cronos doesn't drink, but he stands vigilant while she slowly sips the intoxicating concoction.

When their table is ready, Cronos walks behind her and scans the restaurant for threats, real or imagined. He acts more like a bodyguard protecting his client than a date.

CHAPTER THIRTY-THREE

When Jack pulls up to City Hall, he jumps out of the armored vehicle that he's been driving all day, along with Luis and Conrad, his two companions for this meeting. Ignoring the protests of the mayor's receptionist, they walk directly into Mayor Edwards' office.

"Mr. Mayor, we're here from the First Precinct. Did Detective Inspector Rawlings let you know we were on our way?"

"Yes, you must be Stenhouse. He did call, but the person you're looking for is not here."

"Ms. Singletary isn't here?"

"No, she's currently on vacation, and I don't expect her back until after the first of the year. You can have access to her office, though, and here is her address if you need to visit her condo. I'll have my receptionist show you to Andrea's office, but you're wasting your time. Andrea has nothing to do with all of this."

Lieutenant Conrad remains with the mayor while the detectives follow the receptionist to Andrea's office.

Taking a quick look around the room, they notice no outward signs of anything amiss. There is a desk, two chairs, some artificial plants, and some artwork hung on the wall. Luis begins opening drawers while Jack walks over to the painting on the wall.

"Hey, Luis. What the hell kind of a painting is this?" he calls over his shoulder, as he examines the artwork.

Luis looks up and peers at the painting. "I don't know. It's kinda creepy, though. Looks like some guy eating somebody."

At that moment, the mayor joins them in the office, accompanied by Lieutenant Conrad.

"Detectives, that's a copy of a famous painting by Francisco de Goya, called *Cronos Devouring His Children."*

Staring at the mayor, Jack suddenly makes a connection in his mind and exclaims, "SHIT! We *gotta* speak to Andrea! Luis, you're with me. We're headed over to the East Side."

Running out of Andrea's office, the two detectives leave Mayor Edwards with a puzzled Lieutenant Conrad.

Andrea Singletary lives in the Olympic Towers on Fifth Avenue, in an area called the Museum Mile. The multimillion dollar condo, part of her divorce settlement, comes with a view of Central Park, concierge service, and a doorman, all because her late husband couldn't keep his zipper closed.

As Jack drives the MRAP past Central Park, he longs to get back behind the wheel of his beloved Road Runner. Driving this behemoth through the streets of New York is like driving a '57 Caddy through the narrow, cobblestoned streets of Italy.

When they arrive at "the Towers", piles of snow in the street restrict parking, so Jack pulls up onto the sidewalk as the agitated doorman approaches.

"You can't park that thing here!" he screams.

Jumping out, Stenhouse and Luis flash their badges.

"We'll park it anywhere we want, *sir*!"

Andrea's apartment is on the tenth floor, so they dash across the lobby to the elevator, which opens to reveal a white-gloved elevator operator.

"Which floor, Gentlemen?"

"Ten, please."

In response to this encounter with old-fashioned convenience, Luis glances at Jack and rolls his eyes while Jack just shakes his head.

Within a few seconds, the elevator door opens and the pair exits onto the tenth floor. After getting their bearings, they walk down the hall to apartment 1021, where Luis knocks on the door, but receives no answer.

"Damn!" growls Jack. "If she didn't work for the mayor, I'd break it down!"

"Yeah, I know," responds Luis. "We need to get a warrant or wait till she returns. We can get Conrad to post a couple of uniformed guys here to see if she shows up."

"Good idea, and get a warrant, too. Let's talk to the doorman on our way out. Maybe he saw her leave."

Approaching the doorman, the detectives flash their ID's once again.

"Hi, there. I'm Detective Stenhouse, and this is Detective Luis. We were wondering if you saw Ms. Singletary leave this afternoon."

"Yes, I did. I got her a cab, which wasn't easy considering the difficult driving conditions out there."

"Did she mention where she was going?"

"Said she had a dinner engagement. You can check with Mr. Servilius, our concierge. I believe I saw Ms. Singletary talking with him before she left."

Jack remains with the doorman while Detective Luis leaves to question the concierge, who is sitting at his desk in the marble-floored lobby. As he approaches the large, mahogany temple the apartment operators call a desk, Luis mumbles to himself, "There's more marble in this place than in St. Peter's."

Flashing his badge, Detective Luis introduces himself to Mr. Servilius, who seems bothered by the interruption.

"Hello, there. Can you tell me if you happened to make any reservations for Ms. Singletary today?"

Stroking a pencil-thin mustache, the concierge responds, "Well, Detective, or whoever you are, I'm not willing to share Ms. Singletary's information with you."

Lifting his eyebrows in irritation, Detective Luis bends over the ornate desk to bring his face within millimeters of the concierge's moustache, then gently whispers, "Listen, you little shit. We're investigating a series of murders here. If you're hiding anything from me, I'll rip that little moustache off your face and shove it up your ass. Now, where did Ms. Singletary go today?"

Breaking out in a sweat, Servilius answers haltingly, "I... made a reservation for her... at The Oak Room... at The Plaza Hotel."

"Very good. Now, was that so difficult?" With a slight tap on the side of the concierge's face, Luis turns from the desk and calls out to Jack.

"She's at The Plaza!"

Rushing back to the MRAP, the detectives head south on streets that are finally beginning to get back to normal after the storm.

However, while the light is currently bouncing off the snow like sparkling diamonds, the temperature is forecast to remain above freezing this evening, which will cause the snow to turn into a brown, slushy mess. In fact, a warm spell is predicted for the next few days, which will bring the afternoon temps into the upper fifties.

When the MRAP pulls up in front of The Plaza Hotel, Jack calls Giancarlo before they exit the vehicle.

"Allison, any news on our floater?"

"No, Jack. The M.E. won't autopsy the body until the morning. Assante and I are calling it a night. We're heading back to the First."

"Okay. Luis and I are following up on a lead. I'll update you in the morning."

Ending the call, they enter the hotel and make their way to The Oak Room, where they are stopped by the maître d'.

"May I help you, Gentlemen?"

Jack shows his ID. "Did Andrea Singletary make a reservation this evening? We need to speak with her."

"Why, yes, Detective, she is at the table in the far corner." Turning, he points the way for the detectives.

As unobtrusively as possible, Jack and Luis make their way over to the table and introduce themselves quietly.

"Ms. Singletary, I am Detective Stenhouse, and this is Detective Luis. We need to speak with you, please."

"Why, hello, Detective. The mayor told me you are working on that serial killer thing. Why do you need to speak to me?"

"May we join you for a while, Ms. Singletary?"

"Yes, please, make yourselves comfortable."

The detectives pull out two chairs and sit at the table.

"Thank you, ma'am. While we were looking for locations where the killer may be based, your warehouse building came up as a prime location. We spoke with the importer whose business is located next door to yours, and he told us that he has seen a man at your building who drives a van that matches the description of the one we believe the killer drives. Can you elaborate on this?"

"Yes, I received some properties in the divorce settlement from my late husband."

"You mean the former Governor?"

"Yes, he owned some rental properties, and one of them was the old Remus meat distribution center on the East River. A caretaker watches the building for me, and yes, he drives a white van."

"May we have his name, please, and his address?"

Suddenly agitated, Andrea responds, "I, ah, do not know, umm, where he lives."

"Ms. Singletary, are you feeling all right?"

"Oh, it's just one of my headaches. Ah, I'm okay. His, his name is Theopolis, umm, Cronos Theopolis. He's a Greek immigrant."

Andrea lowers her head into her hands and closes her eyes to try to stop the building migraine.

"I, ah, let him stay at the warehouse from time to time. It's, ah, cheaper than a security guard."

As she continues to hold her head in her hands, Jack and Luis exchange glances, unsure of what to do, until she suddenly raises her head and looks straight into Jack's eyes. Speaking in the first person, she says, "You know, Detective, Andrea is quite upset. I, that is to say, Andrea, needs to leave now. Perhaps we can talk tomorrow."

Rising from her chair, Andrea walks away from the table and leaves the two detectives sitting there alone.

Jack stares at Luis. "What the fuck just happened here?"

"Man, that is one flipped-out broad! We need to get a warrant on her apartment and the warehouse ASAP. And did you catch that name? She said it's CRONOS!"

"Yeah! Gonna be a busy day tomorrow, Luis. Let's get the hell out of here."

In the restaurant lobby, Andrea hooks up with Cronos, then jumps in a cab before Jack and Luis can catch up to her.

Back at the station, Lieutenant Conrad is processing a search warrant for Andrea's apartment and the warehouse, but cannot find a judge on duty to sign the one for the apartment. Placing the paperwork in a file on his desk, he goes home for the evening and leaves the request unanswered until the morning. Meanwhile, Jack turns in the MRAP and asks Detective Luis to drive him home.

At almost seven o'clock, Jack finally walks into his apartment, where he is greeted by Didi with a kiss and a bourbon-and-Coke. While he goes to see a man about a horse, Didi warms up some leftover meatloaf and notices the large case file that Jack has left on the kitchen table. Picking it up, Didi moves it to the coffee table in the living room.

"No police business tonight," she whispers. "Just a little fun time."

Cronos is on his own again, as Andrea's migraine has isolated her from the world. Directing the cab to the warehouse, he places Andrea into bed, then changes into his hunting clothes and takes the van out to find his next victim.

It is a fairly warm night for December. The temperature is in the upper forties and the newly-fallen snow is melting, forming pools of brown, slushy messes.

Cronos soon finds himself trolling on Beaver Street, and it doesn't take long for another hooker to meet her fate in the back of his van.

With his latest prize secured, he slowly drives back to the warehouse.

CHAPTER THIRTY-FOUR

At six o'clock in the morning when Jack's alarm goes off, it shocks him awake like a slap to the side of the head. Struggling to shut the screaming banshee off, he grabs it and throws it up against the wall. Jack is not a morning type of guy.

"Dammit, Jack! That's the third clock you've destroyed!"

"Sorry, Babe. We need to get one that starts off low and gradually increases in intensity." He leers at her. "You know, like me in bed."

"Dream on, Jack. You're a legend in your own mind."

When Didi rushes into the bathroom before him, Jack heads to the kitchen to put on a pot of coffee. He'll drive Didi to the boutique on his way to work.

The city is back to normal this morning. With temperatures well above freezing, the snow is continuing to melt away.

Detective Giancarlo, the first one in at work, stops at Lieutenant Conrad's office to check on the status of the warrants. As she is about to knock on the office door, the lieutenant walks up with his keys in his hand.

"Morning, Lieutenant. Any news on the warrants?"

"Yeah, good news and bad news. I got a judge to issue a warrant for the search of the warehouse, but not for Ms. Singletary's apartment. We won't get that one unless the warehouse proves to be the one we're looking for. As soon as Stenhouse and Luis get in, I want all of you to head down to that building. I called the FBI, and Assante will meet you there with a forensics team."

"Good, I'll be at my desk. Thanks."

When Jack drops Didi off at the boutique, he notices that the sidewalk in front of the store is completely clear of snow.

"Who the hell shoveled your walk?"

"Oh, I forgot to tell you. Father Lucarelli called me about his youth group. He asked if they could clear my sidewalk, and they did a great job. He also said he expects us to be in church this Sunday."

Nodding his agreement, Jack gives Didi a kiss before she exits the Road Runner and joins Sonya, who was waiting outside the store. As he hauls ass away from the curb, he leans on the horn and gives two quick "BEEP BEEPS" in farewell.

When he arrives at the station, he immediately runs into Allison Giancarlo.

"Mornin'. Any news on the warrants?"

"Yeah, we got one for the warehouse, but the other is on hold. As soon as Luis gets here, we'll go there to meet up with the FBI."

Walking in on the conversation, Luis asks, "Who's talking about me?"

Allison quickly turns. "Don't get comfy, smooth talker. We're headin' over to the river. The FBI will meet us there, so let's go."

Giancarlo and Stenhouse pick up the search warrant from Lieutenant Conrad, then climb into the Road Runner. With Detective Luis following them in his car, they should arrive at the warehouse in about fifteen to twenty minutes. Depending on traffic conditions, that should put them there about 8:30 in the morning.

New York City is alive and kicking this morning, and it looks like everyone is up and about, except for Andrea Singletary and Peter Sloan. Andrea is still fast asleep, almost as if she is in a coma, and Peter Sloan is barely clinging to life as he struggles to stay awake, even though he is cold.

Oh, so cold...

CHAPTER THIRTY-FIVE

The '68 Road Runner roars into the parking lot of the old Remus Meat Distribution warehouse with Detective Luis close behind. Waiting near one of the large shipping bay doors is the large black van from the FBI's CSI unit and Agent Maria Assante.

"Been waiting long?"

"No, about five minutes. You got the warrant, Jack?"

"It's in my pocket, but I don't have a key. Looks like the bay doors are locked from the inside. We'll have to breach the front door at that far corner of the building."

Walking over to the CSI van, Maria opens the back door and retrieves a large tactical entry ram to forcibly open the door, like a marauding horde storming a castle. Since Jack is the largest one there, he grabs it, swings into action, and slams it into the door. The first try rattles the frame and loosens the target, but the second shot swings it wide open.

With guns drawn, Jack, Luis, Allison and Maria slowly enter the warehouse. Inside it is cold and musty, with a faint odor of blood and meat drifting across their faces. The building is quiet, except for the sound of the compressors that keep the large refrigeration units cold, humming in the background. As they walk past an office, they enter a large open space with a flight of stairs off to the side that lead to the upper story. At the back of the building are the large refrigeration units that are cooled by the rumbling compressors, and near the first bay door are a boat on a trailer, and a white van.

"Maria, open that bay door and get your van in here. Luis, check out the offices upstairs. Allison and I will check out the van."

As everyone heads to their respective targets, Jack notices a power box on the wall and starts flipping circuit breakers to turn on some of the overhead lighting.

The building is cold and damp, and as the lights cover the area like a warm blanket, rats start running for cover.

With guns drawn, Jack and Allison approach the van slowly and peer inside. Seeing no one, they relax and open the driver's door. The keys are in the ashtray of the center console, and there is a taser on the passenger seat.

"Hey, Jack! Notice anything unusual?"

"Besides a taser? Yeah, it looks like the front seating area is sealed off from the rear of the van."

After taking a quick look around the top floor, Luis returns to the group and announces that the area is empty, then he accompanies Maria to inspect the refrigeration units.

Covering her as she cautiously opens the door and peers inside, he jumps back when she yells, "Over here! We got two bodies!"

Responding quickly, everyone runs over to where Maria is still holding open the large freezer door. Inside, are the bodies of a man and a young woman.

Releasing the door, Maria runs over to the woman, places two fingers on her neck, and exclaims, "Holy shit, she's alive! Get her out of the cold, and call for an ambulance!"

Jack and Luis grab the woman and bring her into the large warehouse area, where Luis lays down beside her to cover her with his body.

"Guys, go get something to cover us up. We need to hold my body heat in until the EMT's get here. In fact, there are some blankets on a cot I saw in the first room at the top of the stairs!"

Meanwhile, at the other body, Jack cries out in recognition, "Holy shit, it's Peter Sloan!" A low, weak moan echoes within the freezer. Jack lies down next to Sloan and tries to warm him up. "Stay with me, Peter, stay with me!"

Realizing that he's no longer alone, Peter Sloan tries to communicate, but he's barely able to breathe, let alone speak. With a raspy voice, he whispers quietly, "I know... that voice... I know... the... killer."

"Stay awake, Pete! Who's the killer?"

Valiantly trying to speak, he says, "And, and, an..."

Then Peter Sloan slips into a deep coma.

Running up the stairs, Allison grabs the blankets and sheets she finds there, and quickly dashes back down to cover Luis, the latest victim, and Peter Sloan. Jack and the others take off their coats and lay them over the blankets, as well.

In the distance, they are relieved to hear the wail of a siren growing increasingly closer.

"You know, I don't know why Sloan is here, but he was trying to identify the killer. Before he drifted off, he said he recognized his voice. He said the word 'and' over and over again, then stopped. Someone needs to accompany him to the hospital in case he comes to, and we still need to check out that van. Luis, did you see anything upstairs?"

"No, just the cot. The second room is locked; I didn't get a chance to check it out."

"Allison, come upstairs with me. Maria, get a hold of Lieutenant Conrad. Tell him that Andrea Singletary needs to be hauled in for questioning, and that we need to get the warrant for her apartment. The FBI techs can handle the van."

Even though the city is equipped to handle difficult weather conditions, unavoidable transportation problems are contributing to a slow morning at the boutique, so Didi and Sonya are dusting and cleaning in an effort to keep busy.

With Sonya busy at the front of the store, Didi decides to catch up on some of the filing in her office, but as soon as she sits at her desk, she notices something on the floor, poking out from under one of the filing cabinets. Picking the object up, she notices that the back of it is marked, 'Property of NYPD.'

"I guess Jack dropped this when he was here," she says to herself. Turning the item over, she notes that it's a photograph of a man with a tattoo on his neck. "Now, that's strange. Where have I seen that before?"

The door to the second office on the upper floor is locked, but Jack puts his shoulder into it and it pops open easily. Allison follows and flips on the light switch, then both of them stare at the walls with mouths agape.

"Holy shit, there's a wall full of photos in here!"

Rushing over to the far side of the room, they gaze in alarm at the numerous photographs of young women.

"I recognize some of them as the ones we already found, but there must be about twenty women pictured here!"

"Jack, where are the rest of these women?"

Looking around the room, he sees a refrigerator and a stove in the corner, and on the wall, the same painting that was hanging in Andrea Singletary's office.

Running over to the fridge, he quickly opens both doors. "Damn, it's empty. I gotta get CSI up here to check out these appliances."

"What for, Jack?"

"See that painting? That asshole *ate* the other victims!"

Leaving Allison upstairs to inspect the office, Jack runs back down to the main area, where he is immediately called over to the van by Agent Assante.

"Hey, Jack, come on over here and look at this! He put exhaust cutoffs on the van and sealed off the rear area from the driver's section. We guess he tasers the victims, then dumps them in the back, and with the exhaust fumes vented into the sealed-off section, they quickly succumb to the fumes and become unconscious."

"Hmm, you're probably right about that, and we just found out that there are more victims than the ones we know about. I need your guys to scope out the second office upstairs for anything and everything. I think this sick bastard ate some of his victims, but I haven't seen any bones anywhere. We need to check out the dump, and get a dive team to check out the bottom of the river. Did we check all the large refrigerator units down here?"

"Yeah, but all we found in them were the young woman and Sloan. The EMT's are transporting them to New York Downtown Hospital, but they don't think they'll make it. I sent one of our field agents along with them in case Sloan does wake up. But how do you know there are more victims?"

"There's a f'kng photo gallery upstairs! Some of the victims' photos are on the wall, but I'll bet most of them aren't."

Jack pulls out his cell phone to place a call to Lieutenant Conrad.

"Lieutenant, it's Stenhouse. Any word on Singletary?"

"Yeah, D.I. Rawlings and the mayor have gone to pick her up; she should be here within the hour. But there's bad news on the search warrant for her apartment. The judge won't sign it unless there's more incriminating evidence that points in her direction. She has friends in high places, you know."

"Yeah, I know. Okay, Luis and Giancarlo can stay here while they check this place out, but I'll be right there. I *have* to question this Singletary chick."

Ending the call, he calls out to the team.

"Hey, Luis! Stay here with Giancarlo. I gotta go back to the First and talk with Singletary. Maria, see if you can get that dive team down here sooner rather than later, and don't forget to call me, even if all you guys find is a fingernail!"

CHAPTER THIRTY-SIX

Jack stares through a two-way mirror, watching Andrea Singletary as she sits in the interrogation room with Mayor Johnsville. Shaking his head, he turns away in disgust.

"Why the hell is the mayor in there with her?" he asks Lieutenant Conrad.

"He says we don't have a shred of evidence of any wrongdoing on her part, so he wants to give her moral support. Jack, she's here to be questioned about her facility manager, and that's all. That's from the mayor himself."

"Okay. I got a strange feeling about this broad, but I'll play along for now."

Walking out into the hallway, he enters the room next door, Interrogation Room One.

Greeting the mayor first, he says, "Hello, Mayor Johnsville." Then, turning to Andrea, he states, "Ms. Singletary, I have some questions for you about Mr. Cronos Theopolis."

Taking a seat across the table from Andrea, Jack places the case file in front of him.

"Ms. Singletary, I just returned from your warehouse on the river, and it was a very enlightening visit. Have you been there recently?"

"No, I don't go there much. I let Mr. Theopolis manage the property. I only go there if he tells me some work needs to be done and he wants approval for it."

"Well, we found some incriminating evidence there this morning. I can't describe what it is, but we need to talk to Cronos. Do you know where he is?"

"Oh, he wasn't at the warehouse? Well, I'm sure I don't know where he is. I'm not his keeper, you know."

"Not his keeper? Where is he from, and when did you hire him? Who is this guy?"

"I volunteer at a local soup kitchen, and he was there to get a free meal. He's from Greece. We started talking, and I felt sorry for him, so I hired him to guard my property. Since he was homeless, I let him use the building as his living quarters."

"So what you are telling me, Ms. Singletary, is that you had no idea what kind of man he was but you hired him anyway, because you thought you could get some brownie points by giving a stranger a job? And are you also saying that you've never seen anything unusual at your warehouse and that you've never been in his living area? I guess everything is just peachy over there, right?"

"What are you driving at, Detective? Andrea already told you she doesn't know anything. Go find this Cronos guy yourself!"

Jack opens up the file folder and shows Andrea a photograph of Lana Jenkins, the "Venus De Milo" victim.

"It's funny that the painting in your office is titled *Cronos Devouring His Children*, and this girl here, named Lana, has no arms, just like the painting. Furthermore, our suspect signs his name 'Cronos' in the notes he's been leaving on his victims. *What are you hiding, Andrea?*"

Jack's question causes Andrea to lean on Rod Johnsville's shoulder and begin to cry, which elicits a strong reaction from the mayor.

"We're done here, Detective! Get out there and find Cronos!"

Grabbing Andrea's elbow, the mayor escorts her out of the room in a huff, leaving Jack at the table, shaking his head.

As soon as the departing couple is out of view, Lieutenant Conrad flies into the room and demands, "What the hell, Jack?"

"Lieutenant, Andrea just doesn't pass the smell test. She's involved in some way, and when I find Cronos, we'll know how."

"Yeah, well, you either find Cronos or a better connection to Andrea, because the mayor just placed her off limits to any further questioning!"

Upset and disappointed, Conrad storms out of the room, leaving Jack alone once more. He remains there alone, silently contemplating his next move, until his cell phone startles him back to reality.

"Yeah?"

"Jack, this is Maria. You need to come down here. We got something."

"Great. I need some good news right about now."

Sneaking a peek at his watch, he notes that it's now almost one o'clock in the afternoon.

"You guys eat lunch yet? No? Then I'll pick up some pizzas on the way down. See ya in a bit."

On his way out of the building, he is stopped in the front entranceway by D.I. Rawlings.

"Jack! I just heard that Peter Sloan died en route to the hospital! They tried to revive him in the emergency room, but he never came around. What the hell was *he* doing at the warehouse?"

"I don't know, Boss. Maybe the killer invited him there. But he's dead? Dammit! He was trying to tell me who the killer is! I didn't like the guy, but I didn't want to see him dead, either. I need to check his phone records to see if they can tell us anything. Listen, Inspector, we're going to need your help with the politics on this one. I know that Andrea Singletary is involved somehow, but the mayor is all over her like stink on shit."

"I got your back, Jack. Now go and wrap this thing up."

CHAPTER THIRTY-SEVEN

Agent Assante calls everyone together for a quick lunch when she sees Jack walking into the warehouse with five liters of Coke and five large pizzas.

"Before we start, Jack, I need to brief you on what we found."

"Wait, before *you* start, I need to tell you that Sloan is dead."

"Aww, crap! That's a damn shame! We have to find out how he got involved. I'll get the Bureau to look into his phone records; maybe it was Cronos who lured him into this mess."

Grabbing one of the pizza boxes, Maria continues. "So now you need to listen to what we found. Our dive team is still in the river, but they reported seeing human bones on the river floor. We plan to collect DNA samples from those bones and also from an outdoor gas grill we found at the back of the warehouse, near the wall overlooking the river. We also got fingerprints from the van, the living quarters, and the grill, and they seem to be all the same."

"So, there's only one set of fingerprints?"

"Well, so far, it looks like there's only one set. Why?"

"Not sure, but I'm workin' on that. Let's eat outside, so we won't contaminate the crime scene. Besides, it's a nice day."

Gathering together, the cops take a break in the snow-cleared parking lot while the Feds crowd around the seawall and pass pizzas over to the dive team in the patrol boat.

"How did your interview go with Singletary?" asks Detective Giancarlo.

"She didn't pass the smell test, and the mayor sat right next to her the whole time; he seemed to be protecting her. He ended up shutting down the interrogation and made her off limits to us."

"What do you mean, 'she didn't pass the smell test'?" questions Detective Luis.

Before responding, Jack swallows a mouthful of pepperoni and wipes his mouth.

"Um, either she knows something, or she's dumber than a box of rocks. It's going to be awhile before fingerprints and DNA are analyzed, but I need to find the link that ties her to the victims. I don't know, I can't put a finger on it, but something's not right."

At the boutique, the ladies have not had much to do all day. Business has been very slow, so Didi offers Sonya the chance to leave early. However, Sonya knows that her boss doesn't like to be in the shop alone, so she volunteers to work the entire day.

Grateful for the company, Didi decides to use the quiet day to do more of the paperwork that's been piling up in her office, but as soon as she sits at her desk, she catches sight of the photo that Jack left behind. Gazing at it thoughtfully, she suddenly blurts out, "Oh, *SHIT!* Now, I know where I've seen this before!"

CHAPTER THIRTY-EIGHT

With the pizzas gone, Detectives Luis and Giancarlo leave the warehouse for New York Downtown Hospital. They've been sent there to check on the status of the last victim while Jack remains at the warehouse with the team from the FBI.

Standing at the seawall, Jack and Maria watch as the dive team brings up a multitude of bones from the various skeletons they found on the river bottom. Turning away from the gruesome scene, Jack stares at the gas grill.

"This is one sick bastard," he mumbles.

Maria turns away as well and asks, "Did you check out the living quarters upstairs? Whoever this guy is, he's not right. There's a wall of women's photos up there. It's like a trophy room, and he's got that poem plastered all over the walls... 'Winter's gray will take its toll on the unsuspecting few.' "

"Luis said he spoke with the warehouse manager next door. I want to go over there and talk to him. Maybe he can give me more insight into what was going on over here. When do you think you'll get some info on the fingerprints and the DNA?"

"We should have answers on the prints tomorrow. The DNA usually takes about a week, but I'm going to have them work twenty-four seven on this one. I hope we can have some answers with seventy-two hours."

"Good. I'm going to put this place under surveillance. This Cronos Theopolis guy has got to show up sometime. Run his name through your database, and link up with Homeland Security and INS for me, okay? Our records check came up empty, like this guy's a ghost or something." He scans the action briefly. "Okay, I'm done here. I'm going next door, then I'm going home."

"No problem, Jack. Say hello to Didi for me."

Before leaving, Jack calls the station to arrange for surveillance, then he heads next door to Simcona Imports. When he walks into the small lobby, he is greeted by a pretty young receptionist.

"Welcome to Simcona. May I help you?"

"Yes, I'm Detective Jack Stenhouse. Is the warehouse manager in?"

"Oh, you mean Mr. Simcona. I'll call him for you."

While Jack waits, he wonders why the warehouse manager has the same name as the business.

Within a few minutes, a tall young man in his twenties walks into the lobby.

"Detective? I'm Frank Simcona. Can I help you?"

"Yes, Mr. Simcona. Do you own this business?"

"No, not yet. It belongs to my Dad. How can I help you?"

"Detective Luis said he spoke with you recently. Can you tell me what you said to him?"

"Oh, sure. I told him that I think a facility manager is living in the old building next door, and that he drives a white van, a Ford, I think. I'm not sure about that."

"Is there anything else you can tell me about that guy? Habits, routine, anything?"

"No, he pretty much stayed to himself. I'd wave hello once in a while, but he never acknowledged me. Nothing unusual over there, though. He'd barbecue outside from time to time, but he never bothered anyone."

"Have you ever seen anyone else at the warehouse besides him?"

"Yeah, sometimes I'd see a woman walking around; it looked like she was inspecting the place. Not bad looking, either; long red hair, high heels. Funny thing though, I never saw her arrive, and I never saw her leave. I'd just notice that she was there. I guess she came and went by cab because there was never another vehicle there, except the van. Oh, yeah. I'd also see him washing down a boat, but not often. Boy, you must think I'm a snoop and have nothing to do but look around, but as warehouse manager, I'm always at the shipping doors, and our dock has a perfect view of the warehouse."

"Was he there year-round?"

"I assume so, but I never really saw him until the wintertime. He was always around in the winter, maybe once or twice during the rest of the year. I thought that was odd for a guy who was supposed to be taking care of the building."

Jack sneaks a peak at his watch and notices that it's after four p.m. He hands Mr. Simcona a business card and tells him they will probably talk again, then walks over to his Road Runner and fires up the beast. Giving two quick beep beeps of the horn, he heads over to the boutique to pick up his fiancée.

While Andrea lies in bed watching Rod put his pants back on, her thoughts are interrupted by the mayor's ringing cell phone.

"Johnsville... Yes, I'll be back in the office in about twenty minutes. Thanks for the update."

Turning to Andrea, he says, "I have to get back to the office. Rawlings wants to give me an update about your warehouse. They're going to put an undercover surveillance unit there to wait for that Cronos guy to show up."

Bending over the bed, he gives her a kiss. "I'll call you later."

Andrea remains in bed while the mayor leaves her apartment, and when she hears the front door close, she breaks out in uncontrollable laughter.

Detectives Luis and Giancarlo are standing in the hospital corridor, sipping the almost undrinkable hospital coffee as they wait for the attending physician to give them an update on the Jane Doe they found in the freezer. After a long wait, a doctor finally approaches.

"Hello, Detectives. I'm Dr. Patel, and I have some encouraging news for you. Our patient has good eye movement and good response to pain, so if she continues to show satisfactory improvement, you may be able to speak with her in the morning. She is slowly coming to, but the next twelve hours will be critical. Right now, she is drifting in and out of consciousness, but she is aware of where she is."

"Did you get a name, Doctor?"

"No, not yet, but she said she was hungry. Come back in the morning. I believe she will be able to communicate better then."

CHAPTER THIRTY-NINE

There is virtually no parking available on a snowplowed street, so Jack double- parks near the boutique and puts the blue light on his dashboard before walking up the block to pick up Didi.

As he approaches the front door, he sees a teenager standing nearby, someone he has seen before. But before he can say anything, Father Lucarelli walks around the corner toward the young boy, and when the priest sees Jack drawing near, he calls out, "Mr. Stenhouse! How are you? I've missed you at church."

Jack walks up to the priest and greets him with a handshake.

"Hello, Father. What brings you out here?" While talking to the priest, he looks at the young boy and tries to remember where he has seen him before.

"We're here to see Ms. Lee. I believe you've met this young man before, Jack. Do you remember Dwayne Thomas? He has joined my youth group and was the leader of the crew that shoveled this sidewalk. We're here to pick up your donation."

Looking at Dwayne, Jack says, "Yes, I remember. Good job, kid. Is the Father keeping you out of trouble?"

"Yes, sir, and again, I'm sorry about what happened."

"Yeah, me, too. It's never a good thing when a young person dies. C'mon, let's go inside."

Jack puts his arm around Dwayne and escorts him into the boutique. As they enter the store, he calls out, "Hey, Babe! There's someone here to see ya!"

When Didi walks out from the back, she is dressed in skinny jeans and a sweater that appears to be two sizes too small. While Dwayne stares at her like a deer caught in the headlights, Jack laughs out loud, and Father Lucarelli attempts to return him to reality.

"Dwayne! This is Ms. Deidre Lee. She owns this place."

Deidre smiles, hands Dwayne an envelope, then bends down to give the young boy a peck on the cheek.

"Thank you for clearing my sidewalk, Dwayne. You did a very good job."

Dwayne is still speechless, so Father Lucarelli responds.

"It appears that Mr. Thomas is a little shy. Thank you again for allowing us to clear your sidewalk, Ms. Lee. It's important to keep these young men busy. On another note, I do hope to see both of you in church this Sunday."

Smiling at Didi, he adds, "Dressed a little more modestly, I hope."

Didi returns the priest's smile, and pats Dwayne's shoulder while the group exchanges goodbyes.

When the door closes behind the priest and Dwayne, Jack locks it, then turns to Didi. "That kid is the friend of that punk I killed in front of your shop. It looks like he's trying to straighten out his life."

"Yes, I know; I don't think I'll ever forget his face."

Suddenly remembering the photo Jack left in her office, Didi turns and runs toward the back of the store.

"Where the hell you runnin' to?"

"Be right back! I have something to show you."

When she returns, she hands the photo to Jack.

"This must have fallen out of your folder when you were in the office."

Pointing to the man in the picture, she adds, "You see this tattoo? I've seen it before."

CHAPTER FORTY

The next morning, Jack is the first one to arrive at work. While he waits for the rest of the team, he brings a cup of vending machine coffee into the situation room to review the case file without being interrupted. He works undisturbed until detectives Giancarlo and Luis arrive.

"Morning, Jack," says Giancarlo cheerfully. "I have some good news for you! Our Jane Doe should be well enough to interview today!"

"That's great news! I have some good news, too, but I'm going to wait until the Feds arrive before I spill it."

"Spill what, Jack?"

"You'll see. Hey, did you catch the news this morning? They had a story on Sloan."

The conversation is interrupted when Lieutenant Conrad walks into the room.

"Morning, everyone. How are things going?"

"Morning, Boss," responds Jack. "There have been some new developments, and I'm going to need your help with a couple of things later today."

When Agent Assante arrives with the head of the crime scene unit, the meeting begins.

"Now that everyone's here, let's start with the team at the warehouse. What did you guys find out over there?"

"Golly gee, Jack, no 'good morning, how are you all today'?" taunts Maria.

In response to Maria's teasing, Jack rubs his middle finger on the side of his nose.

"Look, I have some interesting news I need to share with everyone, but I want to hear from all of you first, so you're up, Assante."

"Right. First, if you don't already know, our dive team found human bones on the river floor at the base of the seawall at the warehouse. We took DNA samples from the bones, and also from the gas grill that was outside the building. We don't have the results yet, but I hope to have something within twenty-four hours. We also dusted for fingerprints and got some off the back compartment of the van. Many different sets were collected in that area, but they're probably from the suspect's victims. We found no prints in the driver's area at the front of the van, but we did get prints in the warehouse, in both of the upstairs rooms and on the doors, and they are all the same – they all belong to Andrea Singletary. Her fingerprints were in our database because of her stay at that mental facility, but to our surprise, we found no other prints there except Andrea's and the victims'."

Jack walks over to the white board, where he places the photo that shows the tattoo on the back of the suspect's neck.

"You've all seen this photo of the tattoo on our suspect. When I was on administrative leave, I brought the case file with me to study at my fiancée's boutique, and the photo must have fallen out there. When my fiancée found it, she told me that she's seen the same one on one of her students. She teaches a course in pole-dancing for 'fitness.' "

Ignoring the snickers from everyone in the room, he adds, "The student was Andrea Singletary."

The snickers fall silent immediately.

Turning to his boss, he continues, "Lieutenant, this is where you come in. I need you and the deputy inspector to convince the mayor to bring Ms. Singletary in for more questioning. We also need that warrant for her apartment. Her prints put her at the scene and I need to talk to her about that tattoo."

"What are you implying, Jack?"

"Nothing, Lieutenant. Not yet, anyway."

Looking at each team member in turn, he hands out the day's assignments.

"Assante, push Forensics on that DNA, okay? Luis, circulate some photos of Ms. Singletary and bring one over to Simcona. Maybe they can shed some light on the warehouse caretaker. Also take a photo to the surveillance team that's watching the warehouse. Giancarlo, you and I need to visit our Jane Doe with a sketch artist to see if she can come up with a face. Oh, by the way, if it hasn't been acknowledged already, nice job on locating that warehouse, Luis. I think this whole thing is going to come to an end real quick. The key seems to be Singletary."

As the team files out to begin the day's work, the last words from Peter Sloan run through the depths of Jack's mind:

And, and, and.

CHAPTER FORTY-ONE

Lieutenant Conrad waits in Rawlings' office while the D.I. phones Mayor Johnsville.

"Mr. Mayor, this is Gene Rawlings. I'm calling to inform you that Ms. Andrea Singletary has become a person of interest in the Poetic Killer case. Since you seem to have an interest in her well-being, I thought you might want to accompany me when I go to her apartment to bring her in for more questioning. No, sir, I cannot reveal at this time what leads us to believe that she is important to this case, but I will fill you in when we arrive at the First... Yes, okay, I'll await your call. Thank you, Mr. Mayor."

"What did he say?"

"Johnsville isn't too keen on the idea of us questioning Andrea again, but he said he'll let her know we're coming over. He'll call me back after he speaks to her."

Conrad remains in the office to discuss the case's progress while they wait for the mayor's return call.

After about ten minutes, the phone on the deputy inspector's direct line rings.

"Hello, this is Rawlings. Yes, Mr. Mayor. ...Really? Well, if we get a warrant, we'll be in that apartment anyway. Sir, I'm sure you realize that we're going to have to find her and bring her into the station. Yes, okay. Goodbye, sir."

After hanging up the phone, he looks over at Lieutenant Conrad.

"Well, either she's not home, or she's not answering the phone. We need to find out which one it is ASAP."

At that moment, Detective Luis pokes his head into the D.I's office.

"Sir, I got a warrant to search Andrea Singletary's apartment."

"Great timing! Head on over there now; I'll have a couple of uniform units meet you there. And Luis, give Stenhouse a heads-up."

"Hello, this is Jack. Yes? Great! I'll meet you there as soon as I'm done here."

Hanging up from the call, Jack continues, "That was Luis, Allison. He got a warrant to search Singletary's apartment. As soon as we question Jane Doe, I'm going over there. You stay here with the artist."

After a short wait, the police sketch artist joins Jack and Allison in the hospital lobby, then the three officers enter the elevator for the ride to the third floor.

When the elevator door opens, Dr. Patel is standing at the nurse's station. When Allison sees him, she calls out, "Dr. Patel! Good morning! How is our patient doing?"

"You mean Kelly Anderson? Well, she's doing just fine."

At the warehouse, all is quiet, but in the unmarked car where two plain-clothed officers are keeping watch, there is a whirring sound as a photo of Andrea Singletary prints out from the computer.

As the officers study the photo, a cab pulls up in front of the warehouse and a red-haired woman climbs out and pays the driver. The officers look at the woman, then back at each other, and in surprise, announce, "That's her!"

Quickly exiting their vehicle, the officers approach Andrea as she walks toward the building's front door.

"Ms. Singletary, we're with the NYPD. You need to go to the station for questioning."

"What? Do you know that I work for Mayor Johnsville? Andrea does not like this, and neither will the mayor."

"Ms. Singletary, we can either do this the easy way, or the hard way. Please walk to our car voluntarily, or we'll have to take you there in handcuffs."

Staring at the ground for a moment, Andrea lets out a sigh and seems to make a decision.

"Very well. Lead on, gentlemen, and please let the mayor know where I will be going."

As the two officers escort Ms. Singletary to their car, one of them calls for a uniformed unit to pick her up and bring her to the First Precinct police station.

While she awaits her fate, Andrea sits quietly in the backseat of the unmarked patrol car and stares at the bright blue sky.

Accompanied by the police sketch artist, Jack and Allison enter Kelly Anderson's hospital room, where they find a dark, slender male sitting at the foot of her bed.

"Hello, Kelly. I'm Detective Giancarlo, and these are Detective Stenhouse and Officer Vasquez. We need to speak with you, if that's all right."

Before Kelly can respond, the dark gentleman glares at her and snaps, "You don't have to say nuthin', understand?"

"It's okay, Hon, be cool," she replies soothingly.

"Kelly, who is this guy?" asks Jack. "I'm guessing that he's your, ah, business partner. Am I right?"

Directing his gaze to the mystery man, he adds, "Hey, Slick. Go get yourself a cup of coffee before your day turns ugly. Capeesh?"

After the man reluctantly leaves the room, Detective Giancarlo approaches the crime victim.

"Kelly, we don't want to take up too much of your time, but we need your help in tracking down the man who assaulted you."

As she presents one of the stills from the security camera at Bowery Park, she asks, "Does this look like the guy?"

"Well, that photo was taken a little too far away to be sure, but it could be him."

"Do you feel strong enough to talk with Officer Vasquez? He's a police sketch artist. We're hoping that he can draw a sketch of your assailant from whatever you can remember about him, how tall he was, what color eyes, things like that."

"Yeah, sure, I'll give it a shot. He was about your height, but I don't know about hair or eye color, 'cause he wore a hoodie and sunglasses. I'll tell you whatever I can, though."

The jangling of Jack's phone interrupts the conversation.

"Okay… right. I'll meet you there."

"I gotta run, Allison. The surveillance guys at the warehouse just picked up Singletary, so I'm gonna catch up with Luis at her apartment, then head over to the First to question her. When you're done here, meet me at the First."

Exiting the hospital, he drives to Olympia Towers, on the Upper East Side.

The plowed snow is still in piles along the sides of the streets like miniature flood dikes, but some of the major businesses and landmarks, like Olympia Towers, have paid to have the snow walls removed. Because that street is clear, Jack is able to pull the Road Runner in front of the building.

Before leaving the vehicle, he places the police beacon on the dashboard, then joins Detective Luis in the main lobby.

"Hey, Luis! Been waiting long?"

"About fifteen. Let's go; the CSI crew is here."

Luis holds up a key to Andrea's apartment and leads the way to her unit. He received the key from Rod Johnsville so that they wouldn't have to break the door down to gain entrance.

Upon entering the apartment, the officers are taken aback by what they're seeing.

"Look at all this shit!" Jack comments. "This place looks like a mythology museum!"

Shaking off their personal opinions, the group sets about searching for anything they can find that may incriminate Andrea in the murders.

Within a few minutes, Luis finds something interesting.

"Hey, look at this plaque in the hallway! It's the poem that our killer quotes from!"

In the master bathroom, Jack is surprised by his own discovery. Written in lipstick on the bathroom mirror is a note: MEET ME AT THE WAREHOUSE. YOURS FOREVER, CRONOS.

"Hey, Luis, come over here and take a look at *this*!"

When Luis pokes his head into the bathroom, he exclaims, "What the fu... Jack, what do you make of that?"

"I don't know, man. This whole place don't pass the smell test."

"Detectives, we got something," interrupts one of the crime scene techs.

Following the tech into the bedroom, they watch as the CSI guys shine a black light over the bed sheets to illuminate the evidence of at least one roll in the hay.

"It looks like a Pollack painting over there," he says.

"Now I know why Johnsville had a key," smirks Luis.

"Okay, I've seen enough," declares Jack. "I'm going back to the First to talk to that broad. Stay with these guys, Luis, and catch up with me when they're done. Oh, and check with the cab company. Get the records of pickups and drop offs from here and the warehouse."

CHAPTER FORTY-TWO

Jack stares through a two-way mirror at Andrea Singletary, who is sitting alone in the interrogation room. Standing alongside him are Lieutenant Conrad, D.I. Rawlings, and Mayor Johnsville.

"What's your plan, Stenhouse?"

"Well, Lieutenant, I got a theory about all this, and I'm gonna let it play out. I just need more confirmation before I spring the trap."

"Be warned, Detective," says Johnsville. "I'm not just the mayor on this one. I'm Andrea's friend, and also her lawyer."

Before exiting the observation room, Jack calls over his shoulder, "You're more than friends, Johnsville."

As he takes a seat across from Andrea, Jack begins his interrogation.

"Looks like we meet again, Ms. Singletary. So let's get right down to it, shall we? Is there any special reason why you were at your warehouse today?"

"No reason. It's my building; I can go there if I like."

"Yes, I suppose that's true. And where is Cronos today?"

"I'm sure I don't know."

"Were you going to meet him at the warehouse, Ms. Singletary? By the way, can I call you Andrea?"

"Andrea is fine, and no, I wasn't planning to meet him."

"No? Then can you explain the message he left you on your mirror? Oh, you look surprised, so let me explain. We obtained a warrant to search your apartment today. Does Cronos always leave you love notes?"

"He has a key to my apartment, and he doesn't like to wake me up."

"I see. He never heard of a post-it note? What are you hiding, Andrea?"

Before she can respond, Mayor Johnsville barges into the room.

"As her attorney, I advise her not to answer that. You need to charge her with something, or let her go."

"Look, we got her fingerprints, and nobody else's, all over that warehouse."

Rising from his seat, Jack walks behind Andrea and lifts her long, red hair off the back of her neck.

"And she has the same tattoo as our suspect. So yeah, she's hiding something."

"Millions of people have tattoos, Detective. This is ridiculous!"

"Well, then, I'm going to hold her for being a hostile witness, and impeding a criminal investigation. Do I need to read her her rights?"

"No need. I'll have her out in twenty-four hours."

The interrogation room door opens, admitting Lieutenant Conrad and a uniformed officer to the room. But before the officer can escort Andrea to the Booking area, she turns to the mayor and says, "Andrea is not pleased about this."

The mayor nods and follows them out, leaving Lieutenant Conrad in the room with Jack.

"You got twenty-four hours, Officer. What's your angle?"

"I got no real proof yet, but I'm working on it. Here's a clue, though. The last word Sloan kept repeating was 'and.' Mull that around in your mind awhile."

Jack exits the room, leaving Conrad alone. The Lieutenant remains there for a moment, thinking about what Jack said, when suddenly a bell goes off in his head, and he realizes what Jack meant.

Jack is sitting at his desk, impatiently waiting for updates from the team, but he doesn't have to wait long. FBI

Agent Maria Assante soon walks up, announcing, "Jack, we have some news from the warehouse."

"No hello, no big hug and kiss?" he asks with a twinkle in his eye.

Smiling, Maria rubs her middle finger along the side of her nose as she says, "No, Jack, although there *is* room for a little excitement here. The samples we took from the gas grill proved to contain human DNA, and woolen fibers we found on the taser are probably from gloves worn by the killer. However, we found no gloves in the warehouse or the van."

"DNA in the grill? UGH! Look, get in touch with the surveillance team and the uniformed officers who brought Andrea in, and ask them if she was wearing gloves at the time. If she was, check them out, and let me know what you find on them. Did your guys run a background check on Theopolis?"

"Yeah. The guy's a ghost; there's no record of him anywhere. I'll go check on the gloves. Oh, one more thing. The DNA in the grill matches one of the victims – Lana Jenkins."

"Oh, man," moans Jack, rubbing his eyes. "Now we know where her arms went."

CHAPTER FORTY-THREE

Detective Luis is at the office of the Yellow Cab Company, speaking with the dispatcher.

"Now that I've given you the two addresses, can you bring up the pick-ups and drop-offs for Olympia Towers and that old Remus meat warehouse?"

"Sure, let me search my database."

Luis waits while the dispatcher inputs the information.

"Okay, here ya go. The latest pick-up and drop-off was earlier today, and there have been several round trips in recent weeks." He peers closer. "Wait, here's something odd. There have been many pick-ups at the corner of Montgomery and Madison, with drop-offs at Olympia Towers. Montgomery and Madison is a few blocks west of the Remus warehouse."

"Thanks. Is there any way I can speak with the drivers?"

"Yeah, this must be your lucky day, Detective. Mahmoud Kaleed was on duty for some of those fares, and he's here this morning. I'll page him for you."

Within a few minutes, a small, dark-skinned man enters the dispatcher's office.

"Pleez make it fast. I need to go now."

"Mr. Kaleed, I'm Detective Luis with the NYPD. Please sit down. I have a couple of questions for you. It won't take long."

"Okay, but how you say? Make snappy?"

"Yes, okay. The dispatcher says that you've made several pick-ups at Madison and Montgomery, and that you usually dropped the fares off at Olympia Towers."

"Yes, the same person every time, a female."

Luis takes out a photograph and asks Mahmoud if he can identify the person in it.

"Yes, yes, she is the one. Anything else?"

"No, that will be all. Thank you."

Jack is on his third cup of coffee when Allison Giancarlo returns from the hospital with the police sketch artist.

"Hey, Jack! We got a sketch of our killer. It really doesn't show much, though. There's a hood covering the head and sunglasses covering the eyes."

Jack stares at the rendering, which is very unsettling. It seems to present an eerie presence of evil, along with beauty. Jack hands the sketch back to Detective Giancarlo.

"Get it circulated. That sketch is.... whatever. We got Andrea in lock up for twenty-four hours, at least."

"Why is she in lock up?"

"She knows something and ain't talking, and now the mayor is her lawyer. I got her in for twenty-four hours, but I'll bet you a steak dinner that she walks out of here early."

"You're absolutely right, Jack. She's gone," says Lieutenant Conrad as he joins the discussion.

"Oh, crap! The mayor didn't!"

"Yeah, he did. He vouched for her cooperation, and said she's going to stay at his place. Sort of a high-level house arrest."

Before Jack can comment, his phone rings.

"Go ahead."

"Hello, Jack? This is Rob Stacy in Forensics. The DNA on the bed sheets belongs to the mayor."

"Ha! I guess Andrea is a great lay. Thanks for the quick work, Stacy."

When Jack hangs up the phone, he faces his boss.

"What the hell did that mean, Jack?" asks the Lieutenant.

"That was Forensics. They picked up DNA from Andrea's bed sheets earlier this morning, and it belongs to Johnsville. This whole thing stinks."

Detective Luis walks in and joins the conversation.

"What stinks?"

"Andrea Singletary."

"Yeah, she sure does. I spoke with a cabby who picked that broad up more than once from the corner of Montgomery and Madison Streets and brought her back to her apartment. He ID'd Andrea from her photo."

"So what do we have? The warehouse has her fingerprints all over the place, but no one else's, and she took many cab rides from the warehouse to her apartment, and back. Then, there's all that weird mythology shit at her place, the tattoo, and Cronos Theopolis, a ghost who doesn't seem to exist, but there he is, cropping up all over the place."

"That's all very compelling, but none of it provides a direct link to the killer," states Conrad. "Should Andrea Singletary have been let go? Probably not, but we got no reason to keep her here."

"But Lieutenant, what about Sloan's last word? And we still need to find out if Andrea was wearing woolen gloves."

"She probably was; I saw her put gloves on before she left the station today."

"Damn! The FBI got some fibers off the taser, woolen fibers. If they match..."

"If they match, Jack, I'll bring her in myself," replies Conrad. "I'll get them from the mayor's place, so we can test them."

"Okay. Assante can call me if the fibers match. Right now, I'm going home, but when the team is with their reports for the day, ask them to come over to my place so we can talk. I'll call Assante and ask her to join us there."

Lieutenant Conrad walks up to the door of Mayor Johnsville's home and presses the doorbell. After a few minutes, the door is opened by the mayor's assistant.

"Hello. How may I help you?"

"I'm Lieutenant Conrad from NYPD's First Precinct. I need to speak to the mayor."

"The mayor is getting ready to go to Gracie Mansion for an event this evening. He is unavailable at the moment."

"Look, I wouldn't be here if it wasn't important. Go get the mayor. I'll wait."

"Very well, Lieutenant."

The assistant motions for the Lieutenant to enter the house, then closes the door and leaves Conrad waiting in the entranceway for what seems like hours. Finally, a door opens, and the mayor appears.

"Yes, Lieutenant? This better be important."

"Mr. Mayor, I've come for the gloves that Andrea was wearing today."

"Why?"

"The FBI found fibers, woolen fibers, in the warehouse. We want to see if they match Andrea's gloves since her fingerprints were also found in the warehouse."

"I don't see how this is going to help you, but I'll get them. Andrea is sleeping right now. It'll just take a second."

The mayor returns within a few minutes, and hands the gloves to Conrad.

"Here you are, but you're barking up the wrong tree. I will be speaking to Rawlings about this."

"I'm sure you will, Mr. Mayor. I'm sure you will."

Conrad takes the gloves and walks back to his car mumbling, "I bet he has to take his hat off just to take a piss."

CHAPTER FORTY-FOUR

"Jack? What are you doing here so early? Is there something wrong?"

"No, Babe. I just decided to leave a little early. Can you get Sonya to close up? A few of the guys from the First will probably stop by later. We're going to finish up work back at our place. We can pick up some fried chicken and beer on the way home."

"Okay, give me a couple of minutes. I may as well close up now, even if it's early. It's been slow due to the weather, so I guess it's okay. We can drop Sonya off on the way home."

Didi and Sonya quickly shut down the shop, then the trio piles into the Road Runner. They drop Sonya off first, then make a quick stop for provisions before heading home.

When Detective Giancarlo arrives, she helps Didi set up the buffet. Not long after that, Agent Maria Assante and Detective Luis arrive together.

"Hey, this ain't the Ritz!" announces Jack, as his guests make themselves comfortable on the couch. "Grab yourselves some chicken! The beer is in the fridge."

Gathering around the table, the group fills their plates, and gets their beers, before re-settling themselves in the living room.

As they begin to eat, their chatter dies down, but Allison re-starts the conversation with a compliment.

"Mmm, this chicken is great, you guys! Where'd you find it?"

Giving her a sideways glance, Jack replies, "I thought you New Yorkers knew everything! Didi found a little Cajun kitchen near her boutique. The food there is outrageous."

Didi is uncomfortable around the team while they're doing their "police thing," so she tells them to enjoy the chicken and cold Bud while she finishes her dinner in the kitchen. The officers understand, and thank her for her hospitality.

"So tell me, Luis, any new info from the cabbies?"

"Yeah, I confirmed that Andrea has made numerous trips from her apartment to the warehouse, and I got a couple of confirms on her photo from the drivers. I also got confirmation of her being at the warehouse from a couple of the men at Simcona."

"Good. Anything new from Ms. Anderson?"

"She remembered that our suspect was wearing wool gloves, but not much else. She did say the van smelled funny, though."

"Okay. Maria, what hast thou brought?"

"What is that 'hast thou' shit? The gloves we got from Conrad, Andrea's gloves, match the fibers found on the taser."

Jack lays a photograph of Andrea on the table and places the artist's rendition of the suspected killer next to it. Then he takes a marker and draws a hood over Andrea's head and sunglasses over her eyes.

As the officers stare at the doctored photo, each of them in turn becomes increasingly astonished.

"Goddamn, *she's* the killer!" exclaims Jack. "The last words Sloan said to me were 'AND!' He was trying to say, 'Andrea!' Who has the number to the D.A.?"

"Jack," responds Assante, "the D.A. is at a cocktail party tonight at Gracie Mansion with the mayor and other local dignitaries. They're having an auction for The Wounded Warriors Project. I know D.I. Rawlings will be there, too, along with the top NYPD brass and the commissioner."

"Ha! I always like to crash a party. Any takers?"

Giancarlo raises her hand while drinking the last of her beer.

"We're partners, aren't we? Besides, I've never been inside Gracie Mansion."

Jack grabs all the case file information and the forensic records, and turns to Giancarlo with a smile. "Let's roll, partner."

CHAPTER FORTY-FIVE

With Allison riding shotgun, Jack pulls out onto Suffolk Street. He points the car to East Houston, but it's the evening rush hour, and traffic is insane. Grabbing his portable radio, he calls for a uniformed unit to meet him when he reaches FDR Drive. That little blue light on the dashboard isn't going to cut it at this hour of the day.

They silently buck the traffic for almost twenty minutes before they pick up their escort. With lights flashing and sirens blaring, the two cars head north to Gracie Mansion, the official residence of New York City's mayors. In recent years, however, the city's mayors have not lived there, enabling the city to transform the mansion into a museum with guided public tours.

Just before seven o'clock, Jack and his police escort pull up in front of the mansion, where the guests have just started to arrive. After climbing out of "the beast," Jack gives high fives to his uniformed *compadres* as thanks for their help.

Their euphoria is short-lived, however, as they are blocked at the entrance when they attempt to enter the building.

"Good evening, sir, and madam. May I see your invitations, please?" states an off-duty officer.

Flashing their badges, Jack and Allison state, "Here are our invitations. We need to see the D.A., and we know he's here tonight."

Clipboard in hand, the officer reads down the invitation list.

"Yes, you're in luck. He just arrived with his wife, but he's gonna be really pissed off."

"Yeah, well, better to be pissed off, than pissed on."

Now cleared to enter the mansion, the detectives follow the invited guests as they are directed to the main ballroom on the second floor, where a bar and buffet have been set up for their enjoyment.

Ignoring the refreshments, Jack and Allison peer through the crowd, searching for the D.A. like submarine captains staring through their scopes. Within seconds, Allison tugs on Jack's arm.

"Got him."

The D.A. is standing with Deputy Inspector Gene Rawlings and Police Commissioner McQuade, Jack and Allison nonchalantly walk over and interrupt their conversation.

"Excuse us, sirs."

"Stenhouse and Giancarlo?" says a surprised D.I. Rawlings. "Out on a date tonight? What the hell are you two doing here?"

"We're here to see D.A. Collins about our serial killer."

"You two decided to bother me tonight?" asks the annoyed district attorney. "This couldn't wait until the morning?"

"No, sir. We got the killer. We just need you to review the evidence and issue an arrest warrant. The mayor wants this done quickly, but once you see who it is, you'll realize the urgency of our request."

"All right, tell me who it is."

As he is about to spill the beans, Giancarlo stops him.

"Not here, Jack. Mr. Collins, let's speak in private, please."

The three of them walk quickly out of the ballroom and head down a side hallway where they can be alone.

"Jack, I'll stand guard and not let anyone down this hall while you tell the D.A. what we have."

"Okay, thanks."

When Allison is blocking off the hallway, Jack looks directly at the D.A. and asks, "Ready?" Pausing for effect, he adds, "It's Andrea Singletary."

"WHAT? Johnsville's press secretary? No way!"

"Oh, yeah. She has the same tattoo as the killer, her fingerprints are the only ones at the warehouse, the fibers on the taser match her gloves, and for the punch line? The last victim didn't die, and the description that she gave to the police sketch artist strongly resembles Andrea."

Jack shows him the two photos of Andrea, along with the artist's rendition, and his doctored photo.

"We also have taxi cab records of Andrea getting picked up and dropped off at her apartment and the warehouse, and her photo and ID were verified by the drivers. So I think this is important enough for you to see."

Collins is agape and just stares. Jack continues anxiously. "Here are all the files. She's been staying at Johnsville's apartment, and with the DNA evidence we found in Andrea's bedroom today, it seems that Johnsville has been, shall we say, dipping his wick. And another thing... The last word Peter Sloan spoke before he died was 'and.' We believe he was trying to say, 'Andrea.' "

Collins stares at the photos, thumbs through the file, and shakes his head in amazement.

"Holy shit! This is really hard to believe, but okay, I'll review all of this tonight. But based upon what you're saying, it looks like we'll be bringing her in tomorrow. I know she had some mental issues after her breakdown, so I'll talk to her shrink in the morning. Give your team my thanks for a job well done. I'm going to keep a lid on it until tomorrow, however. The mayor's too close to this."

"Collins, you don't know how close. He's also her attorney."

"You've got to be kidding. Well, wait till he hears this shit. He's a politician; he'll dump her like a bad habit."

Stenhouse and Giancarlo follow Collins out to the main ballroom and watch as he collects his wife and leaves the party. Also watching the D.A. is Gene Rawlings, who makes his way over to the detectives in a flash.

"What the hell is going on here?"

Jack gives a nod to Allison, who whispers, "Andrea Singletary is the Poetic Killer."

As Rawlings' mouth flies open in astonishment, his drink slips from his fingers and falls to the floor.

CHAPTER FORTY-SIX

On this typical December morning in New York City, the warmth of the sun is hidden by the gray clouds that are taking their toll on the unsuspecting few. The temperature, hovering between the high twenties and low thirties, is providing the perfect condition for the snow flurries that are sprinkling the air.

The quiet of the morning is like heaven to the sleeping Jack and Didi, until it is shattered by the sound of a ringing telephone.

Jumping out of bed, Jack doesn't bother to cover his naked body as he grabs the phone with annoyance.

"Yeah?" After listening to the speaker on the other end of the phone, he responds, "Yeah, okay. I'll be in after I do my three S's."

As Jack looks at Didi lying there in her red teddy, he is reminded once again of the front bumper of a '58 Caddy. Slipping on the pants that he left on the floor the night before, he bends over and slaps her on the ass.

"Gotta go, Babe."

Awakening with a jolt, Didi sneaks a peek at the clock on the nightstand.

"It's seven a.m., Jack! How the hell am I going to get to work?"

Reaching into his pants, Jack pulls out thirty bucks and throws it on the bed.

"Call a cab and buy yourself some lunch, okay? I gotta go in and end this case."

Didi puts on a robe and turns up the heat while Jack is in the shower. Within twenty minutes, he has his pea coat on and is giving Didi a farewell kiss as she drinks her morning coffee.

Even though it's early, Deputy Inspector Rawlings and Lieutenant Conrad are at Mayor Johnsville's house, knocking at the door in unison. Because his assistant hasn't arrived at work yet, the mayor himself answers the door.

"Rawlings, Conrad?"

"Mayor Johnsville, we need to speak with Ms. Singletary."

"She's in the kitchen, but you can speak with me, as her attorney."

"Very well. We need to speak with her together with you, then."

Not waiting to be invited in, the pair push past the mayor and walk into the house, with the mayor following them and protesting all the way.

Andrea is looking out the bay window of the kitchen when D.I. Rawlings approaches.

"Ms. Singletary, we have a warrant for your arrest on multiple counts of murder in the first degree."

As he reads the Miranda Act, Lieutenant Conrad places her in handcuffs while the mayor shouts, "You have this all wrong! I'll have your badges for this!"

Andrea just smiles.

Looking at the mayor, Rawlings says, "Go ahead and speak to the D.A. about our badges, but first, get me an overcoat to place over Ms. Singletary's shoulders."

It's after eight o'clock, and Jack is in the small room adjacent to Interrogation Room One, waiting for Andrea Singletary to arrive at the police station. With him are Detective Giancarlo and two representatives from the FBI, Agent Maria Assante and Agent Lew Donnelly, the profiler.

"I want you guys to observe while I interrogate her," explains Jack. "I'm going to wear this earpiece, so if you need to coach me, Lew, or you need to tell me something, you can do it through that mike on the table near the mirror. Oh, look! They just brought her into the room, and Johnsville is in there with her. I'm going to let them stew in there for a while, so how about another round of coffee?"

When Jack leaves to get another round of coffee and some donuts, the remaining three persons fixate on the images they are seeing through the two-way mirror – Mayor Johnsville holding Andrea's hand, and Andrea smiling like the Cheshire Cat.

Looking at Donnelly, Maria asks, "What the hell is she smiling about?"

"I don't know, Maria. Not yet, anyway. I do have a hunch, but I'll bet we're about to find out for sure real soon."

"Hi, Sonya, it's Didi. Thank goodness I caught you before you left. Jack had to rush into work early this morning, and I'm running late; I'm still waiting for a cab. I didn't want you to think there was something wrong."

"No problem, Ms. Lee, I'll see you at the store."

Didi hangs up the phone and pulls the collar of her coat closer around her neck while she continues to wait for her cab ride to work. *Thank God I found Sonya,* she muses. *She's turned into a tremendous asset.*

CHAPTER FORTY-SEVEN

After Jack and his posse finish the second round of donuts and coffee, he gathers up the case files and heads for the door to the interrogation room. But before he exits the room, he turns to the crew with a grin. "This is going to be interesting," he says.

Jack enters the interrogation room slowly and sits across the table from Andrea and her lover and attorney, Mayor Johnsville.

"Ms. Singletary, I'm very curious as to why you have decided to talk with us. Usually, when a person is charged with a crime as heinous as this, they do not want to cooperate."

"I am sure I have nothing to hide, Detective. I am innocent. I did not kill anyone."

"Really? Our prisons are full of people who claim to be innocent." Jack takes out a mug shot of Kelly Anderson and shows it to Andrea. "Do you recognize this person?"

"I am sure I do not."

"Well, this is Kelly Anderson, the last person you tried to kill. Unfortunately for you, she is still alive and recognizes you."

"I do not know her."

Jack takes out photos of all the other victims and scatters them across the table.

"How about these women? Do you know any of them?"

Andrea shakes her head no.

"This Cronos Theopolis guy you said was the caretaker for your warehouse. Where is he?"

"I am sure I do not know."

"You don't know, because he doesn't exist. He's a ghost, a phantom. There are no records of this Cronos guy coming into this country; no trail, no links. The people at the shelter you said you met him at don't recall ever seeing him there."

Andrea turns toward the mayor, who responds for her. "He is your killer, Detective. Find Cronos and you'll solve this case. Ms. Singletary has nothing to do with any of this."

"Nothing to do with this? Her fingerprints are the only prints we found at her warehouse. Fibers found on the taser used to knock out the victims match her gloves, and cab records put her at the warehouse the night Kelly Anderson was abducted. So if she didn't actually commit the murders, she was there when Mr. Theopolis did. However, there doesn't seem to be any evidence that this Cronos guy actually exists, except for a message on Andrea's bathroom mirror, and her own testimony. So I ask again, Ms. Singletary, what are you hiding, and why are you taking the fall for Cronos?"

Leaning over, the mayor whispers into Andrea's ear.

"You don't have to answer those questions."

Andrea squeezes the mayor's hand and looks straight into Jack's eyes.

"You're very good, Detective, but Andrea is getting tired of all this."

When he hears Andrea's comment, Agent Donnelly jumps up, shouting, "I gotta get Jack!"

Opening the interrogation room door, he signals for Jack to leave the room.

At the sight of Donnelly at the door, Jack says, "Okay, you two love birds. I'll be right back."

Picking up the case file, he leaves the photos of the victims on the table, and exits the interrogation room.

Back in the observation room, he questions Donnelly.

"Why the hell did you pull me out of there?"

"Ms. Singletary responded in the first person."

"Yeah, so what? She's done that before."

"Don't you think that's a little odd?"

"A little odd? It's kinda creepy, actually."

As the detectives and the FBI agents stare at Andrea through the mirror, Agent Donnelly offers a suggestion.

"Jack, I think someone else should interrogate her for a while, preferably a woman. We need to ask more personal questions about her relationship with Cronos."

"You mean like a girlfriend to girlfriend talk? That's a good idea, Donnelly. Allison, you're up."

Jack hands the case file to Allison as she walks past him toward the door, but before she exits the room, Donnelly has another idea.

"Wasn't Ms. Singletary institutionalized because of a breakdown? Let's bring the psychiatrist who treated her here to observe her behavior."

"What are you getting at?"

"When I'm sure, I'll let you know. Before I give you my opinion, I need to observe more of our honored guest."

Anxious to help, Agent Assante pipes up.

"I'll contact Pilgrim Hospital to find out who treated her, and I'll get a squad car to pick him up and bring him in."

With a nod from Jack, Maria walks out into the hallway to place her calls, leaving the rest of the team to watch Giancarlo begin her line of questioning through the observation room mirror.

CHAPTER FORTY-EIGHT

In the middle of her morning rounds at Pilgrim Hospital, Dr. Joanne Larkin is beckoned by an aide from the nurse's station.

"Dr. Larkin! Come into the patient lounge! You need to see this news conference!"

The doctor leaves her clipboard at the nurse's station and walks over to the patient lounge, where she is immediately held captive by the content of the news broadcast.

".....Deputy Inspector Rawlings of New York Police Department's First Precinct has announced that through the efforts of his staff, and with the help of the FBI, they have made an arrest in the Poetic Killer case that has captivated the city. Ms. Andrea Singletary, the late Governor's ex-wife and the current press secretary to Mayor Johnsville, has been charged with multiple counts of first-degree murder, and one count of attempted murder, and is currently being interrogated at the First Police Precinct. District Attorney Collins released a statement indicating that Ms. Singletary will be booked and arraigned later today and that he will petition the court to impose no bail. Mayor Johnsville's office indicates that he is not available to make a statement at this time, but we have been told that Deputy Inspector Rawlings will hold a press conference at noon today. This is Michael DeSantis, ABC News."

At the end of the broadcast, the aide turns to Dr. Larkin, who is quite pale.

"She was my patient," she states quietly.

Just then, a page is heard over the hospital intercom.

"Dr. Larkin, please report to Mr. Thorpe's office... Dr. Larkin, please report to Mr. Thorpe's office."

"Ms. Singletary, I'm Detective Allison Giancarlo. Would you like some coffee or something cold to drink?"

"Coffee will be fine. Black, no sugar, please."

"Sure. As you may already know, this conversation is being monitored and recorded, so someone will bring your coffee in shortly. I have a few questions to ask you now, so let's begin. How well do you know this mystery man, Cronos Theopolis?"

"As I have said before, he is a caretaker for my warehouse and I let him live in the building."

"Okay, Ms. Singletary. Can you explain why the only fingerprints found in your warehouse were yours?"

"I am sure that I do not know. Perhaps Cronos is very neat."

"So neat that he uses your gloves?"

At that moment, an officer walks in with Andrea's coffee and places it on the table in front of her. She takes a sip and nearly spits it out.

"This tastes very bad. May I have a soda instead?"

"Look, you want me to give you stuff, but you don't want to cooperate with us. Ms. Singletary, why did you kill all of these women?"

Andrea listens as Mayor Johnsville whispers into her ear, then she turns toward Detective Giancarlo.

"I am sure I do not know what you are taking about. I never saw any of these women before, and I never killed anyone. Where is my soda? Andrea is very thirsty."

Dr. Larkin walks into the office of Benjamin Thorpe, the hospital's administrator. Waiting there is a uniformed police officer.

"Dr. Larkin, I assume you saw the news this morning about Andrea Singletary. I received a request from the FBI to have you monitor her interrogation, and they sent this fine officer to bring you down to the police station. Since Ms. Singletary was your patient, I believe it would be in the best interest of this hospital if you complied with their request."

"Mr. Thorpe, I have rounds and patients to see this morning."

"Yes, I know, but Dr. Longley will cover for you. Here, I took the liberty of getting your coat. Take all the time you need."

Reluctantly, Dr. Larkin puts on her coat and accompanies the officer to the First Precinct.

Detective Giancarlo rises from her chair and looks down at Andrea. "Andrea is very thirsty? Well, Allison is very tired. I'll go see about your soda."

Giancarlo leaves the room and joins Stenhouse, Donnelly, and Conrad in the adjoining observation room.

"What the hell was that all about? 'Andrea is thirsty?' Jack, what do you make of that?"

"I don't know. She went off on me like that before, like she's speaking about herself as another person. I remember there was a guy at the Academy who used to talk that way all the time."

Agent Donnelly interrupts. "Yeah, some people do that, but like you said, they do it all the time. This broad turns it on and off."

Maria Assante pushes open the door and enters the room.

"I called Pilgrim Hospital and got her doctor to come in and observe. Her name is Joanne Larkin. She should be here in about twenty minutes."

"Great, just what we need – more estrogen in the room."

As Giancarlo and Assante stare incredulously at Jack, they simultaneously rub their middle fingers along the sides of their noses.

Jack reacts with a chuckle. "Let's wait awhile before we bring in her soda. I'll go back in when the shrink gets here."

"Jack, I need to talk to you about something," says Donnelly, pulling Jack aside. "I'll walk with you to get her soda."

CHAPTER FORTY-NINE

"Gentlemen, I would like you to meet Dr. Joanne Larkin from Pilgrim Hospital," states Maria Assante as she interrupts Donnelly's and Stenhouse's discussion next to the soda machine. "As you know, she has treated Ms. Singletary in the past."

"Pleased to meet you, Dr. Larkin. My name is Detective Stenhouse, and this is Agent Donnelly, with the FBI. I'm about to question Ms. Singletary, so I'd like you to accompany Agent Donnelly to the observation room. We're pretty sure that you'll quickly realize why you're here today."

Dr. Larkin walks down the hallway with Maria and Lew as Jack enters the interrogation room with Andrea's soda.

"Here you go, Ms. Singletary. Hope you like Pepsi."

"Yes, that is quite fine, thank you."

"Now, I must ask you again," says Jack as he takes a seat. "Why is it that you continue to claim innocence and that you continue to protect your friend, Cronos? He clearly isn't much of a friend, if he's letting you take all the blame. Ms. Singletary, where is Theopolis?"

"Detective Stenhouse, my client doesn't know where Mr. Theopolis is, or she would have told you. Your questioning is getting repetitive. Andrea doesn't know where Cronos is, and she did not commit any crimes. If you cannot produce any evidence that she is involved, then I'm going to have to cut off all further questioning."

"Mayor Johnsville, let me hear Ms. Singletary's response. If nothing more comes out of this, then I will agree to your request. Now, Ms. Singletary, once again, where is this mystery man, Cronos, and why has he abandoned you?"

Andrea sips her soda slowly, then closes her eyes, and sighs. When she reopens her eyes, she stares deeply into the eyes of Mayor Johnsville, then smiles and turns toward Detective Stenhouse.

"Andrea is getting weary of this. No abandonment, Mr. Stenhouse. Everything is as it always will be."

"What always will be?"

"That we will be together."

"Who'll be together, you and Johnsville?"

"Hahaha, no, me and Ms. Singletary."

"Me and Ms. Singletary? Who are you?"

"I am your mystery man. I am Cronos."

Observing in the other room, Dr. Larkin gasps, while the others stare in astonishment.

"So, you are Cronos?" Jack continues. "Where is Andrea?"

"Rhea is in a safe place, away from you."

"You call her Rhea, not Andrea?"

"Yes, she is my wife."

"So was it you who killed all of these young women, and Peter Sloan?"

"Of course! I must protect my wife, Rhea, from her demons. Those women would have hurt her. Sloan was just an annoyance, a fly that needed to be swatted. I won't let anyone hurt me, or my wife. They corrupted the governor, they corrupted her father, and they enlisted her mother. I alone can save her, and I will continue to protect her."

Addressing Johnsville, Jack asks, "Well, Mr. Mayor, what do you think now?"

Agent Donnelly turns to Lieutenant Conrad. "How's that for a confession?"

"It will never go to trial. Dr. Larkin, was there any indication of this personality split when you were treating Ms. Singletary?"

"No, not at all. This is quite disturbing. How long is this questioning going to continue? Ms. Singletary needs therapy and treatment."

"I'll contact the D.A.; he'll have to pursue this with a judge."

Jack continues his line of questioning as Mayor Johnsville stands up and walks over to the corner of the room.

"Now let me get this straight... I am now talking to Cronos Theopolis?"

"It is I, Detective."

"And where is Andrea?"

"She is resting comfortably."

"Does Andrea know what you've done?"

"No, I do not think so. I have not told her anything."

"Okay, Cronos. We've shown you photographs of the victims we know of, but we've found far more bones in the river than would belong to those victims. How many women have you killed?"

"Numbers, Detective, they mean nothing to me; I must protect Rhea. I can take a guess at how many there were, but if you've seen my gallery, you must know that already."

"Yes, we have an idea, but were there any other victims, any others that don't have a photo on the wall?"

"Yes, there were a few others, but those I consumed. So perhaps there were thirty children of the night."

"Thirty, huh? You said you wanted to protect Andrea. Protect her from what?"

"Those women corrupted her father. Those women corrupted her husband. Those women enslaved her mother, but they will not hurt my Rhea anymore. By the way, her name is Rhea, not Andrea. She is one with me."

"Oh. May I speak with Rhea, please?"

"You do not like my company anymore? You insult me, Detective."

"I just want to make sure Rhea is alright. Can I speak with her?"

"Very well, if you must. Just a minute, she will be right here."

Cronos lowers his head and begins to laugh, then suddenly stops, and looks up.

Appearing dazed and unaware of her surroundings, Andrea looks around the room.

"Andrea, is that you?"

"Why would you think it's not me? Rod, why are you standing way over there? What's going on?"

Mayor Johnsville returns to sit next to Andrea.

"You don't know what just happened, do you?"

"What are you talking about? Detective Stenhouse, what's happening here?"

"Cronos was here, Ms. Singletary, and he told us what we needed to know. Mayor Johnsville, the D.A. will be here momentarily. Andrea, you will be booked, and a psychological evaluation will be ordered. Dr. Larkin will be involved with that process. My work is done here."

Jack rises from his chair and walks into the other room to talk with his crew, leaving Andrea and Rod Johnsville alone in the room.

"Well, guys, we got our killer! Now, it's up to the courts to determine if she goes to trial."

"She's nuttier than a fruitcake," asserts Agent Donnelly. "I don't believe she's faking, either. That lady will never see jail time, but she'll never be let out in public again, either."

Addressing Dr. Larkin, he says, "I'm sure this is a classic case of split personality. What are your observations?"

"Well, Agent Donnelly, I concur, unless she's a masterful actress. This is a case of two separate personalities in one body. Christmas time tends to be stressful for some people, and with her deep belief in Greek and Roman mythology, the emotions of the season must have triggered memories of the bad experiences she's had with her father, mother, and ex-husband. It never manifested during her breakdown, so it must have erupted recently. Such a pretty girl, such a waste."

Just then, Detective Luis pokes his head into the room.

"Hey, guys, I was doing a little research on that painting we found — you know, *Cronos Devouring His Children.* Well, it seems that Rhea is the name of Cronos' sister, who ruled with him as his queen. She had six kids by Cronos, but he ate all of them except one — Zeus — because he thought one of his kids would overthrow him, just as he had overthrown his own father! Some nut-case, huh?"

Jack thanks Luis, who nods quickly and leaves.

As the door closes, Jack turns to Agent Donnelly. "Guess you were right about her, Lew. Thanks for all your help." Then he walks over to Agent Assante and gives her a hug, which surprises everyone.

"What the hell, Jack?!"

"Hey, we're old friends. I thought a handshake wouldn't suffice."

"Wouldn't *suffice*? You squeezed my butt!"

With a sly grin, he says, "Yeah, I always wanted to do that."

Next, Jack turns toward Giancarlo, but she quickly backs up.

"You get a handshake *only*! Touch *my* butt, and I'll shoot ya!"

Jack laughs and extends his hand.

"Assante and I go way back. Besides, what she has hidden underneath that FBI suit would stop traffic... Ah, not that yours wouldn't."

Allison shakes Jack's hand, but raises her other hand to give him half a piece sign.

As Lieutenant Conrad gets the final handshake, he says, "You and your crew did a great job, Detective. I'll fill Rawlings in on all the details after the D.A. and Johnsville bring Andrea to Booking."

Turning back to the two-way mirror, the group watches with concern as Andrea weeps uncontrollably while Mayor Johnsville tries unsuccessfully to comfort her.

However, their concern soon turns into astonishment as Andrea suddenly stops crying, looks directly at the mirror, and begins laughing uncontrollably, even as she is being led away by District Attorney Collins and Mayor Rod Johnsville.

EPILOGUE

Spring is beginning to erupt in the city of New York as the trees start to change from death to life. In a small, isolated room at Pilgrim Hospital, Andrea sits quietly, staring at the walls. In a constant battle for survival, she drifts between Andrea Singletary and Cronos Theopolis.

Dr. Larkin enters the room on her morning visit to her newest patient.

"Good morning, Andrea."

"Dr. Larkin, you disappoint me. Rhea is not here."

"Oh, I'm sorry. Good morning, Cronos. How are you today?"

"I am fine, Doctor. Rhea went for a walk before breakfast."

"You know, we need to get Andrea back, in order to assimilate the both of you into one."

"Doctor, I may be crazy, but I am not stupid. If we 'assimilate' our problem, Andrea will go to trial and will be prosecuted for what I did. If I remain in partial control, we will remain here and enjoy your company. There will be no 'assimilation,' for I am Cronos, son of Saturn. HAHAHAHAHAHA....."

Jack and his new bride, Didi, have just returned from a ten-day cruise to the southwest Caribbean, and have a two-day layover in Fort Lauderdale before they return to the Big Apple.

July in South Florida is hot, and Jack is complaining, as usual, but he still decides to take Didi on an airboat ride in the Everglades. Even though he's a Florida boy, Jack has never been to the Everglades, and while Didi grew up in Louisiana, she has never been to the bayous.

It is a "cool" morning for July at Everglades Park in Fort Lauderdale, about seventy-nine degrees. The newlyweds take a private ride on a small airboat instead of joining one of the giant tourist vehicles that holds over thirty people.

As they travel through the river of grass, their driver crisscrosses across various channels and waterways. The Everglades is very quiet, and mysteriously beautiful. Large herons and storks line the channels while alligators and otters swim and bask in the warm sunlight.

After about twenty minutes, their driver stops near a clearing of elevated, dry ground and points out a Florida panther, which quickly disappears into the brush.

As Jack and his bride look across the landscape, Didi pokes Jack on the shoulder and shouts over the din of the airboat motor.

"Jack, what is that on the bank? Is it a log?"

"Wow, that's not a log; it's a snake, a *large* snake. Probably a python."

"Look at that lump, Jack. What the hell did it just eat?"

"Hey!" Jack signals to the driver. "Can you get this thing any closer?"

As the driver complies, Jack calls out, "Holy shit! There's a pair of feet sticking out of that snake's mouth, *human feet*! Get this thing over to the shore; we gotta get that snake!"

As soon as the boat reaches land, Jack jumps out and climbs up toward the large snake, which is not moving. Keeping one eye on the snake, he un-holsters the small 9mm he keeps strapped to his ankle, but when the snake raises its head, he quickly puts a bullet into it.

Wisely waiting a few minutes to be sure the snake is dead, he pulls out his cell phone to make an emergency call.

Hoping that one bar of signal strength is enough, he dials 911, then asks the operator to triangulate his position, and send it to the police.

Didi and the airboat driver are shocked at what they've just seen; however, Jack calmly climbs back into the boat, mumbles about the South Florida heat, and turns innocently to Didi. “I’m on vacation, Babe. I’m not getting involved in this one.”

“Yeah,” says the bride. “Your lips to God’s ears, Jack. Your lips to God’s ears.”

ABOUT THE AUTHOR

Frank A. Ruffolo resides in South Florida, where he and his beautiful wife, Christine, raised two wonderful children.

After taking early retirement from a forty-year career in purchasing and purchasing management, he discovered a passion for writing and took up a second career as an author, independently releasing two novels—Gabriel's Chalice, a science fiction adventure, and The Trihedral of Chaos, an action adventure.

Now Frank is working with Linkville Press to release his first murder mystery, The Jack Stenhouse Mysteries.

Always writing, Frank is busy putting the finishing touches on four more novels while conducting research on a fifth.

Follow Frank on Facebook (Frank A Ruffolo or Frank A. Ruffolo author) and Twitter (@ruffoloauthor) to read about his future releases.

Made in the USA
Charleston, SC
04 February 2015